SUGARPLUMS ON THE SIDE

a novel

Other Books by C. L. Fails

Decoding Joy

A Spoonful of Sugarplums
Book 1

Where Sugarplums Shimmer
Book 2

A Sugarplum Promise
Book 3

Sugarplum Sweethearts
Book 4

So Okay...:
Treasured Stories from the Life of James M. Robinson, Sr.

My Magical Story Journal

The Secret World of Raine the Brain Series

The Ella Books Series

The Christmas Cookie Books

SUGAR PLUMS

ON THE

SIDE

a novel

C. L. FAILS

LaunchCrate Publishing
Kansas City, KS

Sugarplums on the Side
Written by C. L. Fails

LaunchCrate Publishing
Kansas City, KS
info@launchcrate.com
www.launchcrate.com

Ordering Information:
Quantity sales. Special discounts are available on quantity purchases by corporations, associations, and others. For details, contact the publisher at the email address above. Orders by U.S. trade bookstores and wholesalers.

Library of Congress Control Number: 2024910249

Hardcover ISBN: 978-1-947506-40-4
Paperback ISBN: 978-1-947506-39-8

Printed in the United States of America
10 9 8 7 6 5 4 3 2 1

First Edition

The highest form of energy is love. It vibrates at the
highest frequency and reverberates in infinite ripples.
Choose love - all ways.

Everything I ever wanted was right there within my arms as I greeted her at the door. She floated in from the kitchen and nuzzled in for a hug that felt calming. I didn't know what the evening had in store for us, but each moment with Oakley felt like it lasted forever, so this relatively short relationship felt more like a lifetime to me.

Contents

SUGAR
PLUMS
ON THE
SIDE

Chapter One
OAKLEY

I couldn't believe it. The way he looked at me confirmed exactly what I'd been wondering about for so long. Those eyes. That piercing stare. So loving. So open. I felt like I was the only person in the world at that moment. It was the best and the worst thing that could've happened to me.

I knew in my gut that I was tied to his spirit for life. What I didn't know was just how far into the depths of my own despair that bond would take me.

I thought I had it bad a year ago when I saw Charlie again. But that was only me trying to right a wrong. That end was terrible. I wasn't myself. It seems I have this habit of trying to figure out if I'm still wanted when the truth is that I already know when a relationship isn't a good fit. I can feel it in my bones. In the same way that I knew it long before my college sweetheart, Jenson left with all of our money. I also knew it when I first saw Charlie - before we even went on our first date.

In fact, when he came into my life I just wanted to be wanted by someone. I just wanted to be loved. And what I did to feel that love wasn't anything beautiful or loving. Steppin' out on Charlie, a man that loved me whole heartedly with Jenson, the one I used to love who didn't and couldn't love me back. I wasn't malicious on purpose. But that didn't stop people from getting caught up in the tumultuous wake of my actions.

Now, here I was, being pulled into the wake of someone new. I just hoped in that moment that it was genuine. I hoped for the best. I hoped.

The only things I was focused on when we got caught in a trance were those that would help me become a better version of myself. Just two things really. Trap music and therapy. Well, I guess trap music might have felt like therapy, so maybe just one thing. I was working through the angst that had long been trapped inside of me since I was a child being told to stay in a child's place. The result of my parents not hearing me out or listening to my opinion because I was just, insert whatever phrase you want here.

Fast forward to now, in my early 40s, trying to figure out how to unlearn all the things I did to survive childhood, the awkward teenage years, and college when I was trying to find myself. I'm living in the big city, according to my daddy. It's Kansas City, small town feel with citified amenities. I have my own coffee shop. I'm thriving solo, and now that I'm unlearning all the things, I'm mindful of the type of person I want in my orbit. Must be honest. Must be patient. Must know who he is. Must be looking to grow with someone. Now I just have to figure out if this man with the piercing stare is honest and true, or if he's still part of the karmic lesson left for me to learn. Lord, please let him be the first.

Now let's be straight, I wouldn't ask anybody to bring something to the table that I'm not willing to bring myself. So, yes, I'm honest, now. I'm more patient. I'm learning who I am. And yes, I want to grow with someone. That's all I wanted for real.

So back to this man. He's been a regular at my coffee shop, The Fresh Grind since Thanksgiving weekend. Every Monday, Thursday and Saturday he glides back into my life, swagger level off the charts. A tall dark roast, with two splashes of oat milk and one sugar, his hair low and even - tapered slightly at the nape of his neck. His order, simple. One small cup of coffee. Black. Sugarplums on the side. One bear claw. Warmed. I wasn't sure what the sugarplums were for, but they regularly seemed to be the first to disappear, and I never saw him take a bite.

Every order was for here. He sat in the same booth in the back corner of the restaurant where he'd use a fork to delicately dissect his bear claw and chase it with hot coffee and flash a sly smile every time he'd catch my eye. It felt both comforting and invasive at the same time. With Jensen, there was an ease in our conversation. Charlie had so much potential. But I was magnetically drawn to this mystery man in ways that were hard to describe. I've heard people use the term, like a moth to a flame before. That doesn't feel nearly strong enough to explain it. I could feel him before he arrived. It's like his soul was a beacon for mine. I didn't even know I was lost, but I sure felt like it after his first visit to the shop. And for three days a week, if only for a couple of hours, I was home.

January 1st was one of the slower days of the year for us. People weren't typically up and ready to greet the day after staying up for so long the night before. I have to admit, I was feeling a bit tender for that particular swap of the calendar. Just the night before we hosted Charlie and Dr. Chris' wedding reception. It was a last minute request from Charlie, who wanted to celebrate in the place where they met but also wanted to make sure it wouldn't be a problem for me. So we closed early and helped the caterer and wedding coordinator set up shop. There wasn't much foot traffic anyway because of the snowstorm that blew through town, leaving a wake of trapped limos and chaos. Literal trapped limos. I saw 3 on the side of the road on the news, which kept me company until everybody else arrived.

So couple the snow packed roads with the first day of the year and you guessed it. You get yourself a fairly empty coffee shop. I opened it anyway though, because Saturday. I was hopeful that he'd show up.

There I was leaned up against the back counter, watching the news on the tiny tv in the far corner when my beacon started blinking. I felt the stirring and uncontrollably stood upright. It was instinct. My body was at the ready. The door opened. A well-timed gust of wind whipped a tuft of snow up into a swirl. And in the blink of an eye there he was.

"Are you open?" He asked, hope hanging out in his punctuation.

I suddenly couldn't speak. If you know me at all, you know that's hard to come by. A nod and a smile. That's all I could get my body to respond with. A nod and a smile. I met him at the front counter. Not sure how I got there because I don't remember my feet moving. His eyes remained fixed on mine the entire time.

He wasn't from Kansas City. I could tell by his accent. My guess was somewhere east of here. "I was hoping you were open today."

"It is Saturday." I said, hoping he hadn't realized that I just disclosed that I knew his schedule.

His slow nod said that he caught it.

"Happy New Year!" I chuckled in his direction.

He licked his lower lip and tucked it into his mouth just long enough to bare his dimples. I hadn't seen those before today and now I couldn't unsee the charm they added.

"What a great way to start the new year. Happy New Year to you too!"

"So, what can I get for you today? Are you going with the usual or are you trying something new?"

He leaned his weight back on one foot, his right hand covering his heart, "Oh, you know my order?"

"Small coffee. Black. Sugarplums on the side. One bear claw. Warm."

His mouth dropped open. "Wooooooooow! Am I that predictable?"

I giggled at the look of shock on his face. "Order something and let's find out!"

"Okay. Okay. Let me just look at the menu right quick." He said, eyes still fixed on mine.

I looked up in the direction of the menu and allowed my eyes to drop back down slowly, hoping his had followed their path. They hadn't. He was still looking at me. Piercing my soul.

I cleared my throat, mostly to regulate my breathing, "Your order, sir?"

Eyes still locked in. Reading me. He smiled, "Two small coffees. Black. Sugarplums on the side." He popped an eyebrow. "One bear claw. Warm. Two forks." He studied my body language. His breath, steady. Confidence oozing out of his pores.

Normally a move like that would make me nervous,

but his presence felt like home. "Are you expecting a guest today?"

He didn't say a word. Only nodded in my direction as if he knew that I knew who that second coffee and fork were for. He was right, but I was taught not to make assumptions. He was gonna have to ask me to join him like a gentleman.

"So, just a long night then?" I asked him.

"I didn't get into anything last night. I just took it easy. But you look like you could use a good cup of coffee and I'd like to buy you one."

"Well now that was the kindest compliment anyone has paid me yet this year."

He laughed, "I didn't mean anything by it. I'll just take one coffee unless you'd care to join me."

Close enough. "So that was TWO coffees, Black. Sugarplums on the side. One bear claw. Warmed. Two forks. Coming right up."

"How much do I owe you?"

"First customer of the New Year - it's on the house."

His eyes narrowed, like I had ruined his plans. I grabbed a tray from below the counter and placed it in front of the man who was watching my every move. I inhaled slowly then turned towards the pastries and grabbed a bear claw, popping it in the microwave for spell. I pivoted towards the jar of sugarplums, scooping out a spoonful and dropping them into a separate cup and placing that cup on the tray. I glanced at him out of the corner of my eye as I glided towards the hot coffee, filling two cups and placing them on the tray, just as the microwave sounded. I caught a whiff of the bear claw and my stomach howled.

"Looks like that bear claw is right on time."

"I think I'm a little hungry." I said as I grabbed the plate of food from the microwave.

He chuckled, his dimples resurfacing. I slid the tray in front of him and pointed towards his booth in the back. "I think there's a space open in the back there."

"I'll meet you back there."

"You know where the forks are."

He nodded and slowly turned in the direction of his booth, stalling as he hit the area with the silverware. His gaze returned to me as he methodically pulled out one fork and set it on his tray. A smile curled up in the corner of his eye as he slowly grabbed the second fork, raised it in my direction, then set it on top of a napkin on the tray.

I would've thought my body would betray me in a situation like this, but all systems were checking out as normal. My pulse didn't race, my breathing was steady, my palms were dry. By its responses, I was disinterested in him. But that couldn't have been any less true. I was so intrigued by that man. What was so important to him that he risked life and limb in the snow, on New Year's Day, to come have a cup of black coffee that he could probably fix himself at home?

I called myself tidying up the area even though we only had one customer and his order didn't warrant any type of mess. I must've wiped the counter down no less than 5 times. Maybe that was an indication of my nerves. Or I was stalling. Or maybe I was stalling because of my nerves. We definitely didn't need to clean anything and nobody else was on the roads, let alone coming into the shop that morning. I folded the towel and draped it neatly across the sink's edge.

Yet again, I don't remember my legs moving, but I was getting closer to him, so they must have been moving somehow. "Stubborn stain on the counter?" he asked as I slowly glided towards his booth.

"I'm sorry?"

"The counter. You wiped down the same spot at least 10 times."

I paused about 10 feet from his booth. "So...should I be concerned that you were watching that closely or flattered?"

He raised his hands in resignation and chuckled, "Fair enough. You don't know me yet. I mean, maybe I should be concerned that you know my order. Especially when there are usually so many customers in here. You don't even know my name."

His smile was comforting. I returned the favor, hoping mine was as well. I inched towards the corner booth. He stood and extended his hand. "Jason Andrew Mitchell."

"Wow, the full name!" I chuckled at his openness. "It's a pleasure to meet you Jam," I said as I innocently extended my hand for a shake. The energy in the shake caught me so off guard that I gasped. It took my breath away. All I could do was stare into his eyes and continue to shake hands with Jason Andrew Mitchell. I couldn't look away. In an instant I felt like I'd lived a million lives with him. That jolt of energy was replaced with an inexplicable feeling of home.

"Do I get to learn your name too?" he joked.

I blinked out of my trance. "I'm sorry, it's just that I feel like I know you. Have we met before?"

"I feel it too, but I don't think so. I don't even know your name," he said as he stopped shaking my hand and just held on - waiting for me to respond.

"Oakley. Oakley Powell."

"Hmmm...now that's interesting," he said as he pointed towards the booth and helped me into my seat. "See, I gave you my full name for the background check that I know you'll run when I leave here. And you, only gave me two..." he finished as he winked in my direction and sat back down on his side of the booth.

I nodded through my ever-present smile, "Make it to a 5th date with me and I'll give you my middle name."

"Challenge accepted."

"Only 4 more to go, Mr. Mitchell."

"No ma'am. We still have 5 to go. I would never count this as a date. You're on the clock. In fact, it looks like you might have another customer or two coming in."

We both craned our necks towards the front door to see a staggering couple, struggling to hold each other up. I wondered where they were headed and I willed them with every jab step to pass the door of the coffee shop and keep on walking. I've never been glad to see a customer walk on by before, but in this case - I wanted to get to know a little bit more about Jason.

I turned back in his direction to find him sipping on his coffee, still eyeing me.

"So Jason, tell me about you."

"I'm an actuary and it's actually why I..."

"I was an actuary once in a previous life."

"Was this a life that I was connected to or?"

"I'm sorry?"

"Nah, it just feels like I've known you for a few lifetimes, that's all. Is that too much for the first conversation? I'm a straight to the point kinda guy."

"Not too much at all. How long have you felt like that, Jason?"

"Since Thanksgiving weekend. As soon as I walked in the door. You didn't take my order, but I could feel it when we caught eyes. Am I alone in this? You just said you felt like you knew me."

"I felt it when we shook hands. The energy."

"It was crazy right? If I'd been out drinking last night I might think I was still tipsy."

"I get it," I said and just gazed at him. It felt like he was intercepting my thoughts.

"Yeah, so I'm an actuary and it's what brought me here in the first place."

"To Kansas City? You're not originally from this area are you?"

"Bowie," he said stoically.

"Maryland?" He nodded. "Yeah. That accent was thick."

"You're talking about somebody's accent, Miss Oakley?"

I laughed, because I had a feeling he was about to serve me my words on a silver platter at the prime expense of my country twang.

"Itsa pleasureta meetchu, JAAAYAM" The accuracy was impeccable. His intonation was solid. I knew my country accent was thick, but I didn't think it was that thick.

"Really, Jason?" I asked through chuckles as he nodded and popped a couple of stray sugarplums into his mouth.

"Well, you're just lucky you have a bit of charm on your side," I teased as I watched him snicker. "Hey, talk to me about those sugarplums on the side."

"Oh, these are little melt in your mouth delicacies as far as I'm concerned. I love 'em. Where do you get them from?"

I raised my hand.

"You make them?" he asked with wide eyes.

I nodded, "I do."

"Get outta here!"

I started to slide out of the booth which made him laugh.

"Please stay. You make these for real?"

"I do. I can usually batch them once or twice a week depending on the demand."

"I always eat these first. I try to stretch them out but they're so good they just disappear."

"I've noticed that."

"You've noticed quite a bit, I see." His eyes were piercing my soul again when they weren't scanning over my nose & lips. "Do you pay attention to all of your customers this closely? You know my order. You know where I sit. You know what I eat first."

If I could blush, I would have definitely turned red. I think my skin was just brown enough to save me. I think. It didn't stop the giggle though.

"So, that's a no, I take it."

"Well, I think I'd better go check on our other customers," I said, knowing good and well there were no other customers at the present moment.

Jason looked over my shoulder, then out to the barren streets. "Ma'am. Is there someone in the back I don't know about?" My giggling kicked it up a notch. He looked down on the floor underneath the table, then his eyes traced the path back towards the counter and quickly cut back at me. "Some of The Littles secretly living underneath the floorboards? In the walls?" I was in full on laughter at that point. "I mean, what? What am I missing? Are they invisible? Has somebody been sitting in that booth over there this whole time?"

I finally squeaked out a no. "Nothing like that."

"Nothing like thaaayat," he mimicked.

I continued to laugh. "Sir. You got one more time to mock my accent."

He pretended to lock his lips and toss away the key behind the table over his left shoulder.

"So, what brings you out and about today, Jason?"

He looked at me, his lips pursed, and cocked his head to the side, as if to accentuate the fact that his mouth was on lock down.

"Oh, you've got all the jokes today, huh?"

He shrugged his shoulders, and took a sip of his coffee, extending his recent vow of silence. Our eyes locked again in an intimate gaze as I dropped a sugarplum into my mug and used a spoon to help it melt into the light roast that was still steaming in my mug.

He smiled and set his cup of coffee on the table. I tilted my head in curiosity, wondering what he was thinking about in that moment. His eyes were so intense. We must've sat in contented silence, staring into each other's eyes for a good 30 seconds. It felt a little invasive at first - like I was standing in front of him completely naked. I wanted to close my robe to protect my soul. But there was no robe to cover up my insecurities. Instead I had to sit through the vulnerability and own every inch of my bare spirit. I was being tested on all the things I was working to let go of and unlearn.

Part of me felt like that's just how he liked it - the challenge of me sitting through my discomfort and owning the trust fall of locking eyes with a stranger for longer than 3 seconds. It was like sleeping with the light on in a strange space. It doesn't really matter if it's on or off when I'm actually sleeping, but I felt a comfort in knowing that objects in the strange room would be more easily identifiable with the lights on. And somehow, I told myself that I could sleep better knowing that. Knowing that I could look away was my saving grace. Except, I couldn't look away.

Ever gazed out a window with a beautiful view and found yourself getting lost in every inch of scenery? This was that. All fractions of Jason's eyes were different and beautiful, and I was magnetically pulled into the view. I could feel my heart opening up and because I had already gotten used to him seeing my naked spirit, I welcomed the unspoken conversation.

I let out a contented moan. His face perked up, one eyebrow raised, but still not speaking. "Your pupils just dilated. They're like saucers right now," I teased. He nodded slowly and popped both eyebrows in my direction, still not speaking.

I stood up, maintaining eye contact, walked towards his left shoulder, lightly placed my hand on said shoulder, then leaned behind him and grabbed that pretend key out of the windowsill. I tried to unlock his lips with it, but he shook his head no. I sat that fake key down on the table then reached behind him again. I tried the second invisible key, which also didn't work. I leaned further over the seat and he placed his hand on my arm to stabilize me. When I came back up with "the key" and tried to unlock it this time, it worked.

He stretched his jaws out and proceeded to lick his lips. The dimples. Good gravy. He knew exactly what he was doing.

He opened his mouth and let out a shallow breath before he spoke. "You."

I was still standing beside the booth, looking him in the eyes, one hand on his shoulder, trying not to lose my balance after his velvety voice answered one of my questions. Which question I wasn't quite sure, so I asked, "I'm sorry?"

"You. You're the reason I'm here today. You're the reason my pupils look like saucers. It's you."

"I'm. Wait. I." I couldn't get a complete sentence out of my mouth if somebody offered me a million dollars. It just wasn't physically possible in that moment. I backed away from the booth and he gently held my hand, his gaze falling to the floor. That jolt of energy was back.

He was holding on so tenderly, not as if he were demanding that I stay, but like he was asking - quietly. So I waited right there, until his gaze returned to mine.

I had to do a bit of prompting for that to happen, softly calling his name, "Jason."

Everything about him was gentle, his gaze as he looked up at me, his facial expression. He spoke softly, "I love it when you cross my mind, Oakley."

I sat down in the booth beside him before my knees buckled and I ended up on the floor.

"Jason."

"You should've left the key on the floor or wherever you picked it up from because I have a lot to say."

I tried to slow my racing heart. "Jason."

"I'm gonna marry you, Oakley Powell. I can feel it in my bones. I've never been so sure of something in my entire 44 years of life."

Chapter Two
JASON

Damn. It's been a while since I've allowed a person to uproot my soul the way this woman has. And it was instantaneous too. I had one job, to go in person to this coffeeshop on Small Business Saturday and connect with the owner so we could sit down in person and run some renovation numbers to ensure they had the best chance of minimizing risk. That's it.

I've always been a numbers guy. Stats and math were kinda my thing in high school and college. I had the build to play sports, but my family encouraged me to protect my brain at all costs. Even when those costs were dodging verbal bullets from classmates because my big brain intimidated the shit out of them.

Mental warfare. That's what they assailed. And when I came out victorious, I was threatened in other ways. I never did anything to anybody. They just hated that I was so damn smart, and they told me every chance they got. What I got in return was a chance to sharpen my wit. Every insult hurled my way, every joke at my expense made me more and more funny, which came in handy with the ladies.

They swooned at my sense of humor. It probably doesn't hurt that I'm also tall. And now that I've hit my mid-40, my Dad-bod has booted as has my gray hair, and apparently there's "something lovable" about me. I've heard that regularly since my Jackie Robinson year. That was two birthdays ago now, but the more I age, the more I seem to hear it. I've been close to getting married, twice - once in my 20s and once in my 30s, but I'll save those heartbreaking stories for another day. Just know, the last time I was close to proposing, W., was in office and I was still in the DMV for all of the foolishness.

Anyway, I've been in Kansas City for work since Obama's second term and I got to see all the bigotry first hand out here in the Heart of America, so they call it. Can you imagine the heart of something pumping hate fueled blood into the rest of the body? Yeah. It's as accurate a picture as you're thinking right now.

As an actuary, I got to use my stats skills and my charm to assess the probability of events and occurrences, and their financial implications. Insurance companies rely on our accuracy, so I'm well compensated for the amount of work I put in.

It's not something I projected for myself, but I still

enjoy the work. It found me honestly. I was on a job board checking out new opportunities when a friend of mine told me about a woman who had just gotten fired from her job as an actuary because of her fiancé's janky choices. They kicked her up outta that jont and my friend was like, "My dude, you should apply." I didn't even know what an actuary did. I had to google it. But when I did, it felt like a perfect fit for my nerdy ass.

So I submitted my resume, interviewed and was offered the position. The salary was more than double what I was making before. More than double. So I hopped on the chance to stock some cash and I've been here ever since. They keep trying to promote me, but I just thanked them for the raises instead. I don't want any more responsibilities than I already have. They want me to train a team of people. I just want to do the work that I've come to love and go home to my boring life at the end of the day.

That's what I thought I was doing on that day. I had one job. I walked into the Fresh Grind coffee shop and saw her face. That's when I knew that I was gonna marry her. I didn't know how it was gonna happen. I only knew that it was a certainty. It was a "when," not "if." It was like we didn't have a choice in the matter, like it was already written in stone or some shit. One look at her angelic oval face and my world was upended. She was bad, even if she did dress like a Bamma. I thought I was gonna go home to my boring life at the end of the day, but that was about to be shaken up. I could feel it. I was supposed to be in there for work because she hadn't been responding to my emails and phone calls. But work was about to get personal then a mug.

She took my order. Small coffee. Black. Sugarplums on the side. The person in front of me had asked for them in their coffee but I didn't even know what they were. So I decided to try them first. Bearclaw. Warm. "Comin' right up there. What's a good name for us to use when your order is ready?"

I had them use my favorite gag name, Mr. Reeman. Say it all together. Faster. There, did you hear it? Good. I liked to stay incognegro while I was out and about on work. She chuckled when she went to call the order for "Mystery Man," a smirk filled her face as she looked in my direction and hollered it out loud. I thanked her as I picked up my order and found the best seat in the house for observing their daily activities.

The staff was efficient. Guests seemed happy. The machinery was still newish, but she had inquired about a possible upgrade to their tech and the space. Just a quick phone call would've helped me gain a bead on things, but while I sat in the back watching her, I quickly understood why returning email and phone calls could be a difficult ask. She was just as busy as the staff was - which is probably why they were so efficient at their job. But on the flip side of that was a woman who was probably exhausted at the end of the day.

I just knew she had a spouse to go home to at night. One quick check of her left and right hand suggested that I might have made an assumption about that. No ring. No tan line. No indentation. I bet she was too exhausted to go out at the end of the day. I made some notes in my notebook and popped one of those sugarplum things into my mouth. It dissolved on site and was the most delicate and robust whatever it was that I'd ever experienced. In my mind they had to be imported from some high end shop in Italy. I don't know why Italy was the spot in my mind, but it had to be there or England. Either way, they weren't American, and they were so good that I had mindlessly eaten all of them before I realized it.

It was kinda like mindlessly eating chips out of a bag. You reach in thinking there's like 3 chips left only to realize that you just wolfed down the last one and barely tasted it because you ate it so fast. There's a brief moment of, "I would've savored that last one differently had I known," and I had the same sinking feeling in my gut after realizing that I had just swallowed the last one.

I placed my pen on the table and looked down at the bear claw, hoping I wouldn't allow my body to scarf that up so fast that I missed an opportunity to savor the last bite. I used my fork to section off tiny bite-sized morsels so I could slow down. Why am I telling you all of this? Because you need to know how I am. If it's good, I'm coming after all of it. Doesn't matter what it is, if it's good - I'm about to zone the f out and devour every last bit. That's been a hard no for a lot of women. I'm so lovable until they find out that I'm all in. Then I'm too much. I'm overwhelming - and they're just not ready for this type of relationship yet. And that's how I made it to 44 without getting married.

But that is about to shift. I know it in my gut. Because after that first day in the coffee shop, I knew we'd be connected for life. That sounds like a prison sentence, but hell, lock me up and throw away the key. I didn't want anybody else after that. I didn't even know her, but I knew her. I knew that I knew her, and I hoped that she knew that I knew her and that she knew me. I was confident it would click. That's the level of certainty I had after that first visit to the Fresh Grind, speaking of the name - I did make note of the connotations that might be associated with that and the potential risk that might follow it, if it hadn't already happened.

So I just observed on visit one. I told my boss that I was going back in to talk to her on visit two, the following Monday - Cyber Monday. The closer I got to the place, the stronger the heartbeat that surrounded me. It wasn't mine. It felt like the earth's heartbeat or something equally as ethereal and esoteric. I went inside in spite of feeling like I was on shrooms or something, and the pulse got heavier the closer I got to her. I ordered the same thing. She had someone else deliver it to my table in the back. "Here y'go Mystery Man. Enjoy!"

I spent a lot of time pretending like I was taking notes. But I had taken all the notes I needed on visit one. She was too busy again for me to sit down and chat with her, so this visit was merely to suss out whether or not that "thing" I felt the first go round was still present on the second. It was.

I left that Monday and went straight home, to sit with my thoughts. That oversized chair welcomed me home and my cigar was just waiting to relax my energy. I was overstimulated. Just one ever-present hum of energy seemed to fill my body when she was near. It was like she was there to help me find myself. Funny, I didn't think I was lost. In fact I thought I had a pretty solid handle on who I was and what I wanted. But some kinda way I just felt like there was so much more to learn about life and about myself in it. My Momma told me once to just stay open to the things I don't understand so I can grow to understand them.

I took one puff of that cigar, inspected it, and set it down in the ashtray. I knew in my gut that it was the last one I'd smoke. In fact, that was the last drag I'd have of one. I had the same feeling I'd experienced with the Sugarplums. It happened so quickly and was finished before I could even savor the last bit of it. I didn't know why I was done with it, but I knew I was done.

Suddenly I realized that all of my shadow self was about to be confronted. So not only was I about to merge lives with the owner of The Fresh Grind, I was also about to level up individually. I sat there staring at my cigar as the smoke twirled and danced up into the air and wondered about how my life would look at the end of this year. I tilted my head back and let the weight of it rest on the back of the chair. I closed my eyes and that's when I saw it. Just as clear as if it were happening right in front of my face, the two of us - standing at the altar, exchanging rings and looking lovingly into each other's eyes. I squeezed my eyelids tightly to see if I could change the channel so to speak, and it worked. But instead of switching to a different program, there was a voice - "Let her love you."

Momma said stay open so I was bound and determined to learn whatever I was supposed to learn from the woman who was standing at the altar with me. I could see it so clearly. We looked so happy. I wanted the contentment that was in my posture, the stable sense of peace. I realized in that moment that it was that peace and contentment that I considered boring, and that I longed for so much.

I promised myself that I wouldn't go back into the coffee shop until the following Thursday. That gave me four days to sit with everything I'd just experienced. Four days to dig even deeper into the ways we'd help each other live. Thrive. Exist. Four days to get antsy. Four days to return to myself. Four days to create a plan. So when Thursday came, I went back to the shop. Ordered the same thing. Sat in the same booth. But it was too busy. I came back on Saturday. Then again the following Monday. Repeat until the end of the year. Then enter the new year.

I woke up on New Year's Day and grabbed my phone to see if The Fresh Grind was open. It was. I sang terribly in the shower and then got dressed. I looked around my house as I was grabbing my coat and the world seemed to shift on its axis - a tilt if you will. I walked out the door and turned around for one last glimpse. It felt like I had been thrown into an alternate or parallel universe. I didn't know what was going on but there wasn't a feeling of gloom or doom. It was quite the opposite, I felt reassured and confident that whatever was on the other side of that door would be fine and was meant for me.

The streets were filled with snow, so the drive to the coffeehouse was slow and steady. It felt like someone was sending me a message to slow down and pay attention. So I did.

I parked the car and peered in the windows on my way to the door. The space was empty. I half wondered if they were open, then I saw her leaning on the counter watching tv. Just waiting. Her frame looked totally relaxed, at ease, peace filled. She wasn't running around. It was the perfect time to connect with her - not for work, but for my damn self. I had high hopes for us. The highest in fact. But I had just received that message to slow down, so I played it cool - as cool as I could anyway. Inside, I was too hype to finally get a chance to chat with her. Learn more about her. Observe her in a less stressful state. I reached for the door, didn't even have a hand on the handle yet and suddenly she sprang upright. Maybe there was a security camera inside or something. It's like she knew I was there before I could even open the door.

She turned to me and her gaze reaffirmed those high hopes. It wouldn't have mattered if the shop was filled with people. She would've been the only person present to me.

She knew my order - recited that jont back to me like it was hers. And then...you know how it feels when someone you're not sure notices you pulls a move so detailed and familiar that it stops you in your tracks? That's some personal shit. Had me out there feelin' seen and vulnerable. So I joked it off.

Comedy had always been my way of distracting from how wide open I was. I started doing it for smoke and mirrors, but her laugh...and that smile - that lit a fire inside me. We started trading barbs back and forth and she was holdin' her own. Sometimes people hold back to be polite. She was goin in on me in this cute accent. It was so thick.

She had to be from a small town. I'd been in Kansas City long enough to distinguish between their country drawl and those who were raised in neighboring towns.

Listen, people from Kansas City will try to have you believing they don't sound country. Ask any transplant. They'll tell you. Words with an o on the end sometimes end with "uh" - see Exhibit A. Colorado, pronounced Col-o-Ra-do. Kansas City pronunciation, Col-uh-RA-duh. They drop parts of the pronunciation on some words. Hell, even Kansas City somehow has only three syllables when they say it. Now imagine ramping up the country by about 10. That's how Oakley spoke, and when it was something she was passionate about, you could probably amplify the countriocity by at least 15 instead.

None of that mattered to me. The level of cute in her accent was unmatched. Score one. She was going toe to toe with me and I had nothing but respect for it. Score another one. I got a vibe that this was her shop. Ambitious. Score another one. Winning all around. Something in me felt like this was the right time to ask her to join me for coffee. While she was working. Nothing imposing about that. I felt bad about it as soon as I asked for the second cup of coffee and two forks for the bearclaw.

Who the hell was I to put her in such a compromising position? I wasn't her man, yet. And even if I was, to just show up and demand her company, like that. That's not a move I typically make. A lot of my actions were atypical when it came to her. I really was a softy at heart, but something about her presence made my alpha male stand up and show out. It was like I was instinctively trying to impress and protect her. From what? I don't know. But this shit was oozing out of my pores in a way that I hadn't experienced before. I was suave and debonair. Everything I tried so hard to be the opposite of in all of my past relationships. I had been the nice guy. The guy people loved to love in theory but ended up leaving in the friend zone. I guess I had tried to be that person because I didn't think anyone would like this version of me. So maybe she just brought the real me out of the façade. Could I be that comfortable with her already?

All of this was running through my mind while I was waiting to see if she would say yes to my not so subtle ask.

She told me she'd meet me in the back, where I regularly sat. She had been watching me more than I knew. It caught me off guard again. Vulnerable and seen, I meandered my way to the booth in the back where she knew I was going to sit. I took that time alone to settle the internal dialogue that was about to send me back into my nice guy shell. Every now and then I'd look up at her and see about 20 years down the road. She would catch my glimpse and all I could do was smile at her. If she knew what I knew...

The same spot. She was cleaning the same spot on the counter over and over. I wondered if she was trying to stall or figure out how to get out of joining me for coffee. She draped the towel over the counter and headed my way.

"Stubborn stain on the counter?" I asked, so she knew I saw her too.

She stopped about 5 feet from the table and asked if she should be concerned about me watching her that closely. I didn't want her to feel uncomfortable, so I did the thing they taught us to do back in elementary school. Introduce yourself to people so they can get to know you. Here I was envisioning a future with a woman whose name I only knew as wifey in my visions of the future. That wasn't weird at all. I stuck out my hand and gave her my name. My full name. The whole thing. Why? I don't know. She didn't get Andy Mitchell, the name I used for work because on resumes and emails it sounds less threatening. She got my complete government name. Jason Andrew Mitchell. She called me by my initials as she shook my hand. The only other person who called me Jam was my grandmother.

My pop said she's the one I got my quick wit from. We used to roll everywhere together before I was old enough for school. She'd introduce me to people as her Jam. She'd use it to call me in from outside. When she needed to get my attention quickly around a lot of people she'd sing it. She'd been gone for about 5 years and I missed her so much. So naturally, Miss Oakley calling me Jam had me feeling some kinda way.

So there we were, holding hands and not letting go. The energy that surrounded us almost knocked me back into the booth. It was a warm touch full of peace and comfort, and it magnified those 20 year visions. If they were just out of focus before, her touch brought everything into 20/20. It was instantaneous and intense for just a mere handshake, and for a split second I think I could read her mind. I was home and I think she felt it too.

I had to ask for it but, she gave me her first and last names and told me that I had to get to the fifth date before I could get her middle name. Challenge accepted. She tried to count this as one of the dates but I wouldn't hear of it. I wanted to earn it.

We talked about a lot. I tried a couple of times to tell her what brought me into her coffeeshop, but she interrupted with excitement both times. The first time she told me that she used to be an actuary too. I was curious about her shift in careers. The second time she clowned my accent. I gave it right back to her and had to lock my lips and throw away the key when she told me that I had "one more time" to mock her.

She asked me what brought me out today. My lips were sealed so I hoped my body language would speak for me. I gazed into her eyes. She squirmed a little bit, like she was uncomfortable. Then suddenly she settled in and I was in TROUBLE. Mesmerized. I felt like the tables had turned and she was reading my mind. I wanted to tell her everything. I needed to tell her everything. I couldn't move forward with a clear mind without telling her.

"Your pupils just dilated. They're like saucers right now," she exclaimed.

I nodded and popped my eyebrows in her direction. Lips still locked. She pretended to pick up the key from behind me and unlock my lips so I could talk again. I pretended like the first two weren't the right key. She braced herself on he back of the booth so she could lean over even further. I held on so she wouldn't topple over. The energy was back and so strong. She unlocked my lips and stood beside the booth while I stretched my jaws out. I had taken a sip of coffee through my pursed lips so I tried to clear the residual that was just hanging out. Her nostrils widened as she looked down at me.

I breathed as deeply as I could while I told her what was on my mind. Her hand was on my shoulder and I could smell her spicy perfume. "You."

She looked caught off guard.

"You're the reason I'm here today. You're the reason my pupils look like saucers. It's you."

"I'm. Wait. I." She was having trouble finding the words and backed away from the booth. I returned my hand to hers for reassurance and looked away. I didn't want to keep her from leaving. I wanted her to stay. And she did.

She called my name so softly it was almost a whisper.

When I looked up into her eyes again, she was looking at me with a combination of fear and care.

My voice matched hers as I spoke softly, "I love it when you cross my mind, Oakley."

She crumpled into the booth beside me. Her breathing shallow, "Jason."

"You should've left the key on the floor or wherever you picked it up from because I have a lot to say."

She placed a hand on her heart and spoke in a near whisper, "Jason."

I told her exactly what was on my mind then waited. "I'm gonna marry you, Oakley Powell. I can feel it in my bones. I've never been so sure of something in my entire 44 years of life."

I waited for her to blink. I waited for her to move. I waited for her to continue breathing. She wasn't doing any of it.

I ran my fingers through her curly locks and tried to breathe for both of us. I leaned towards her ear and whispered, "If I make it to date five."

She laughed and nestled her head against mine. I, meanwhile, sighed in great relief and chuckled a bit before softly asking when she was available for date number one.

Her voice tickled my inner ear and sent a shockwave up my spine. "What are you doing Sunday?"

"Tomorrow Sunday or next weekend?"

"Tomorrow. I'm taking a day off and closing things down. Sundays are our least busy days and it's the new year. I'm not expecting a lot of people."

I leaned back and looked in her eyes to see how serious she was. I studied her face.

"I think I can make that happen." There was a twinkle

in her eyes. "You thinking a brunch date or something later in the day so you can sleep in? Tell me what time to pick you up."

"There's a cute little brunch spot I can meet you at around 10:30."

I slid my phone in front of her and asked her to send herself a text with the location so I had it too and so she had my number, you know, in case something came up.

She held onto it for a few seconds then tried to pass it back my way. "It's locked."

"112" I said as I nodded in the direction of the phone. She plugged in those digits and waited for the phone to open. I gave her the rest of the passcode, "820."

The phone unlocked and she looked at me curiously. She opened up messages and started a new one, "You trusted me to unlock your phone?"

"I'm an open book. Not trying to hide anything from you."

"So can I poke around in here?"

I waved a hand towards her as if to say feel free. She sent a message and handed the phone back to me.

"Did you save your contact info in it?" I looked at her instead of the phone. She shook her head no and I handed the now locked phone back to her.

Those eyes pierced my soul as she was silently asking me to unlock the phone again. "You got it."

"112" She said as she looked up at me then back to the phone, "820."

"Good memory I see."

"And you're okay with me just having this in my memory?"

"Open book. There's nothing in that phone that you can't have access to."

"Oh you were serious when you said...you were gonna...I was gonna..."

"Never been so sure of something in all my life, Miss Oakley."

She finished saving her name and contact information in my phone, then handed the phone back over to me. She wasn't speaking.

"Uh oh, is there a key I need to find somewhere?"

She shook her head no, then turned towards the door. A new customer. Five of them.

"Happy New Year! I'll be right with you!" she called toward the front of the store. Her gaze returned to me. Eyes apologetic. "I need to go help them, Jason. Do you need a refill on your coffee?"

I shook my head, "Can I help you?"

"I got it, sir." She winked at me as she stood to her feet. "Thank you, though."

"Mmm hmm." I watched her walk away and decided that this was as good a time as any to make an exit. I stood to my feet and put my coat on. "I'll see you at 10:30, Miss Oakley."

She stopped and pivoted in my direction, then took a few steps towards me, "Are you leaving already?"

I was heading in her direction and we met in the middle. I wrapped an arm around her lower back and she reeled me in for a hug. The young crew of five who were waiting patiently all let out an "awwwwwwwwwwww" in the highest pitched tone of their registers. They giggled like we were so cute. I lowered my cheek to her forehead and she nestled in.

"Mmm...how is this just our first hug?" I whispered to her. "Feels so familiar."

"I don't know, Jason. I don't know anything anymore," her chuckle made me smile. Apparently one of the nosey five decided they had to tell everybody what they saw.

"Oh, he LOVES you loves you. Do you see this guys? I want a love like this in my life. I NEED a love like this in my life. I can't wait for my husband to come hang out with me at work."

Another one chimed in, "Umm - you need to keep a boyfriend before you can get to a husband, Mandy!" They all laughed, including Mandy, who wasn't finished.

"You're not wrong. All I'm sayin is I want a love like that. Do you hear me Universe?! Like these two right here."

I chuckled, "They're getting rowdy down there, you should probably go get them some coffee."

She nodded, "Did you look at my contact info?"

I hadn't looked at it and I let her know that. One arm still wrapped around her, I used the other to retrieve the phone from my pocket. She broke from the hug and placed one hand on the phone. "Look when you get home." She caught me in another one of her gazes and popped an eyebrow at me.

"Why can't I look now?"

"At least wait until you leave here. I'll see you tomorrow, Jason."

I nodded at her request, but damn I wanted to kiss her so badly. I had to physically shake my head no to break out of my own trance. I ran my fingers through her hair one more time. "I'll see you tomorrow, Miss Oakley."

We walked towards the counter together and the five young ladies gushed about some glow that they apparently saw hovering around us - like we were Bruce Leroy or something. I wished them a Happy New Year and kept walking as she went back to work behind the counter. I paused at the door to wait until she turned to look at me. Her smile lit me up. I grinned at her and walked through the door. Outside and with the door just a few feet behind me, I stopped within eyeshot of Oakley and opened up my phone to find her contact card.

I looked at it and shook my head. Laughter erupted from deep within my stomach. She had saved her contact in my phone as "Oakley B. Powell-Mitchell." I looked up at her, serving coffee to the five giggly ladies, and waited until she glanced up in my direction. I waved my phone at her and watched as she bit her lower lip and lowered her gaze. Then I walked away, excited for all that the New Year had already gifted me.

Chapter Three
OAKLEY

He found the contact card and waited until I knew that he'd found it. He waved his phone at me and I instinctively found myself blushing internally again. I looked down towards the counter and when my eyes resurfaced, he was physically gone. His spirit was still with me though. And thank goodness, because those giggly girls had questions. LOTS of questions.

"Where did you find a guy that loves you like that?"

"You're not wearing a wedding ring! How long do you have to be married to reach the stage where you're not worried about wearing it anymore?"

"Did you know at first sight that he was gonna be your husband?"

"What do I need to do to deserve a love like that?"

"Here's your coffee ladies. I trust that you had a great

time ringing in the New Year?"

"It was dope! But when are you gonna teach us your ways, sis? We need help!"

"I need help too!" I joked with them in hopes that they would back up. The truth was, it definitely felt true. I was fresh off a night where I had to watch an ex I'd wronged celebrate the start of his new life with his wife...in my business. I didn't want to intervene or anything and I was glad he'd found someone who could appreciate him the way that he deserved, but I'm not gonna say it didn't sting a little. I definitely had an internal heckler that kept talking about how it could've been me if I would've had my stuff together. I don't think it ever would've been me. But I did feel like I didn't have my stuff together yet. I kept waiting for it to feel like I did. Even though I was well into my healing journey, it felt less and less like there was a destination I needed to get to. The journey felt like the destination if that makes any sense. Because of that there was a sense that you just are where you are. So I was learning to make peace with the idea that I didn't know all there was to know in life and that was okay.

They laughed their way to the same booth that Jason had been sitting in. "Maybe it's a lucky booth!" Mandy said as the giggles continued.

About thirty minutes into their visit, when it was clear that there weren't going to be many customers that day, I plated a few pastries and delivered them to their table.

"Ladies, I thought you might need something on your

stomachs." Pointing out a few of the options, "These are gluten free. These are sugar-free. These are gluten and sugar free. And these have all the bad stuff."

They thanked me profusely for the food. I thanked them for keeping me company this morning. Then the ring leader, as Jason quietly named her, spoke up.

"So we noticed that you didn't answer any of our questions. Sorry if we crossed the line back there."

"Girls will be girls. My friends and I were the same way in college. Then I graduated and we kinda lost touch."

"Was it Jason who made you lose touch with them?"

"No it wasn't Jason, but it was a guy - and he didn't treat me right."

"That's his fault!"

"It is. He chose it and I allowed it because I thought that's what you were supposed to do when you love someone - be understanding of their faults. I was blind to them though."

"Is that how you found your way to Jason?"

"Y'all really think we're married?"

They all nodded eagerly, like it was some kinda foregone conclusion that we simply were. I was curious what they saw, so I asked them.

Mandy piped up first. "You're just so comfortable with each other."

Then the long braided one, "It's how he looks at you. Like he just knows he's gonna take care of you forever."

"How on earth does someone look at you like that?" I naively asked. They all gave me the same look at the same time, and it's exactly the way that Jason gazed at me. It's the reason I felt like the only person in the world. Calm and serious with a hint of humor. Full of love.

I laughed at their facial expressions and the giggles returned.

"So how long have you two been married for real?" Mandy asked.

I shook my head.

"You're not married?!" She asked incredulously.

I continued to shake my head no.

"Dating?" She asked with hope in her voice.

"Tomorrow."

"You haven't even started yet and he already looks at you like that?"

I grinned and shrugged, then turned to walk away.

"Sis!!!"

"How?"

"What did you do to him?"

"Were you already friends?"

"Seriously teach us your ways!"

I pivoted back towards the table. "Y'all, if I knew, I'd definitely help you out. I just got his name today. The first date is tomorrow. Come in next week and I'll let you know how it went."

Mandy looked around at her friends who all nodded. "We'll be back next weekend."

And with that, I left them to enjoy the pastries and tended to the excitement that was bubbling up inside of me at the thought of my first date with Jason. It doesn't matter how confident you are, there will always be first date jitters if you care.

And I definitely cared about this one. When he said he was going to marry me I was stunned into silence. I definitely had a feeling about him. I just hoped it was right.

We didn't have too many people stop by for coffee so I closed up shop a little bit earlier than planned. On my way to the house I decided to drive by the cute little brunch spot where I was going to meet Jason in the morning. I wanted to get a sense of where to park and how long it would take to get there to help my anxious mind get a bit more rest. I fixed myself a light dinner and watched my favorite movie to start the new year. Before I went to bed I showered and plaited my hair into flat twists. I picked up the new journal that Dad had given me for Christmas and opened it up to page one. I jotted down the date so I could remember when I started writing in this one. The world moved fast and I knew it would be easy enough to forget the window of time captured within each journal.

January 1, 2021

Today I met him. The man who's been coming into the shop since Thanksgiving weekend. Jason Andrew Mitchell. I've always been drawn to him like a magnet and now I think I know why. He feels like home. He looks at me with so much love. And of all the things for him to say to me, he told me he's never been so sure of something in all of his 44 years of life. He's going to marry me, he said. And the scariest part is I think he might be right. I promised him that he could have my middle name if he made it through the 5th date with me. If we're not already married before the 5th date that is. He calls me Miss Oakley with so much passion.

While I was finishing up my journal entry he sent me a text. "I'll see you in the morning, Miss Oakley."

"Sleep well, Jam."

"Remind me to tell you about that nickname tomorrow."

"Will do!"

"Sleep well, Oakley B. Powell."

I was just about to send the sleeping emoji when I received another message from him. "Oops - sorry, Powell-Mitchell."

" **blushing emoji** Good night sir."

"Goodnight"

I hopped back into my journal entry to finish it so I could get some sleep.

Apparently sometimes he calls me by the name I left in his contacts. I hope I didn't jinx myself. I'm gonna try to get some sleep so I can be well rested for tomorrow. I'm so excited about this date that I don't know how well I'll sleep. We're about to find out. Until tomorrow's entry. Oakley Powell.

I don't know why I signed all of my own journal entries. Nobody else had ever journaled with me, so there wasn't really a need to sign it. At this point I was about 20 years in the game signing my entries. No need to fix something that's not really broken I suppose. Anyway, the bed was calling my name, so I turned in for the night.

When the morning came, I tried my best not to overly hype up the day, but I was still excited. I had dreams about him all through the night. Sweet dreams I might add. And I'm grateful for them. I might've sent a text to cancel if they were any different.

A good dance always helped me work out the anxious

energy, so I turned up the 80s dance hits and jammed to Whitney Houston and New Edition to distract myself. Then came the song that felt like it was speaking to me. Got a Date by Dionne Warwick. I definitely didn't remember this from my youth. That's What Friends are For, yes. Got a Date? No. Except I did. I was getting ready for it and I couldn't wait to look into those eyes again. A quick cardio workout. A shower to get all cleaned up. Moisturized my body, spritzed myself with Nomad, then I put that song on repeat and danced my heart out as I got dressed to go meet Jason for our first date.

It was only a short 10 minute drive away from me, but it felt like the longest ten minutes I'd ever experienced. I missed every light. Pedestrians were crossing the street at random points. It was as if I was being asked to slow down. So I did. In fact, I slowed down enough to question whether or not the experience we'd had before was real or something coincidental that aligned with a story I wanted to be true. Enter a twinkle of doubt. It wasn't much. But it was enough to color the first date experience with a slightly different hue.

JASON

I sent her a message letting her know that I was on the way, albeit just a bit behind schedule, but she was driving - at least her phone told me so by the automatic reply that I received in return. No worries. The street was higher than the restaurant so I could see inside when I parked the car. I loved that she was dressed for whatever. We hadn't talked about anything but brunch. Usually women get all fussy over that meal. We're having lunch? Casual. We're having dinner? Semi-Casual. We're having brunch? Let me do a full makeover right quick. It felt kinda ridiculous to me, but if it made them feel great, go for it I guess.

She was different. I was about to go greet a barefaced, curly haired woman in an oversized sweatshirt, skinny jeans and some Timbs. And I couldn't wait.

I hopped out of the car so fast that I forgot to lock it. I was nearly at the door when I realized it, so I tilted the key over my shoulder in the car's direction and pressed the lock button repeatedly until I heard the horn sound. Key back in my pocket, I opened the door to the spot then it hit me, I was legit about to start dating my wife. I grinned at the thought of it and then grinned even harder when I was standing beside her.

"Well, Good Morning, Miss Oakley!"

"Good day, sir." She was kinda cold. I wondered about a million things in the moment but I only asked one of them.

"Did you sleep okay?"

"Just fine thank you." Her response was curt and I didn't know what to do with it.

"Good. Good. I apologize if you had to wait for a bit. I hope you got my text."

She shook her head and then checked her phone, nodding once she read it.

"There's a 45 minute wait, Jason. I'm sorry."

I rubbed her back and checked in on my app. The next party the host called for was, "The Mitchell's. Party of two?"

I raised one hand to signal the host and held out the other for Oakley. She hesitantly placed her hand in mine as we followed our fleet-footed host back to the table near the window. I thanked the host and waited until she sat down before I took my seat. It was sunny outside but still January cold. Sitting by the window gave us the best of both worlds. We got the heat of the sun but the cold glass didn't let us get too warm. The ambient music of the morning was courtesy of the Smooth Jazz All Stars playing their rendition of Daniel Cesar's greatest hits. I hadn't looked at the menu yet, but I did sit puzzled by the look on her face. I didn't know what was going on, but even her bothered face was cute. She on the other hand had buried her face in the menu. She hadn't looked at me once since we sat down.

"So you said you slept okay, Miss Oakley?" I hoped that would break her out of her trance.

She simply nodded and kept studying page two of the menu.

I picked up the menu and reviewed page two. "So what sounds good to you this morning?"

She shrugged. No eye contact. No words. Just body language that was sending a message all its own - "leave me alone."

I figured out what I wanted to eat so I'd be ready whenever it was time for us to place our order. I set the menu down on the table and watched her for another minute before I put my hand on her menu and lowered it to the table.

She finally looked up at me, but it wasn't a look that said I'm ready to talk now. Instead it was a look of annoyance filled resignation. Think of how a mother looks at her child after they've been calling her name 10 times in a row and she finally choosing to concede, knowing they likely won't stop on their own. That look. That's the one I received from Miss Oakley.

I chuckled. The timing was probably piss poor. Sure. But it was humorous to me that even her annoyed look was still cute.

"What's going on this morning?"

She sucked her teeth. It felt like she was about to lay into me, but that would have to wait. I was saved by the waitress who came over to introduce herself and take our drink order. I motioned to her to order her drink first, then I told the waitress what I'd like. I also told her that I thought we were also ready to order food. So she turned back towards Oakley to get her order. I followed with mine after Oakley shared that she wasn't ready yet. Once I was done she quickly ordered the same thing as me. When the waitress confirmed that we'd made the best choices and placed a hand on my forearm as she exited, I thought Oakley was about to burst a gasket.

"Do you know her, Jason?"

"First time I've met her was a few seconds ago when she came to the table to take our drink order." I paused and waited for her to say something. She just looked at me like she was trying to sift through some bs. "Oakley, talk to me. What is going on today?"

"You showed up late."
        "I sent you a message."

"You showed off your car when you got here."
        "I forgot to lock the doors."

"You somehow got us seated right away."
        "I used an app."

"You had them call us the Mitchells like we're married. We're not."
        "I used my first and last name. They took one look at us and chose to call us the Mitchells."

"You pushed my menu down and demanded that I talk to you."
        "I was trying to see what's going on."

"You forced me to order when I wasn't ready."
        "I didn't force you to do anything."

She paused and looked at me.

"You just refuse to apologize, huh?"

"Help me understand what warrants an apology and I'll definitely do it." She was silent. "I'm not trying to be difficult. I'm just trying to understand what's going on, that's all."

I extended my arm across the table and opened my hand to her, palm up. I hoped it would shake her free from whatever was holding her captive. If she could just feel it again, that warmth, that feeling of home, maybe she'd see us again. I know it was a tall ask, but we were floundering. I was a little bit desperate.

"So holding my hand is supposed to fix everything?"

I closed my hand but left it on the table.

"I don't know what you want from me right now. You're not willing to hear a perspective that's different from what you experienced so there's not really room for me to help you understand. You're not willing to share what's really going on, so I can't truly understand what's going on. I'm feeling a little stuck here, Oakley."

"I don't know if you'll ever understand."

"You gotta give me a chance to try."
"I don't."

She was right. I made an assumption that she felt what

I felt and I hoped that it was enough to carry us through the challenging shit that showed up. But she didn't owe me anything.

"You're right. You don't." I left it at that and chose to sit in silence instead of trying to hear and then be heard.

She was still looking at me, clearly frustrated. But she wouldn't offer anything, and I wasn't trying to force her hand. So I just picked up my phone and started doom scrolling.

A few minutes later the waitress brought our waffles to the table. I thanked her with a smile, which was apparently too friendly for Miss Oakley. She huffed and ate the waffles seemingly in protest.

Halfway through my waffles, I was starting to get angry and I gently set my fork down on the side of the plate. Hands folded in front of me, hovering just above the food, I looked at her. She wouldn't return the glance. I cleared my throat and spoke softly, "Oakley."

She sliced off a piece of waffle and pierced it with her fork, then picked up part of her over-hard egg in the next stab. "What kind of monster mixes their waffles and eggs together?" I thought to myself. That thought brought a slight chuckle, which led to an eye-roll-huff combo as she stuffed her fork into her mouth. She even chewed with an attitude.

The waitress who was either messin' with us or had the worst timing in the world, sauntered over to check on things. I told her that my food was good and I thought my date was enjoying hers as well by the bulge of waffles and eggs that were in her cheek. Humor. Apparently it was well timed for the waitress, who laughed, but Miss Oakley did not appreciate that I had somehow managed to find joy in this situation.

When the waitress left, she let me have it. She went on and on about how I was a pretentious, inconsiderate, arrogant, smug son of a biscuit. She literally called me a son of a biscuit. I tried not to, but I couldn't help it. I laughed. I hadn't heard that since I was like 12.

"First and foremost. I apologize for laughing. I'm sure the timing was off, but I wasn't expecting to be called a son of a biscuit today and it caught me off guard. I wasn't laughing at you or your emotions or your feelings and I certainly hope it didn't feel that way. I'll do a better job of checking myself in situations like this."

She nodded. "It felt like all of that."

I reached for her hand and held it in my grasp. "I'm so sorry, Oakley. I'll do better."

"No Jenson. You won't!"

There it was. We were starting to scratch the surface.

I spoke softly and caressed the top of her hand, "Miss Oakley. Tell me about Jenson."

Chapter Four
OAKLEY

I had just called him Jenson. I don't know what triggered it, but I called him by the name of the man who'd hurt me the most and there was Jason, sitting across the table, trying to calm me and help me sort through what was going on. I wanted to run out of there as fast as my legs could move and that's exactly what I did. Instead of facing it, I ran. I just left him sitting there. I was standing just outside the doors of the cafe about to hyperventilate when I felt a hand at the small of my back.

"Hey." The sound of his voice calmed my anxious energy instantaneously. "You don't have to tell me what's going on. But running away from it won't make it go away." I couldn't turn to face him but nodded at his words. "When you want to talk, I'll be there."

I opened my mouth to speak but I couldn't get out

anymore than a whisper, "Okay."

He left me standing there on the corner. I was just about to return to the restaurant to grab my coat when the flirty waitress brought everything out to me - leftovers included. "He took care of the bill and asked if I could make sure you got your things before you left. I don't know what sea you found that fish in, but hold onto him Momma."

I was angry. Angry at myself for not dealing with my own stuff. Angry at Jenson, for what he'd done to me all those years ago. Angry at Jason for being so steady. I know, that sounds dumb, and it is. But I was just angry and that emotion spared no one.

Also, I still thought Jason was kind of a jerk the way he showed up late and flashed off for people. Then he wouldn't even hear me out when I called him out on his crap. "That's why I walked out," I tried to rationalize with myself. *I don't know who he thought he was foolin' but it ain't me. I'm not about to be the same person I was when I was with Jenson.* I felt it that whole time, but I didn't want to acknowledge it. I knew that doing so would mean the end of the relationship I had so heavily invested my future self into and no matter how bad things were, I didn't want to admit defeat to myself.

Even when I called Jason by the wrong name, I was still blaming Jenson for what he did to me. The truth is just like what I told the giggling ladies yesterday, I allowed it. In order for me to be ready to welcome anybody in my life I had to accept responsibility for my own stuff. That was my priority. I falsely thought today's date would have been the start of our lifetime of love together. I still had some work to do.

The next day came before I was ready for it. I went back to work and opened up The Fresh Grind. I didn't even think about the fact that it was Monday until he walked through the door. I asked one of my team members to take his order and I went to the back. I didn't want to see his pretentious self in my restaurant, but also, business is business. I stalled in the back for a solid ten minutes, hoping maybe today he'd gotten his coffee, bear claw, and sugarplums on the side to go. My hope was not fulfilled. Instead I walked out and checked his booth to find him staring straight at me, bright smile still present. His sugarplums were missing. I decided to see if he'd eaten them or if he'd decided not to order any.

"Good morning to you, Miss Oakley." *Pretentious.*

"Good morning, Mr. Mitchell. How was your order today?" I asked. He looked a bit taken aback by the formality of my approach.

"The sugarplums were delicious as always. Everything is, actually." He gazed deeply into my eyes, "How are you?"

I fought for my life, "I'm well, thank you for asking."

He was stoic at the table, "Good."

My breath began to calm down. "Indeed."

"Oakley."

"Jason, I stand by what I said yesterday."

"I stand by what I said on Saturday." *Arrogant.*

"We went out on Sunday."

"We did," he said as he stared into my soul again.

"I-"

"I think it's safe to say date one didn't go as planned for either of us."

"Understatement of the year."

"Well, we're only a few days in so..." he laughed. I did not. Damn those dimples. "Okay so I'm thinking we need a redo."

"You want me to go out with an arrogant son of a biscuit?"

"If that's how you see me then yes. Give me a chance to show you that maybe I'm not who you perceived me to be on Sunday."

"Yeah, I don't know that I'm interested in that."

His head tilted in curiosity. His voice filled with quiet reverence, "What happened from Saturday to Sunday that shifted things so much for you?"

"What do you mean?" I asked. He turned his phone around to show me the contact card that I'd added on Saturday. I couldn't say anything.

"You went from this," he said while point at his phone, "to calling me a son of a biscuit for something I didn't maliciously do."

"But you did it."

"I don't deny that I was late, but I told you as soon as I knew I wasn't gonna be on time."

He had done that.

"You laughed at me."

"Yes, and I apologized for chuckling at how cute you looked when you caught me off guard and called me a son of a biscuit."

He had done that too.

"I really think if we talk through this we can find the break in communication, Oakley. I still stand by my words from Saturday," he said as he tugged on the hem on my shirt sleeve. I don't know why that move felt so intimate, but I felt exposed in a room full of customers. I didn't like that he could take me out of myself like that.

"I don't know about another date, Jason."

"I can understand why you would feel like that. Are you

open to a simple phone call in lieu of a date?"

I was heavily considering it. "I've been told I'm a great listenerd."

"You mean a listener?"

"No, I meant what I said." *Smug*.

"You're a nerd?"

"When it comes to listening, yes. I want people to feel heard when they talk to me."

"I definitely didn't feel that way."

"I understand and I'm sorry. I want to make it up to you. Could we start again, please?"

"I don't think I want that right now."

"Fair enough. Let me ask you this. Does my presence here bother you? I can leave if need be."

"I just assumed you loved our coffee."

"You really don't believe me, do you?"

"I don't."

"I haven't given up. I'll give you some space. Call me when you're ready."

"Okay, sir." With that I walked away, again.

JASON

That date left me more intrigued than ever. When she walked out of the cafe the waitress looked at me with these apologetic eyes. I asked if she could do me a huge favor and take care of my future wife. I paid the bill, left her tip, then plated her food inside the box and wrote a note on the lid that I'd be there to talk when she was ready.

When Monday morning arrived, I had to decide whether or not to stick with my routine and head into her coffeeshop. Ultimately my craving for those sugarplums won out. I hopped in the car and slushed through the streets on the way to get my Monday morning cuppa Joe. When I parked the car and got out, I saw her say something to the barista then disappear into her office.

Once it was my turn to order, I was asked if I wanted my regular. I nodded and asked if she could repeat my order to me. Oakley had told the barista what I wanted and said it was on the house. I didn't get to ask her if I was going to get to pay for my order at any point this year, but that was twice in 3 days that I didn't get to. Maybe it was a peace offering. Maybe it was a proverbial olive branch. I was going to ask her about it but when she came back to the booth to check on me she was still kinda cold. The feeling of home was still there. I felt compelled to touch her but didn't want to cross a line of any kind, so I tugged on her sleeve. I watched her breath change when I did it. She looked a little unnerved which is the opposite of what I wanted, so I let go just as quickly as I had started. It felt like she wanted me to know that she saw me but she also wanted me to know that she wasn't ready to chat yet.

I didn't know what was left for me to say or do so I left an open invitation for her to contact me if and when she was ready. I wasn't going back into the coffeeshop for personal reasons. Unless she contacted me and extended an offer to be in her physical presence, I didn't have a reason to connect with her - well, except for work. I still had to figure out how to handle that. It was the entire reason I ended up in her space to begin with. I still had one more attempt to connect with her before the agency made their decision based on the evidence I'd gathered without her help. I opened my laptop and sent one more email her way.

OAKLEY

It was almost time to close up shop for the day and I had just reached a point where I could open my laptop and check email. There it was. Yet another email from Andy Mitchell. I hadn't replied for a few reasons. The first, the day always seemed to get away from me before I could reply. Then time would pass and it just felt rude to respond so late, so I wouldn't. I was definitely overthinking that part. More than anything though I think

I didn't reply because I wondered about whether or not he was the actuary who had taken my job when I was let go after Jenson did me dirty. There he was again, coming up in stuff that was present day even though he'd done his damage twice, years and years ago. Our email signatures told people how long we'd been with the company and his was in the same year that it all went down. It was a rabbit hole of crap that I needed to figure out. Instead of ignoring that email I sent a reply.

"Hello Andy,

I thank you for your patience as we worked through the busy holiday season. I would be happy to schedule a time to chat with you about our request and will yield to you for next steps. I'll keep an eye out for your reply.

Happy New Year,
Oakley Powell"

I closed my laptop, locked up shop and scooted across town ready to wind down for the day. I had hoped the drive to my house would be peaceful. Instead my brain kept filing through all of the ways Jenson was still impacting my life. It was overwhelming. It nearly broke me as tears filled my eyes on that 10 minute ride. I pulled into the garage and sat in silence until the light inside the garage automatically turned itself off. I opened and closed the garage door again so I wouldn't have to stumble my way into the house. I stopped in the kitchen, mentally exhausted from trying to speed process all that stuff in the car. It's like I was trying to purge all of it at once. We'd spent years together. That was kind of an unreasonable thought to entertain. So I shut it down and opened the fridge to see what I didn't have to cook. The box of leftovers from my date were still inside. A waffle sounded great. I pulled it out and grabbed a plate from the cabinet so I could pop it into the toaster oven and reheat it. When I opened the box I nearly dropped it on the floor. There was a handwritten note on the lid from Jason.

"Whenever you're ready to talk - Call Me."

I popped the food onto the plate and placed it into the toaster oven, then went to the bathroom to center myself. While I was washing my hands I decided that the best things to do was to change into something more comfortable, eat my dinner and call someone who was willing to listen. My family didn't want to hear anymore about him. They'd made that clear. My therapist was okay with me talking about the situation because, well, she's getting paid to do it. Enter Jason, who - now that I think about it - didn't trip when I called him by another man's name. He just asked me to talk about him and I ran away.

Sweatpants and a hoodie on, I went back to grab my waffle and sit down at the table. I said a quick prayer over my food and then studied the handwriting on lid of the box. It hadn't been written in haste. He had taken his time to write it. I could suddenly hear his voice from that day.

So stoic and open, "Oakley. Tell me about Jenson." Even today I got more of the same from him. "I haven't given up...call me when you're ready."

I looked at the phone sitting beside me and pulled up the last text I'd received from him, "Apologies if you end up waiting for me. Running about 10 behind but I'm on my way. See you soon."

The first thing he did was apologize. I missed it. I was scared to death that he might just be it for me and I talked myself right out of a good first date on the way to the date. He apologized to me, but I actually owed him several. That Saturday he had felt like my everything. That just goes to show you how we can talk ourselves into seeing things the way we want, for better or for worse - and this was definitely a situation of the latter.

I picked up my phone and started typing out a long text. My brain kept telling me something different though. *He told you to call him. <u>Call him</u>.*

I took a deep breath and hoped that he wasn't still at work. Then I convinced myself that maybe it was better if he was at work because then I could leave a message and it wouldn't be as bad as trying to apologize on the phone. I dialed his number and the phone rang one time before he answered.

"Miss Oakley, are you okay?" His voice. There was something in his voice that was music to my ears. It calmed the storm within me. Softened me.

"Hi Jam," I paused so I could catch my breath.

"Hmmm...I didn't get to tell you about that name during our date. Don't let me forget to do that some day okay?"

"Okay."

"So I think I missed your answer. Are you okay, Oakley?"

"I didn't answer that one. I'm okay."

"It's good to hear your voice. It calms me." He paused and I grinned. "Not that I was anxious about anything. I just feel more grounded and settled." *What on God's green earth?* "Was that a smile I heard?"

Heck yes, "it was." I was stupefied!

"What are you laughing at?"

"I was thinking the same thing you just said out loud and it made me smile. That's all."

"Oh okay. So you're feeling okay. What's up?"

"I owe you several apologies."

"What?"

"I wasn't listening. I got scared and I freaked myself out. I treated you pretty terribly today and yesterday. I apologize for all of it, and for running from you."

"You don't have to apologize for that, Oakley."

"I want to though. I have some stuff to sift through over here and I think it's best that I don't date anybody until I can work through it."

"Ahh." He was silent and I wasn't sure how to read it.

"Yeah, I just think it was too soon for me to start trying to date."

"Too soon after what?"

"Well..." I stopped to think about it. It had been a couple of years since I messed up things with Charlie and nearly a decade since things had blown up with Jenson.

"Are you still there?"

"I am."

"Too soon after what?"

"I don't think it was too soon now that I'm thinking about it."

"Okay."

"I think I've just been running away from my feelings for a while."

"For Jenson?" He'd remembered his name.

"For what happened in that relationship and after."

"Ahh..." there was a silence that just kinda hung out with us for a while. I didn't know what else to say and it felt like he was trying to decide if he wanted to say what was on his mind. "Is there anything you want to talk about?"

"Well, if you're still okay hearing about Jenson, I'd like

to talk about it."

"I'm not."

I was stunned. I didn't know what to say. I wasn't expecting that to be his response.

Out of nowhere, his throaty chuckle entered the chat. "I'm kidding of course. We can talk about whatever's on your mind, even exes."

"You sure?"

"Tell me about Jenson, Miss Oakley."

Suddenly I felt like I'd returned home.

"Well..."

He interjected "I'm sorry. Hold on, I have another call."

"Mmm hmm." I was just waiting for him to switch over when my phone beeped. Jason had invited me to FaceTime. I answered it, suddenly aware of how I was dressed.

"Is this okay with you?" he asked, his voice calming me again.

I nodded. "Don't get all quiet on me now Miss Oakley."

I smiled, "Was this your other call?"

"Absolutely."

"I love that so much," I said through a chuckle of my own.

He grinned into the phone's camera. "Are you eating dinner right now?"

I nodded, a slight smirk graced my face. I sliced a piece of waffle and stacked it on top of my eggs, then popped it in my mouth.

"Are those your leftovers from brunch?" he asked.

I nodded again.

"I have questions."

"Ask away," I told him.

"One, how on earth do you eat eggs and waffles at the same time. You did that when you were frustrated with me and I thought you were a monster."

"Not a monster!" I laughed.

"Definitely a monster."

"I've been eating them like this since I was little."

"Ahh...old habits die hard."

"I suppose they might."

"Okay. Question two."

"Yes?"

"What made you call me?"

"The leftovers. It was the note you left on the lid of the box. It looked like you took your time to write it, which meant that you weren't in a hurry and you weren't writing it in anger. Then I started replaying our date and how I showed up for it."

He exhaled and a crooked smile filled one side of his face. Damn, those dimples.

"I wasn't angry at all. I figured when you called me by somebody else's name that meant you were dealing with some stuff that was related to him, not me."

"You were right. Are you eating dinner right now?"

"I am. Also leftovers from brunch."

I hadn't seen him take anything with him. Then again, I also hadn't turned in his direction. I just stood there, locking in the sensation of his hand on the small of my back. So familiar and new.

"Microwave or oven?" I asked him.

"Toaster oven reheat for a waffle for sure."

"Definitely." We laughed together.

"So Miss Oakley, can we consider this an extension of

the first date? Can we finish it?"

"I think I'd like that, but you're over there and I'm over here."

"I'm okay with FaceTime or..."

I was curious, "Or?"

"If you want, we can meet at another restaurant or you can come here. I'm open to how that looks."

"Would you be open to coming to my house Jason?"

"I didn't want to be presumptuous and just offer that as an option, but yes."

"What part of town are you in?"

"Are you trying to decide how much time you have to clean up?"

"No. It stays tidy around here. I was thinking more about changing clothes."

"I'm in joggers and a hoodie. Do I need to change?"

"Me too, Jason."

"Drop a pin in your location and I'll head out from midtown to get to wherever you are."

I dropped a pin to him in messages and he chuckled.

"Miss Oakley." He paused, that grin widening by the second. "I think we're neighbors."

Chapter Five
JASON

She dropped the pin and I almost fell out of my chair. We weren't more than a 5 minute walk away from each other. I sent her a pin so she knew where I lived, then walked two blocks over, wondering the whole time if I've seen her before and not known it. I wondered how many times I'd passed by her while we were driving. There's nearly no way we could live that close to each other and not have crossed paths at some point.

I knocked on the door of her Craftsman house and could hear her feet running towards the door. She didn't saunter or walk. She definitely ran. The door swung open and there she was.

"Hi neighbor!"

"Hi."

"Welcome home. I mean. Welcome to my home."

I smiled at the sound of her saying welcome home. Damn I couldn't wait until she was my wife. God bless the person who invented joggers for women.

"Thank you!"

"Please come in, Jason."

She snagged my coat and offered me some covers for my shoes. She laughed when I told her I had on clean socks. I was having a hard time grasping the thought that I was not only in her house but that we lived so close to each other. This would either be really good for us, or one of us would need to find another neighborhood.

She grabbed my leftovers and popped them into the toaster oven for a few minutes, warming them back up for me after my chilly walk on this January evening.

"Would you like to eat in the kitchen or by the fire?"

"I'm open to whichever is most comfortable for you. You were already at the table."

"I wasn't dating myself though. Fireside would give you a little ambiance."

"What if we eat at the table and then chat by the fireside afterwards?"

"Sounds like a plan to me."

So we ate at the table and I told her more about how I'd found my way to Kansas City from Maryland.

"It was June of 2008. I'd had a good feeling about things with my then girlfriend. She was my match. I thought we had so many things in common. We were vibin' on the same level. The way she loved me was big. I love hard. We even ate the same breakfast. A solid match, right? So I thought when her job was moving her to Kansas City that we'd survive the distance for a little bit. I found a spot for us to share together where she could stay by herself until I got there. I flew down with her. Helped her move in. Spent the first weekend with her and then flew back to DC. Before I left, she begged me not to go. Said she didn't have a good feeling about being out there. I was gonna be paying half the rent on that space, plus rent for the place I was living in at the time so I had to stay at my job until I could find a gig in KC and move to be with her. Every phone call was the same. She hated the job. She hated the city. She hated the people. "When are you moving?" she'd ask me. She just wasn't happy. I always told her that I'd be there soon. This went on for months. I came home from work one day and she was in my apartment. In DC.

No warning that she was coming. Not even so much as a text the morning of her flight. Just boom - in my space. I was happy to see her and also kind of confused. Turns out she just wanted to feel some sense of normalcy again, so she came back for the weekend. That was a good weekend. She was happy. Things felt like they were back to normal while she was there.

Then tears all over the place when she had to go back. Tears from both of us."

Recalling that made me emotional all over again. I just let the tears roll down my cheeks as I continued to tell Oakley about my trek to Kansas City. She placed her hand on top of mine as I spoke.

"We had a serious talk about marriage on the way to the airport. She didn't want me to propose just because of the move. She asked me instead to move in with her, in the apartment I'd picked out for us in Kansas City. Move all my stuff across country without a job. She told me we were a team and that she could cover us until I found something. I believed her. I submitted my two weeks notice and the company decided to downsize me instead, not because I'd done something wrong, but so they could give me a severance package to help me make the move across the country. Talk about some good people.

So I packed up all my stuff and moved to middle America. We had elected a black president. There was hope. I thought we'd be fine. Turns out there was some stuff she was leaving out. She'd been door knocking for the Obama campaign and some of the neighbors had asked her to deliver their choice words to the then Senator, some even extending their threats to all black people in America. When I moved in, some of their threats subsided, but we realized were living in a complex state - one that elected a Democrat as governor by double digits, but somehow couldn't accept the same campaign promises from President Obama, and instead throwing their votes behind McCain. Their bigotry was on full display and my city girl was caught off guard by all of it. She stayed through his inauguration. But by the time Valentine's Day rolled around in 2009, she announced that she was moving back to DC and she wanted me to follow her. There wasn't a conversation. No discussion. Just, I'm moving.

I don't know if you've had a chance to experience this, but I'm not the running type. Bigots, challenge, change - it's everywhere. I'd already decided that they were gonna have to get used to my ass not moving out of the way for them. So I didn't move back. I found a job to tide me over and eventually one of my friends sent me a position description for an actuary and I've been working for the same company since I applied for that job."

I was just about to tell her the original reason that brought me into The Fresh Grind when she interjected. "I can't believe it. What happened to the two of you?"

"She called me selfish for not moving back with her. It was honestly okay with me. Once I moved in, I realized that a lot of the things that I thought we had in common, we actually did not. She'd just pretended to like the stuff I liked. Later on I found out there was a co-worker of mine in DC that she thought was interested in me. Instead of just talking through it, she tried to control and manipulate me so the other person could see that she was the one I wanted to be with. She was with the person I wanted to be with, but she couldn't see that through her desire to "win" me." I shrugged it off.

Oakley was shaking her head. "I'm sorry you had to experience that, Jason. You've been in Kansas City for a long time now."

"I have." I nodded just thinking about all of the things I'd experienced in the time I'd been in KC. "Distance fades. The heart grows stronger. The longing stops if you're willing to take the lesson and apply it to your life. And - Kansas City kind of grew on me." I looked down at her arm stretched across the kitchen table. Her hand resting on top of mine. That energy made me stand up from my seat to do something else.

Dinner had been finished for quite some time by the time I finished telling her about my cross country journey. I helped her clear our plates from the table and then asked where the bathroom was. By the time I returned, she had set up shop on the floor, by the fireplace, with some oversized pillows. I asked if the plates had been washed yet. When she said no I asked if she'd mind if I washed and dried those first so we could fully relax and talk. She extended a hand in my direction and I helped her up off the floor. I thought she was going to take a turn in the bathroom but she'd asked for help up so she could wash the dishes with me. I washed. She dried and put them away since it was her space and she knew where everything went. I watched closely so I could learn.

She topped off my glass with fresh ice and more water from the pitcher in her fridge, then excused herself to the bathroom. I headed back into the living room to settle into a seat on the couch pretty close to where she had been lounging on the floor.

When she returned from the bathroom, she plopped on the other end of the couch and smiled at me.

"Thank you for this. I didn't see any of this coming today when I woke up."

She spoke softly, "Me either. But I'm glad it did."

"So, are you ready to tell me about Jenson?" I asked. She nodded confidently. I settled into the couch and she struggled to get comfortable. "Do you need one of these big ass jonts from the floor?" She laughed and shook her head no. "Just thought I'd check. You look a little uncomfortable."

"I am. I'm not sure if it's related to what I'm about to share with you or the spot I'm in on the couch. Face to face feels so vulnerable."

"Do you want me to turn around?"

"Can we sit back to back while I tell you this story?"

I didn't say a single word, I just appreciated that she was creating space to share this with me, so I turned around - my back waiting to receive hers. I heard her turn around and felt her scoot closer to me on the couch. I waited for her to prop herself up against me, but she didn't. So I scooched back just a bit until I found her.

"Is this okay?"

"I think we need a pillow," she said before finding a

throw pillow and placing it between the smalls of our backs. "That feel okay?"

"Works for me. Does it feel okay to you?"

She didn't respond right away. Then I heard her giggle.

"Well, now I know who I'm workin with," I said as she laughed even harder. "I had that one coming. You good?"

"I'm good."

"What were we even supposed to be talking about again?" she asked me.

"Jenson."

"Ahh, that's right. Jenson. Where do I start?"

"How about the beginning?"

Chapter Six
OAKLEY

I opened up about Jenson, hoping that doing so would help me release some of what I was still allowing to hold me back.

"He and I had dated since college. We met during our sophomore year at a mixer in the residence halls. I was there with my roommate, Jen, and she kept motioning to this strange guy in a bucket hat.

'What are you doing?' I asked in exasperation.

Giggling an iron-willed call of submission in my direction, she waved at him once more, further solidifying my desire to request another roommate.

'He's coming this way, girl! Get your stuff together,' Jen strained through her toothy grin.

'I'm done with you. Who is that? I can't even see his face past that bucket on his head!' I sighed.

'Excuse me ladies. I couldn't help but notice the two of you from across...'

'Stop it.' There was no way I was letting him finish that statement.

'I'm sorry?' he asked, raising one eyebrow and flashing a crooked smile.

'You have the nerve to come over here and act like you and Jen weren't signing to each other all night. I'm not a fool. Don't try to run game on me,' I insisted, cracking a smile at the two of them.

He laughed with a rumble so deep I thought I could feel it in the pit of my stomach. Turns out, those were the butterflies that always seemed to take flight after he flashed that crooked smile of his. I turned away from him, hoping to hide the flushed look on my own face. I had a sneaking suspicion that this was going to be one of those relationships that would define a pivotal moment for me. I was right.

'Jenson Norris." he said, extending a hand to shake mine. It was warm and firm, yet his touch was soft. So was my heart and we were pretty much inseparable after that.

Football games, watch parties, study sessions, breakfast, lunch and dinner in The Caf, movie nights, casino night, parties in the Union, house parties, Black Student Union meetings, you name it, we were there together. Jenson was my safe place, my home away from home, the first person I would call when I passed a test or struggled with a term paper and he did the same with me.

We spent our Christmases with my family and our New Year's Eves with his. His sister became my sister, and my younger brother looked up to him like he was the best man in the world, often calling him to talk about the game or how to approach a girl he liked at school. It all seemed so natural and easy. We talked often about the type of jobs we would have once we graduated, the type of city or town we would live in, how big our first, second, and third house were going to be, our future children, Kerry and Corbyn, and where we were going to retire for both the warm and cold months. I'd had a bit of anxiety leading up to the end of my senior year because after 3 years of routine, relative safety and contentment, things were going to change. They had to.

The day of our graduation he was more quiet than I've ever seen him. His ceremony was first so our families (his and mine) all went to the coliseum at 8:00 in the morning to cheer as he walked across the stage. We popped over to our favorite hamburger joint, a hidden treasure from the main row of eateries in this college town, for a quick lunch afterward. He was still quiet. The weeks leading up to commencement he had stopped talking about the future. I didn't know what to make of it. All I could do was reassure him where

I stood with respect to our relationship, but it didn't feel like it made a difference to him. So I didn't bring it up when we were at lunch. We just ate and smiled awkwardly at each other, then returned to the coliseum at 2:00 for my ceremony.

I stood with the other graduates in my college and nervously got in line to shake hands with the deans and grab the degree I was merited. The closer I got to the front, the more nostalgic I became. Every step sent me deeper into a spiral of memories until my eyes had glazed over with thoughts of the good and bad moments that I was about to leave behind for true adulthood. Tears began to build in my eyes and I thought about venturing into that world without Jenson.

I remember hearing them announce my name, 'Oakley Powell, Bachelor's of Science Degree, Accounting.' I remember walking confidently across the stage in what felt like slow motion; nodding at the department head, shaking hands with the Dean of the College of Business, hearing my family and Jenson's shouting congratulations, spotting them in the crowd, smiling and waving at them, pausing for a photo, then off the stage. Those ten seconds felt like ten minutes. I can still feel every blink, every inhale, every exhale, the motion as I ambled down every step in my heels, the tug at my heartstrings when I realized that Jenson wasn't sitting with our families, the warmth of the tear that fell from my left eye and coursed its way to the floor, the walk back towards my seat knowing that we were done, the joy I felt in seeing his face as the graduate in front of me turned towards our row, the smile that creased my face from ear to ear and I got closer to him, the moment my heart skipped a beat as he dropped down to one knee and extended a hand to me, the sound of the collective "woo" of the graduates immediately beside us he knelt down, the moment he held my hand while down on bended knee. At that moment, time stood still and though I know there were graduates behind me, I don't remember them passing me at all. I just remember his face, so serious and full of anxiety.

'You and me, Oakley,' he paused, choking down the emotions causing a lump in his throat. 'That's all I've known for the past three years. That's all I've felt each day we're together. That's all I want in the future. You and me, raising Kerry and Corbyn, retiring and spoiling our grandchildren. But I can only have that if you want it too. We can only have that if we work together. Will you take this adventure with me?'

I cried like my dog had died. Suddenly the thoughts I had about everything coming to a close had vanished. They had been replaced with the promise of the future we had crafted together.

'Oakley, will you marry me?'

I couldn't get any words out, but I looked him in the eyes and nodded, sniffling away any potential disaster created by a runny nose.

'I need to hear the word, Oak,' he said with that crooked smile.

I shouted, 'Yes!' The graduates beside us cheered, so too did the crowd to our left after Jenson removed the ring from its black velvet box and slowly slid it over my knuckle and onto my finger.

I was ready to face the world with him. My confidence had been restored.'

I paused briefly when I heard Jason say "awww." I suddenly started critiquing whether or not I had included too many details. He seemed to be really invested in this part of my life.

"Was that all?" he asked, snapping me out of my internal monologue.

"No. Sorry. Jenson had received a job offer in Kansas City that provided enough for him to take care of both of us while I found work. He didn't have to carry me for too long though. I found a job within two weeks of graduation which meant I only had a week between our move and when I started work myself. Since we were now planning a wedding, we shared a place together and also opened a joint bank account. That all made sense at the time, but in hind sight that was probably the worst thing I could have done.

None of what happened next was anticipated. In fact, things had felt the same as they did in college. We'd talk about each other's day, but this time instead of being centered on our classes, discussion was about what we were learning on the job. Mine was going exceedingly well. Just four short months on the job and

I was receiving high praise from my supervisors. They were connecting me to people who would be willing to serve as my mentor, then before I knew it, the bottom fell out.

I had gone out to lunch with a few co-workers for Taco Tuesday and tried to use my debit card to pay (only for my meal mind you) but it was declined. I had them try once more, and again it was declined. Thankfully, I had a co-worker spot me a lunch until I could figure out what was going on with the bank. As we drove back to work I called Jenson to give him a heads up, but he didn't answer the phone. While it wasn't uncommon for him to answer his phone during a workday, that non-answer was actually the start of my downfall. I left him a voicemail and finished the rest of the work day. When I got home I received my third surprise for the day.

As it turns out, Jenson had failed to ever pay the rent on the house we were staying in and I came home to an eviction notice posted on the front door, while my clothes and other belongings were in boxes on the front yard. Tears welled up in my eyes as I tried to figure out what was going on. I called Jenson again, and this time the phone went directly to voicemail. I called my Dad to get his help on what to do and he encouraged me to visit Jenson's job to connect with him and figure out what on earth was going on. I hopped back in my car and hustled across town to his office, where I discovered my fourth surprise for the day. One was tough enough to manage. Two of them were stressful to say the least. Three was about all that I thought I could take, and then that theory would be pushed to its limits. When I arrived at the office I was greeted by the front desk attendant who remembered me to be Jenson's fiancée. His eyebrows turned in towards each other like they were about to give each other a high five. That mystified expression let me know that something was off. I braced for impact as he opened his mouth to speak.

'So, are you applying for Jenson's position or...' he paused waiting for some sort of confirmation.

Now it was time for my eyebrows to fist bump in solidarity. Confusion written all over my face.

'Oh, sorry honey. I assumed he told you about what happened.'

I slow blinked to catch my breath before my knees bucked and I passed out. In chatting with the attendant I was informed that Jenson had been fired from his job 3 months to the day that I showed up.

I booked it over to the bank before they closed and found surprise number five. Jenson had cleaned out our bank account. I sat sobbing in the guest chair in the office of the branch manager and asked what I was able to do.

'I wish I had better news for you honey,' she started. 'With him listed as the head of household on your account there isn't anything that he needs your permission for. The opposite though is true for you.'

'Can I stop my checks from being deposited into the account?' I asked, hoping for some reassurance that they could redirect them into a different account.

'Unfortunately we are unable to do that unless the two of you sign a specific form together to do so.'

I was outdone and so very confused. I thanked her for her time and stood up, realizing in that moment that I was homeless and penniless until my next paycheck hit, which would be another 15 days. I called Jenson's mom. No answer. I called his Dad. No answer. I called his Sister, my sister for the last 3 years. Nothing. I searched for them online and couldn't find any of them. I had been blocked.

I called my Dad with an update and will never forget the words he said to me in that call, 'I know you're thinking the worst in this, be patient until you see what happened.'

I returned to work, the only place I knew of where I could stay in peace. When I arrived, Jerry at our front desk made a phone call with a serious look on his face - one that said I was guilty of something.

'She's here. Yes, I'll hold her.'

I thought this had to be a dream.

'Jerry?' I quivered out through shallow breaths.

'Where's your badge Ms. Powell?'

Before I could finish asking Jerry what was going on, the door to the lobby swung open with a force so hard it hit the wall. Out stepped my supervisor who asked me to sit down.

'We had high hopes for you Oakley. Unfortunately we cannot take the risk to continue your employment with our company.'

'What risks?' I asked, just as confused as I was when my debit card didn't work at lunch.

'We received a note from your fiance requesting the immediate creation of a life insurance policy on you so that he could take out a loan,' she sighed then continued, 'I don't want to tell you how bad that looks, but that you would choose a partner like this also speaks to your level of discernment.'

'He did, what?' another bombshell. It was during this conversation that I felt my soul leave my body.

'Unfortunately in a job where your discernment has an immediate impact on our bottom line, we're going to have to let you go. Security is bringing down a box of your personal belongings. I will need your badge though.'

I could feel the heat from my anger seething through the skin on my face. I was beyond hot, and embarrassed, and because I no longer had a soul, my heart went to a really petty place and just hung out there for a spell. I had been an empty shell ever since, hopping from person to person, and job to job in an attempt to fill my life up with meaning again. Then along came Charlie, who was pretty much the exact opposite of Jenson and I thought I needed him in my life to feel like I was worthy of the type of love I thought I had with Jenson. I should've been honest with Charlie from jump. I thought I fell in love with him but I think I fell in love with the idea of him. He didn't deserve what I did to him."

Jason, dropped his head backwards onto mine and suddenly I realized we were rocking from side to side. I told him that I couldn't tell if I was moving or if he was. "It's me. Just trying to provide some comfort," he said before quietly asking a question that burned me in my gut. "What did you do to him Miss Oakley?"

Oof. What did I do to him? It wasn't anything I could escape. I mean I had just admitted to doing something to him but it felt different entirely when someone asks you what you did to another person, especially a person as good-hearted as Charlie.

"Well, I had received an email from the man who disappeared without a trace and with all of my money.

It read:

Oak,

I know I'm the last person you probably expected to hear from. I can explain, but we need to talk about it in person. Let me know when you're free to talk and if you have the same phone number.

I'm sorry,
Jenson

An email, from Jenson. Charlie and I had talked about what happened in my last relationship. He knew I was engaged. He knew that Jenson disappeared without a trace or so much as a word. We both thought that I had received closure, but the way I felt after that email said I didn't. I wanted an answer. I deserved an answer. I couldn't bring myself to tell Charlie about it. I just wanted to confront Jenson, find out what happened, get it over with and move on.

I replied:

Jenson. My phone number is the same. Call me at 8:00pm tonight to get an address of where we can meet. It will be a public place so I am not tempted to seek revenge.

Oakley

Before I could close my email app, I received a reply. Will do.

I timed my work break for 7:58 so I could have enough time to find a quiet spot to listen. My phone rang right at 8 o'clock. I didn't recognize the phone number, but I knew the only person who would be calling at that time was Jenson.

'Yes?' I answered firmly.

'Oak. I'm sorry.' It sounded like he truly was, but I had placed a wall around my heart when it came to Jenson.

'Meet me at The Fresh Grind Coffeehouse anytime between now and 10:00pm. I'm at work.'

'Tonight?'

'Yep. Tonight or not at all.' I hung up.

I went back to work behind the counter. That call took all of 2 minutes. Twenty minutes later the door to the coffeehouse opened up and I knew it was him. His eyes scanned the entirety of the coffeehouse in search of me. I motioned for him to get in line to place an order.

'Could I have a large coffee? Black.'

"Uh oh. Maybe I should start asking for oat milk," Jason joked as he reached back to hold my hand through the telling of the rest of this ridiculously long story. I couldn't figure out why I felt so comfortable telling him all the grisly details. It definitely didn't show me in my best light. But for whatever reason I wanted him to know.

"Please don't change your order for that dolt, sir. The barista prepared his coffee and Jenson paid at the register, looking me dead in my eyes without saying a word, only a nod and a $10 tip. I motioned with my head towards a booth in the back of the coffeehouse. The rage that I imagined I would feel was non existent. Instead I was filled with curiosity.

He sat in the back, nursing his coffee and every so often glancing my way. Once things slowed down, I meandered my way back to his booth and sat down.

'Talk.'

'You look good, Oak.'

'Not that. You don't get to...'

'I'm sorry. I wish I could have. Pause. I wish I would have told you what was going on with me before I left.'

I looked at him stone-faced, guarding my heart.

He shared everything that happened in his words. He was blackmailed by someone who got him fired and then asked for more money than we had available. He thought he would be able to get a new job, but found out that his name had been blackballed in his industry. He told me that he had instructed his family not to answer any calls from me, so that he would have time to fix things. I listened and believed him. That one-time visit to explain what happened turned into regular drop-ins to see how I was doing. Before I knew it we had reconnected and things began to escalate. You know how you exercise and lose weight, then when you stop exercising your weight comes back ten-fold in far less time than it took for you to lose the weight to begin with? It was like that. It all happened so fast that I didn't have time to tell Charlie about it, at least that's what I told myself."

I could feel the emotions stirring up inside my soul as I started retelling this part. I hadn't really told this part to anyone other than my therapist and my Daddy.

Jason, still as sensitive and as understanding as ever asked, "Is it okay if I turnaround?"

"Mmm hmm," I offered, feeling more confident that I could look him in the eye and tell him about what happened. I sat upright and rotated my body in his direction as I felt him do the same. He moved the pillow from between us and stretched out his legs, then scooted off the couch and onto the floor with the floor pillows. His back leaned up against the couch and arm stretched across the cushions, he tapped me on my leg and motioned for me to join him on the floor. I sat mostly beside him, my back slightly overlapping part of his chest. He reeled me into his grasp and pressed his face against mine for a few seconds.

"So, you told yourself you didn't have time to tell Charlie about it?" he asked, prompting me to finish telling the story.

"Uh huh. I fell into a pattern where I would tell myself that I'd talk to Charlie that night, then that night we would talk about the future and he would look at me with the same gaze from New Year's Eve. Then I couldn't bring myself to hurt him. About a week before Christmas, Jenson picked me up on my lunch break and surprised me with a trip to a jeweler. We were "just looking" at rings when he asked the jeweler to size the one that I wanted. As the jeweler came in from the back, in walked Charlie. I was still beaming from the shock of Jenson's surprise when I turned and saw his face.

'Mr. Hughes! I have your ring in the back. Just let me finish sizing this couple's ring really quickly and I'll grab it for you,' he said to Charlie before turning to Jenson and I to chat about the selection waiting in the back. 'This guy must REALLY love his woman! Three carats, this guy!'

'Congratulations, my man!' Jenson said, genuine excitement flowing from his lips. I squeezed him to stop him, in hopes of communicating to him that this was Charlie, my Charlie. His face was devoid of emotion. It looked like someone had ripped his soul from his body, just as had been done to me. Unwittingly I had just put him through the same thing as I felt because I couldn't be honest with him when I received the email.

He stormed out of the jewelry shop before I could say anything. I tried to follow him, but I still had the freshly resized ring on my finger. I tugged and tugged, but it had cooled around my finger and I couldn't get it off quickly enough. By the time I could, Charlie was gone, out of my life for good. I tried to call him. I sent emails that bounced back to my account. I sent unreturned texts. I hoped he would come see me at work so I could explain myself, especially since it wouldn't be a good idea for me to show up at his school. I had become the very person I loathed, just a few months before. I owed Charlie an explanation, but most of all I owed him some space. The space to be hurt, to be angry, to hate me, to miss me, to want an answer.

I owed him all of that, no matter how much time it took, and no matter how much I wanted to explain it now. So I gave Charlie time and space, and he didn't return.

I never fully believed Jenson, I only wanted to feel like I was still special to him. So the thing that broke up Charlie and I, ended up being a flash in the continuum of time and not even worth the energy I gave it in the first place.

I had a hole in my soul again, but this time, I had done it to myself. That's what happened with Jenson and Charlie. I've forgiven myself for what I did to Charlie, but allowing Jenson to hold so much space in my mind has taken its own toll on me."

He exhaled deeply, his body softened. His head tilted on top of mine but he didn't say a word.

Chapter Seven
JASON

I was stunned into silence. I had been trying my best to hold it together while she was speaking. She'd dropped so much on me all at once. She'd had her heart shattered into a million pieces by a man who was incapable of loving her. She'd cheated on her last guy with the man who broke her heart. I understood it from a human perspective - wanting to be wanted, but she made the choice out of so much pain. All of that was terrible and heart wrenching and I was amazed at how poised she was as she told the story. Then it struck me. The story had felt familiar as she was telling it and in a flash of understanding I realized it was because my friend told me about the reason my current position had become available. There was a high probability that I had stepped in to fill the position she had been asked to vacate. And she STILL didn't know the real reason that took me in to see her on Small Business Saturday. In about 30 seconds time I realized there's a delicate line that I was gonna have to walk while I told her. Not only might it send her back to that moment in time, but I'd also be inextricably linked to her in the timeline of her broken heart - as the one who took her job.

I wasn't ready for that. It didn't matter how sure I was that I was gonna marry this woman. I still had to treat this situation with kid gloves. I was processing all of this internally when I realized that I hadn't said anything at all after she'd just shared one of the most personal parts of her story.

"Oakley, I know it took a lot to share that with me. Thank you."

She didn't say anything. Only bowed her head in response. Suddenly her head fell on my shoulder and I could feel her body begin to quake. I knew she was crying. I didn't need to look at her to see that much.

Her face was close so I didn't need much volume. "What do you need?"

She continued to shudder and wrapped as much of herself around my arm as physically possible. Still no words, but that didn't mean she hadn't sent a message. So we sat, on the floor, all snuggled up beside the fire until she no longer needed me. Without words my senses worked overtime. Her soft curls smelled like sweet potato pie. Her oversized hoodie smelled of her spicy perfume. I don't know why I called it spicy. It had notes of cinnamon or ginger, or maybe both, mixed with some cardamom and black pepper plus some sort of citrus and a hint of vanilla.

Deliciously spicy, and it took everything in me not to kiss her forehead in that moment. This was not the time, even though she had us sitting by the fire, to do anything other than support her as a friend.

She'd already admitted to feeling like she wasn't sure she should be dating right now. I couldn't make this a romantic situation. It didn't matter how much warmth I had in my heart for her. I could know where we're headed from my perspective, but putting her in a position she's already said she doesn't want at the moment would be flat out wrong. So I needed to hold tight to everything that was inside of me.

Now no one should live with words unsaid, so I knew at some point I'd have to tell her everything. But this, this was not that point in time.

Instead I just held her. Poured my unconditional love into her through touch. I was present in the moment as I stared into the flames that jumped and played in the fireplace.

Her voice was warbled as she broke the silence, "Jason." She cleared her throat and called my name again, "Jason."

"Yes, Miss Oakley?"

"I'm sorry."

"For what?"

"For cheating on him." The remorse that hung out in her tone was thick. "I never meant to hurt him."

"Did you ever get a chance to tell him that?"

Her voice, a near whisper, "Yes."

"Good. I'm sure he appreciated it."

One good cleansing breath escaped her body. "I hope so," she said, her body starting to lose its tension. We sat in silence for a few minutes, breathing together, holding each other.

"Oakley?"

"Yes, Jason?"

"You made sure I was well hydrated during dinner."

She chuckled. "Do you need me to move so you can use the bathroom again?"

"I don't want you to move because I'm thoroughly comfortable right now. But if I don't, we'll have an entirely different situation to deal with." Humor worked every time. I got the chance to see her face light up again as she leaned over, both in laughter and to give me the chance to stand and head towards el baño.

When I returned, she was still on the floor, a blanket draped around her shoulders. She looked up at me with eyes that looked like they were asking to be accepted. I leaned over, kissed her widow's peak and thanked her on my way back to the floor.

"Are you cold or tired?" I asked.

"I'm emotionally drained but not tired. The blanket is for security and comfort. I'm a regular Linus over here."

"I see," I said while making a face as I waited for her to suck her thumb.

"No I'm not a thumb sucker," she said and paused, like she was alluding to something. I wasn't touching it. Under different circumstances I would've fed right into it. But not today. Not after she shared what she just shared. No. No. No. No. No.

"Mmhm," I said.

She was feeling vulnerable. I could see it all over her face as she leaned in closer to me and draped the blanket on my shoulders.

"Oh, this is one of those weighted jonts." Its heft caught me off guard. "I can see why people sleep better with these."

"Are YOU getting tired?" she asked me, scootching in a little closer.

"I'm here as long as you need me tonight. I'll pull from whatever energy reserve I need to so I can be here for you." She grinned up at me. There was that twinkle in her eyes again. It was almost mischievous.

"Thank you, Jason. Can I get you anything?"

I scratched my neck and started twitching. "Actually, yeah." I waited for her to ask.

"Whatcha need?"

I amplified the twitching and scratching, "You got any of them sugarplums?"

She bolted from the floor into the kitchen. "Actually I do!" She opened up what looked like a tall cabinet door and then disappeared inside. I was curious so I stood up and followed her in there.

"What in the magic snack pantry is this?!" She hadn't heard me follow her into the kitchen and I startled the jar of sugarplums right out of her hand.

"Good gravy, Jason. You scared the bejeezus outta me!" she said as she picked up the jar from the floor.

"Oh no! Not the bejeezus. How do we put it back in you?" There was that smile again. Then she laughed, with her entire body. Her head tilted back behind her. Eyes closed. One hand protecting her heart, the other soothing her contracting abs. She doubled forward and heaved for air.

"Here's your sugarplums good sir. Now pardon me while I take a trip to the bathroom. I think you might've made me pee a little bit." I hadn't seen that one coming. Now it was my turn to double over in laughter. I stepped out of the pantry and out of her way - apologizing as she ran by. The only thing I'd hoped was for her to feel comfortable in my presence. Safe to say I think she did. I didn't know where to go to wait for her. If she needed to change into something else I didn't want her to feel ashamed or like she had to hide anything. So I stayed in the kitchen. The door to the pantry still open. My eyes locked on the number of sugarplum options she had stashed away inside the space that couldn't have been more than 4 feet wide, wire racks that ran part of the way up one of the long walls and the wall opposite the door.

The actuary in me hoped that she didn't make those here at home and then take them into the coffeeshop. The risk started automatically tallying up in my head. That reminded me that I still needed to tell her about my first visit. I was so lost in thought trying to figure out how to tell her with care, that I missed her re-entry into the kitchen.

She cleared her throat as she was all leaned up on the door frame. The hoodie was the same but she had changed into some running shorts. I dropped the jar of sugarplums onto the floor.

"I don't think these want to be eaten today," I told her.

"Should we get you some different ones?" she asked. I didn't respond. I was too busy trying to distract myself from lookin at her curves. She walked right past me leaving a scented trail for me to follow back into the pantry. "How about some top shelf ones?" she said as she balanced on her tip toes and tried to grab them herself. The running shorts. Sheesh.

Internally, I started to recite The Lord's Prayer.

Our father,

She stretched even further trying to grab a new jar of sugarplums to replace the ones we'd already dropped twice.

Who art in heaven,

Another stretch, her hoodie raised just above the waist of her shorts.

Hallowed be Thy name,

"Jason, can you come help me?" that damn frisky twinkle was back in her eye and I was in trouble. I could feel it coming.

Thy Kingdom come,

I took one step closer to her, my back to the shelves. I tilted my head back to see what she'd been trying to grab and there was nothing up there. Literally nothing on the shelf.

Thy will be done...

I felt her step in front of me. Sweet potato pie and spicy perfume. My. My. My. My head lowered and I watched as she pointed to the top shelf, those big beautiful eyes that I just wanted to swim in looked me over. "What do you need?" I whispered into her ear. Eyes closed, feeling out the moment with my energy.

Thy will be done...

I'd forgotten the rest of The Lord's Prayer. She leaned closer, her face resting against mine and whispered, "The sugarplums - from the top shelf."

Thy will be done...

I wrapped my arm around her waist like we were dancing and spun us around inside the tight pantry. Her back was now against the shelves, my body sandwiched her in. "What shelf are they on?" I asked as her chest began to heave with each labored breath she took.

Thy will be done...

She wrapped her fingers around the nape of my neck. "The top shelf, Jason," she said before she slowly pulled my face in for a kiss. I didn't know up from down. I didn't know left from right. I was completely discombobulated as she pulled me into her world.

Thy will be done...

I wasn't thinking straight. I had to tell her first. I couldn't continue to suck on those supple lips. I had to tell her. She was going to hate me, but I had to tell her.

Thy will be done...

"Mmmmmiss Oakley." I tried to stop but I couldn't pull away. We were like magnets, stuck to each other for the moment.

"Shit Jason" I could feel her smile while she kissed me and it felt so good.

"mmmm MmmHmm?" I whimpered. Instinct began to kick things up a notch as I placed the twice fallen jar on the shelf and let my hand caress her face while we continued to neck in the pantry. Why were we in the pantry?

"I know what I need," she said as her hand traced down my spine.

Thy will be done...

I forced myself to be attentive as she spoke. "What's that Miss Oakley?" I asked her as I placed my hands on her shoulders and created a bit of physical space between us. She bit down on her lower lip. "What is in this pantry?" I asked her. "Something's got us all worked up. Is it the sugarplums?"

"Jason, I need..." I looked at her, begging her with my eyes not to say what I thought she was going to say. I placed a finger up to her mouth before she could finish that thought.

"Can we step outside the pantry first please?" She nodded and followed me out - our fingers laced between each other's.

On Earth as it is in Heaven.

"Thank you," she said as she fidgeted with the pocket of her hoodie. I nodded.

"Give us this day, our daily bread." I said aloud.

"Were you reciting The Lord's Prayer in there?" she chuckled.

I nodded again and scratched the back of my head, "Yeah but I got stuck on, 'Thy will be done.'"

She leaned in and kissed me again, leading me backwards out of the kitchen and into the living room. "Couch or floor?" she asked me between breaths.

"I'm sorry, what?"

"How are you this cute? Couch or floor?" she asked again.

"You choose," I said, then watched her spread a blanket on the floor and have a seat.

I sat down on the couch.

"Jason - " she started

"Yes ma'am?" I asked, my arms folded across my chest, trying to restrain myself.

"I need you."

Chapter Eight
OAKLEY

He didn't say anything. Just took one massive gulp of air and swallowed it. I'd just told him that I needed him and he didn't say anything. I felt so vulnerable. Naked and exposed. I needed his help. I needed his patience. I needed his heart. I needed his love. He'd shown me all of that in one short evening as we continued our date and I knew I didn't want to live my life without him.

"Jason. If it's too much for one night, we can call it."

Still nothing. He just stared at me and I was having a hard time deciphering his facial expression.

"Jason?"

"Miss Oakley. I have something I need to tell you before you kick me out of your house."

That sounded serious and I didn't know what to do with it. And yet somehow, I wanted him now more than ever.

"I'm listening." He inched closer to me and sat down on the floor.

"Promise you'll let me get this out. Don't kiss me until I finish, okay? Then you can decide what to do next."

"Scouts' honor," I told him.

"You've just shared a lot of very personal stuff with me and I want to honor that. Part of what you shared is that you were in love with the idea of Charlie because you were in a space where you wanted to be wanted. I understand how you could feel like that after the way you were mishandled by Jenson. Sharing what I'm sure was probably kept close to your heart might leave you feeling a bit exposed. Naked. Vulnerable even, maybe? All with good reason if you're feeling like that. What I don't want is for the two of us to enter into a relationship when you're in a similar state to when you first met Charlie. Before I came over tonight you mentioned that you weren't sure you should've been dating yet. I respect that too. So, if I need to wait a while for date two, I can do that. However long it takes, I'll wait. You don't have to worry about rushing through the process before someone else comes into the picture because I don't want anyone else. I want to earn my way into your life - the right way. So if we need to just be friends for a while - not friends with benefits, just friends that hang out sometimes, I can do that. Also, I need to tell you about something else."

"No more Jason. Stop." He was right. He had named every emotion I was feeling.

"No, I have one more thing."

"No - you're right. I definitely feel all of those things right now. I'm also magnetically attracted to your soul."

"Come here," he said as he reached out for my hand and nudged me to come closer to him.

"Let me finish, Jason." I said as he nodded. "You know me and I know you. I know you can feel it. I can see it in your eyes. You look at me like you're just waiting for me to figure it out."

He grinned.

"I figured it out, okay? I see you. I've seen you since you came in on Small Business Saturday."

"That's what I wanted to talk about."

"I'm not finished, sir." I watched him sit up and pay attention. A mix of love, passion and intrigue filled his face before I continued, "You feel like home and I don't know why. That's not the same thing I experienced with Charlie. I need you to understand that I feel the difference."

"I feel you."

"Do you?"

"I want to."

I studied his face. I didn't know how to shush the internal dialogue that was calling on me to attend to *all* of my needs. Instead I just wanted to follow it and see where it took us.

"Damn. Tell me how you really feel."

His head cocked to the side, he whispered, "Come here."

It was like a call of the wild. I sat beside him, shoulder to shoulder. I lowered my head to the shoulder nearest me and he dropped his on top of mine.

I whispered back to him, "I need you, Jason."

"You can't be whispering that kinda thing in my ear without some clarity." I giggled.

"You know what I mean."

"I do not want to make that kind of assumption. I don't even know your middle name yet."

"It's —"

"Aht! Don't you say it. I still have 4 dates to go before I earn it," he said to me. "Let me earn it Miss Oakley!"

"You have 3 dates to go."

"I thought this was a continuation of the first date."

"That was a bad date. Let's leave it by itself. Let this one be a do over."

"A do over of date one, right."

"No, date two."

His warm laugh made me smile and filled my soul with light. I whispered into his ear, "Jason."

He whispered back, "All this whispering into my ear is gonna start something that I don't think we're quite ready for yet. If you don't knock it off I'm gonna have to go home."

I whispered again, "Take me with you."

He blushed, "One of these days. Not tonight though." He stood up and asked if I could walk him out. According to the clock it was nearing midnight. I grabbed his coat and draped it across my shoulders. I could smell his musk and cologne combo on it and it wasn't doing us any favors.

He stepped back and looked at me in his coat, "I think it looks better on you than it does on me." I laughed softly. "You know what? This cold air might be about the same as a cold shower tonight. Hold onto that for me?"

"Jason, no - it's too cold for that. You need to put something on."

He shook his head. "I'll be fine. It's less than 5 minutes

and if I'm cold I'll walk even faster."

He kissed me on my widow's peak again. That's what set me off the first time. It was such a nurturing kiss. I felt seen and understood when he did it the first time. And this time when he did it, it felt like, "I'll be back."

"Please text me when you make it home."

He did me one better and shared his location with me.

"I'll see you soon, okay?" he said. I nodded.

He stepped outside and waved as I closed the door behind him and immediately began to watch him on my phone. He made it to the end of my street and made a left. He walked two streets down then made another left onto his street. I stopped watching my phone and walked into the kitchen instead, peeking into the pantry and reminiscing while I snuggled up in his coat. I placed my hands in the pockets and felt something jingle. I said a quick prayer that he had a second set in his joggers or another type of entry, because I definitely had his keys in this coat.

I looked down at my phone to see his location. His dot was moving quickly back towards my street. I opened the front door just as he ran around the corner. He stopped and slowly looked around at his surroundings. He looked bewildered as he gazed towards the house, but he didn't move. I motioned for him to come back but he still didn't move. I ran outside to grab his hand and guided him into the house. He was shivering as I propped the door open for him to come inside. I pulled him in as close to my body as possible and locked the door. I walked him near the fireplace and asked him to sit down on the floor. I ran some hot water in the kitchen sink and filled a bottle with it. I handed it to him and asked him to hold onto it so his fingers could warm up. He nodded through his shivers.

"When I opened the door I had just found your keys in the pocket." He nodded. "Jason, you're still shivering. This hoodie is freezing cold. It's not gonna warm you up. You need outta these clothes."

He looked at me and shook his head no.

"Hypothermia sound better to you?" I asked him.

He shook his head no again.

"Will you let me help you please?" This time he nodded yes.

I raised his hoodie over his head and found that the t-shirt he was wearing underneath had been partially covered in sweat - likely from his run back towards my house. It's exactly what was keeping him so cold.

"Jason, I need to take this off too. Let me grab a towel for you."

"I don't need a towel, just take it off," he said through clattering teeth. I peeled his t shirt off and set it to the side.

"How are your feet and legs?" I asked and watched him

shake his head no. I took that as a "not good" and unlaced his boots and removed his socks, then took off his joggers so the heat from the fireplace could get directly to his skin.

Turns out that was a "no, please don't take my joggers off for another good reason" - one that I didn't discover until I sat on his lap to share my body heat with him.

He whispered, "I'm sorry."

"No, don't. Just lean in. Let me warm you up."

"Too late," he joked.

"Jason, no humor right now. I'm really worried about you."

He rested his head against my neck and I could feel the cold transfer begin. I was still wearing his coat so I had become a human incubator of sorts. My backside felt like it was cookin', but after a couple of minutes the trembling stopped. I looked down to make sure he was still breathing. Our breaths had synced. He looked up at me and nodded.

"Are you okay?" I asked him.

"Yeah - thank you."

"I'm so glad. You scared me."

"I see. I'm sorry. I should've -"

"Stop. Don't. Just keep thawing out."

"Oakley"

"No. Don't say anything, Jam."

"Just let me speak. I almost slipped into a hypothermic coma!"

"That's definitely not a thing." I chuckled.

"It's a thing, but maybe I wasn't that far gone yet."

"You're still cold. Stay close to me."

"Is this real life?"

"Mmm hmm"

"I'm not dreaming?"

I pinched his arm. "Could you feel that?"

"Barely."

I ran my fingers across his chest. "Can you feel this?"

"Hmmm. Sorry."

"I guess we got our answer."

"Did you really just save my life?"

"No. Stop it."

"How's this for a first date story?"

"You're on the third date, sir."

"Am I?"

"Can we kiss on the third date?"

"When we're both fully clothed and not loopy from a near hypothermic coma, yes."

He paused, brandishing a sheepish smile, "Hand me my sweats."

"Uhh no. They're still cold, Jason." He set the bottle of warm water beside us on the floor and wrapped his arms around me.

"Hey."

"Hmm?"

"Thank you."

"Anytime neighbor."

He held on so gently. His touch, so tender. "I guess you got your way, huh?"

"Indirectly. But I'd much rather not have to worry about hypothermia. Why did you go out there without a coat?"

"I thought I'd be okay and I was almost all the way back to the house. I didn't start to get cold until I hit my porch. I tried the keyless entry. It malfunctioned. Then I was cold and I realized that you had my keys. I tried to get back as fast as I could."

"That's when you started running?"

"Yeah. That was probably the worst thing I could've done because my body started sweating."

"Oh, Jason."

"When you came out to grab me I was so confused. I couldn't figure out why I was on this street. I couldn't figure out how I was looking at you..."

"I could tell."

"...in my coat."

"When I thought you were in trouble, I received confirmation of just how much you mean to me." I asked Siri to play some music and Bridge Over Troubled Water came on. I teared up and lowered my forehead to his.

His kiss was soft and reassuring.

"I'm okay, Miss Oakley," he said. I kissed him again so he could feel how much he meant to me. "Shit. I'm no good for making rational decisions right now. You're gonna have to stop us."

I continued to kiss him and let things escalate.

"Please just wait." His insistence halted me. "I don't want the first time to be linked to trauma, Oakley. I know it's gonna be beautiful. I want us both to fully enjoy it."

I smiled at him and nodded. We were caught in another gaze and I saw another twinkle in his eye. "Your pupils sir."

"I can't help it. I...mmm, I'll tell you soon." I couldn't say anything. I just cried some more.

"Soon?"

"Mmhm. Promise."

One more kiss of reassurance from Jason and I knew the coat had to come off. I turned off the fireplace and helped him up off the floor. I hooked his pointer finger with mine and guided him into the bedroom.

Chapter Nine
JASON

"You can sleep in here tonight. I'll sleep on the couch." That's what she told me, then tried to ease out of the room.

I still had a hold of her finger. I wouldn't let her walk out of the room without a quick tug. "I'm not completely thawed out yet. Will you cuddle with me?"

"We're just cuddling?" she asked me innocently. It was a fair question. In hindsight I probably should've just tried to finish the date on facetime and planned for something else. But I didn't. Now I'm standing in my skivvies asking her to cuddle with me through the night.

She nodded and offered me a spare toothbrush. I washed my face and brushed my teeth, then returned to the bedroom where she was already waiting for me. She had changed into flannel pants and an old t-shirt and I felt like I was at a severe disadvantage.

"Does it get cold during the night?"

"Why do you ask, Jason?"

"You're wearing flannel pajama pants, ma'am."

"I'm trying to be good, that's all. I don't have anything that will fit you. Your clothes are still a little damp so probably not a good idea to sleep in those. That means you have to sleep in the boxers. So I have to modify my nighttime attire so I don't put us in a compromising position."

I chuckled at how thoughtful she'd been and the way my mind was set up late at night. "It's past midnight, which means I'm a little bit loopy so forgive me in advance," I said. "I don't think the clothes you wear will dictate what we do. Honestly it's just more to remove."

She laughed and covered her face. "You are loopy, aren't you?"

"Maybe just a little bit. Is that a problem?"

"Absolutely not."

"Okay good."

"Big spoon or little spoon?"

"Well, considering that I almost froze, I think I need

your body heat on my vital organs."

"Loopy."

"So, BIG SPOON ME!"

"Wait, you want me to be the big spoon or the little spoon."

"I'm the big spoon."

"Okay, well it's time for bed."

"Yep. Here we are."

"Jason, is this gonna be okay? I have extra blankets and the couch is super comfy. I really can sleep out there."

"No ma'am. Come warm me."

"You need to close your eyes sleepy man."

I giggled like a 7 year old boy laughing at a fart joke.

"They're closed."

"Good night, sir."

"Good night, ma'am."

"Little Spoon me!!" she shouted, mocking my loopy blurt from a few minutes prior.

I buried my face into her hair and tried to take in the scent.

"What are you doing?"

"You smell good. I'm just trying to soak it up while you're near." She eyed me suspiciously. "We're closer to the morning now. It'll be time to get up before you know it."

"Good night, Jason."

"Good night, Miss Oakley."

I wrapped my arm around her waist and pulled her in close, wasting not an inch of space between us. She felt so good in my arms. So natural. This felt like our 100th night together instead of the first.

"Does it feel like we've done this before to you?" she asked me.

"I was just laying here thinking that."

"You were?"

"I was."

"Why are you still awake?"

"Because even though it feels like the 100th time, it's just the first and I want to remember everything about it."

The moonlight shone through the sheer window coverings and I found myself even more attracted to her as her face bathed in the delicate and moody blue rays of the moon.

She whispered, "Jason" into my ear and my soldier saluted. I backed up a bit to give her some space but she eased back into me as soon as I moved.

"I'm trying to remember everything about tonight too. Just be. It's okay. The body does what it's meant to do. Trust me."

"Are you trying to tell me something?"

"Go to sleep."

"Ha ha. Okay Miss Oakley. Good night." It was the last thing I remember saying to her before closing my eyes for two minutes and waking up as the sun began to rise.

Chapter Ten
OAKLEY

I blinked my eyes rapidly and tried to piece together the difference between the dream state I was leaving and my current reality. The grogginess was thicker today than normal, an indication that I'd slept particularly well the night before. I felt protected and covered.

There was an atypical heft around my waist. Before I could blink myself fully awake, I realized that the newfound heft belonged to a person. A random arm, wrapped around my waist. I continued to blink rapidly to see if I could become coherent enough to figure out why there was an arm that didn't belong to me holding me close.

I could feel his breath, its rise and fall easy - not labored. The fingers reached for mine and intertwined themselves. Their gentle grasp, familiar. Home. I didn't even realize it, but I heaved an exhale.

He whispered, "You awake?"

I nodded, knowing exactly who was behind me, holding me through the morning light. It was his energy, so warm. Home. That Mystery Man. Suddenly the events of the night before came flooding back to my mind. He had scared me so badly. I thought hypothermia was about to set in. Without any warning, I loved him with my entire being and now here he was laying in my bed - mostly naked. The warmth had definitely been restored to his body.

Still whispering, "Good morning."

The shockwaves that rolled through my body actually made me quake right into him. He giggled, "Be careful there ma'am. You okay?"

I laughed, "I am. How about you? How are you feeling this morning?"

He nuzzled his face into my neck and mumbled, "mmmguuud"

"Now what now?" I joked.

He backed away, "I'm good. All thawed out."

I rolled over to sneak a peek at his face. His eyes seemed to ask if it was okay that he was laying in my bed in this moment. I was so glad to see him alive and kicking.

He smiled as he looked down at my face, "Hi."

Damn, those dimples. "Mmmm. Good morning, sir."

He ran his hand across the top of my hair, smoothing out my bed head, then closed his eyes and lowered his forehead to mine. It was such a peaceful way to begin the morning.

"I'm sorry about last night," he spoke softly.

"What do you mean?" I asked quietly.

"I didn't mean to worry you like that. I didn't mean to create a situation where I ended up half naked in your bed." He chuckled.

I didn't say anything, only nodded.

"How early do you need to get up to open the cafe?"

"I should've been up a few hours ago, Jason."

"Oh no. Let's get up then!"

"Two more minutes, Jam?"

"As much as I'd love that, I have a coffee date at this cute little corner restaurant that I need to keep."

"Oh? Who's the luck coffee date?" I snickered.

"The most beautiful woman in the world," he said as he nuzzled noses with me.

"She must be pretty amazing for you to be so excited this early in the morning, Jason."

"I mean, she aight. She does make me laugh though."

"Is that important to you?"

"The utmost. If we can't laugh together, how the heck are we gonna handle all the hard shit?"

"Damn."

"I want us to inspire more joy in each other."

"I love that."

"Okay? So you feel me? Let's get up and start the day then."

"So you can go off on your coffee date?"

"Yes ma'am. Can you get up first though? I don't exactly have any pants on."

I couldn't help but laugh at his response. I slid out of the bed and headed towards the bathroom, sifting through about 5 different plans that could give him an excuse to exit without feeling any sort of guilt or hard feelings. Nothing happened. Just two emotionally exhausted people resting in the comfort of each other's company. There really wasn't anything for him to worry about. Or me for that matter. I didn't want him to walk home thinking that I didn't enjoy his company. That feeling of home just kind of lingered and I found myself thinking about his touch, the way he'd held me so tenderly. Suddenly there was a knock on the bathroom door.

"I'll be out in a minute," I called to him.

"No need to rush. I'm gonna head back to my place to handle business. I'll give you a call a little later, okay?"

"Okay."

"I'll see you soon, Miss Oakley."

"See you soon, Jason."

I'd done all of that worry-warting for nothing. He was gone without so much as a hug. I knew I needed to get my head back in the game. I was a couple of hours behind schedule and The Fresh Grind was waiting for me. Sometimes owning the business was exhausting, even though I knew it was worth it in the long run. In a perfect world, I would've been able to sleep in and play hooky with Jason today. But there's only this world, the one we exist in within this moment, so thinking about the "wouldn't it be," felt a little bit like self-torture. Nothing I want for myself.

I got cleaned up and headed off to work. Walking into the shop only about 30 minutes later than normal I felt a rush of pride. Most of the extra time I was missing that morning was taken from exercise and moving at a more leisurely pace. Enjoying the morning was important to me because the days were so long. So while I was missing it today, I knew I'd be sure to incorporate more intentional time tomorrow. Fortunately for me, our end of day rituals also include a bit of set up for today. The only thing left for me to do was a quick check of the inventory, making sure the trash bins were empty and readying the staff for any abnormal scheduling - events, etc. There was none of that planned for the week, so we were basically ready to open. I took a few things back to my office then hung out in the back until it was the time to flip the sign. Right on time I found my way to the front and unlocked the door. Our first customer walked in just after I turned the sign to open.

"Good morning, Miss Oakley."

Chapter Eleven
JASON

I was glad she made her way to the bathroom. It gave me a chance to hustle back to my house and get cleaned up without extending the chances of us skipping work today. Waking up with her in my arms felt a little too natural and I was ready to wake like that for an eternity. I didn't want to scare her away though, so when I got the chance to say goodbye through the door and slide out, I took it.

I put my coat on and walked back towards the house. The world felt so much bigger in that moment. So much space to explore. So many opportunities to find. Anything felt possible in that short window of time, and I soaked it up, every second of that brisk walk down the street and around the corner.

I took my time getting ready, being sure to feel the moment - the excitement I felt knowing that we'd found each other again. I just knew that we'd spent lifetimes with each other before. And there she was again. I was so grateful when she said she felt it too, otherwise I was gonna have to be extra patient while she figured it out.

I hopped in the shower and let the warm water soak through my bones, while my favorite podcast played. Then I layered up for the day, cologne, thermals, work clothes, thick socks and boots. Winter coat. It was supposed to reach a high of 50, but it was only 20 degrees to start the day. Typical midwestern temperature swing from what I could tell. I grabbed my keys, sipped my pregame coffee - two creams, one sugar, then hopped in my car to start the day.

It was Monday so I made my way down to observe the client I'd been observing for the last two weeks. I knew if things were going anywhere between us that I needed to tell her today. I'd been trying for the last few days but she wasn't listening to me. *She didn't hear me when I was trying to tell her that I was the guy who'd been emailing her.* But today would be different. I could feel it. The odds were in my favor.

I was the first customer of the day. She'd just flipped the sign around and turned her back to walk away before I got to the door.

"Good Morning Miss Oakley," I called to her as I opened the door.

She lit up like the New Year's Eve decorations that still adorned the coffee shop and I was so glad to see that gorgeous face. Peace calmed the nerves that had started to rise to the surface and I stepped inside. She rushed to me and held me close. It was more than a hug. I could feel her love through her touch. She was definitely telling the truth when she said that she knew. I could feel it.

"Good Morning, Jason," she mumbled into my chest.

I kissed the top of her head. "Is there somewhere we can talk?"

Her pupils dilated as she nodded, a grin spread wide across her face. That smile took me somewhere else every single time. "You're on the clock," I thought to myself. I had it on internal repeat. She tucked her lower lip underneath her teeth and squeezed, that plump lip puckering out with the slightest pressure. *You're on the clock, Jason.* Her pointer finger snagged mine and she led me towards the back like a seductress. I was falling under her spell with each and every step. And when she looked back over her shoulder, her eyelids low and sultry, I paused - my feet seemingly cemented in place. Our fingers stretched to their limit as she kept walking. *On the clock.* "What about your customers?" I asked her. She stopped momentarily.

"It's okay, Jason. The team is well trained to take care of any customers."

I nodded. My feet quickly caught up with hers as she continued her stroll towards the back. Having long legs was a distinct advantage that was working in my favor in that moment. "Miss Oakley..." I whispered near her ear as we entered her office. She closed the door behind me, using the weight of her body to hold it closed. Her fingers were spread wide, palms flat on the surface of the door as if she were willing it, or maybe herself to stay right there. *On the clock, Jason. On the clock.*

I couldn't help myself. I tried. I walked back towards the door my hands wringing themselves, a sign of an internal war that was raging within. "Come here," I whispered. She bit her lip again and I could feel a smile burning one side of my face.

"Uhn uhn," she said, shaking her head no while one eyebrow raised on her face.

"Come here," I repeated in the deepest voice I had. My words like a fishing lure, hooked her. My gaze, reeled her in. Magnets. My good conscience tried to persuade me to be noble. But the other side tried to rationalize that "we'll be gentle." I placed my hands on her hips and slowly pulled her close. Her arms draped around my neck. Her fingers slowly caressed the area where my hair faded into skin. My breathing shallowed. *You're on the clock.* I inhaled sharply, trying to steady myself. *We'll be gentle.* I whispered as I exhaled. "Can I kiss you?"

She leaned near my ear and whispered my order, then pointed towards her desk. There it was, waiting for me. One small coffee - black. *On the clock.* To the left of that, one cup of sugarplums on the side. *On the clock.* To the right of the coffee - one bear claw, warm. *On the clock.* Two forks.

"I'll be gentle..." I whispered.

She nodded and I kissed her soft and slow, trying to help her feel my love. Her fingers continued to caress my scalp while she leaned in hard, all of her weight resting on my body. I held on tight as I felt my soul dance with hers. That was the first time I've ever had an out of body experience while I was kissing someone. It's like I was watching myself in action, kissing her good morning. When she let her hand move down my back and squeeze, my good conscience came bolting back to the surface.

"Well...good morning to you." I chuckled as I kept her gaze and let my spirit return to my body.

"Good morning, Jam."

"Did you know I was coming in today?"

"I was hopeful that I was your coffee date," she said, then smiled bashfully.

"I KNOW you're not about to act all coy after kissing me like that!" I teased her.

"Not coy, just curious."

"About what?" I asked her.

"How you instinctively know how to kiss me...I've never been kissed like this before. It felt so good, my soul...this sounds stupid - never mind."

"Say it."

"No, it's okay."

"You felt like your soul left your body?"

She looked at me, a mixture of perplexed and feeling seen and curiosity. "How on earth did you know that?"

"It felt like we danced with each other for a bit and then I was watching us kiss."

"I felt that too."

"I mean I'm kind of glad. Otherwise I would've been more than a little concerned about my mental state." We laughed together, her hand draped across my heart. "You can tell me whatever's on your mind, Miss Oakley. No judgement here."

She nodded again then nuzzled in for some standing cuddles, her head now resting where her hand had just resided. I kissed her widow's peak again and she looked up at me. It was in that moment that I saw 7 year old Oakley, just hoping to be loved. And in that same breath, I knew that I needed to tell her what I'd been trying to share from jump.

"So, this is date number five."

"Date two."

"Date five."

"Date three?"

"My middle name is..."

She was about to tell me her middle name and I couldn't let her say it. I spoke loudly, but didn't yell. "No! No! No! Not yet!" Her smiled turned into a laugh. I attempted to back away but she slowly followed me. I bumped into her desk. I was stuck.

Lurking ever closer, "It's date five, Jason."

"No. Date three, max!" I replied, turning my body sideways trying to dodge her as she returned to the standing cuddles.

"My middle name is..." I panicked and placed my finger on top of her lips, like that would be enough to somehow seal them and keep her from sharing her name before it was time.

"Miss Oakley. Please don't."

She nibbled on the tip of my finger and I removed it before she could pull the whole thing into her mouth.

"...Brooke," she said with a gloating smile. Even that smile still pulled me into her world. I wished she hadn't told me because I knew it was only gonna make things that much more difficult once I told her the truth.

"Oakley Brooke Powell," I said matter of factly.

"Mmmhmm," she said through a closed lip smile.

"You down with OBP?" I joked. Her teeth shone through.

"Hey, hey, that's me!" She went tit for tat with me on the jokes and I loved every second of it.

On the clock, Jason. On the clock.

"Okay Miss Oakley Brooke."

"Yes Jason Andrew?"

She held onto me and looked up at me with adoring eyes. I was about to melt under her power but I knew that I needed to hold on, for the sake of business.

"I need you to have a seat so we can talk."

She looked puzzled, "Oh, you were serious about finding a place to talk."

I nodded, as serious a look as I could muster on my face.

She sat down in her seat and pointed towards the seat on the other side of the table. "I'm not about to be the only one seated. Please sit down."

I sat and she handed me a fork then picked up the other one and tapped them like we were clinking glasses. "Don't let your coffee get cold, Jam," she said as she sliced a corner of the bear claw and took a bite.

"I won't, Oakley Brooke." I said as she smiled at me.

"So what's up? What's goin on? Tell me why we're sitting down."

"Well..." I cleared my throat, then continued. "I've been trying to tell you the reason that brought me into The Fresh Grind, but something always interrupts it."

"It's me isn't it? I've been interrupting you. Is it me?"

I nodded and laughed.

"Oh shoot. I just did it again, didn't I?" She said, her face changing colors to match her embarrassment. She cut another corner of the bearclaw with her fork, this time much larger, then took another bite. I guessed that maybe she thought if her mouth was full that she wouldn't be able to interrupt me.

"It's okay. Just please let me get this out and then I'm all ears, no matter what you feel the need to say." She nodded at me and stuffed more bear claw in.

"Well, you already know that I'm an actuary," I started trying to set up the blow as gently as possible. She nodded, then grabbed a sugarplum. "So, after hearing you talk, I think I might have been your replacement. The timing seems to align with that being the case." Her eyes widened and she grabbed my cup of coffee from me then took a long swig.

I watched her, waiting for her to say something. She

pursed her lips together like she was making sure that she wasn't going to interrupt me this time. I got the sense that she wanted me to continue, so I did.

"I wish that was all, but it's not." I said as I watched her shake her head from side to side as she snuffed out another piece of bear claw - it was halfway gone at this point. Truthfully, she could have it all as long as she didn't hate me. She waved me on and I spoke again. Slowly. Methodically. I was pacing myself so I said it correctly.

"You should have received some emails from me recently. In fact I know you have because you just replied to one the other day." She looked stunned. Totally frozen in place. I continued, "Andy Mitchell ring a bell?"

Chapter Twelve
OAKLEY

Andy Mitchell. Andy. Mitchell. Jason had just told me that he was Andy Mitchell, the guy who was supposed to schedule some time to come check out the "inherent risk" associated with my business. Andy Mitchell, the guy who I stalled in replying to because I just knew in my gut that he had replaced me at work. Andy Mitchell was the guy I'd just given my middle name to. Andy Mitchell was the guy I was kissing on this morning. Andy Mitchell was the guy I'd let sleep half naked in my bed last night. Andy Mitchell was the guy I'd fallen in love with when I thought he was about to go into a hypothermic coma. Andy Mitchell was the man I'd grown to trust and now I didn't know if he'd done all of that to get me to respond to his email or if it was real. I didn't know what was real anymore.

I couldn't even speak.

But Andy Mitchell did, "I understand if this is causing confusion - if you need me to leave." He studied my face. "I'll just go."

"You think you can just waltz in here and shatter the lenses on my rose colored glasses and then just get up and leave?" I was hot and bothered, and not in the good way.

"I didn't know what you wanted me to do. I'm right here. We can talk about whatever."

"Why didn't you tell me?"

"I tried to Miss Oakley."

"That's a fast conversation to have, Jason. Andy. I don't even know what to call you right now."

"Fair. Call me whatever comes to mind. I tried to tell you at least three times and you interrupted me every time. Then you'd say something and follow it with that damn smile and I'd lose focus."

"Don't try to sweet talk me, now."

"I know you probably don't believe it right now. But I promise this is all real for me."

"Mr. Mitchell."

"Don't do that."

"Mr. Mitchell, I've just had the blinders taken off of my

eyes."

"You're right. I apologize."

"...and you're sitting over there talking about losing focus when I smile."

He reached out and held my hand. I pulled away. "I do lose focus when you smile. I get lost when I look into your eyes. I just physically watched myself kissing you. That's not a normal thing for me."

I wanted to believe him, but all I could think of was Jenson and how I blindly trusted him and got crushed in the process.

"I know this probably feels like the whole Jenson situation all over again, but I can assure you that I'm not like him. I tried to tell you the truth on several occasions."

He had tried to tell me the truth, but I was so excited to connect with him that I wasn't listening. I found myself feeling scared of how much I felt for him. It was such a pure love, not all consuming, but I felt in my soul pretty early on that this would either completely ruin me or we'd get our happily ever after. Now I was sitting across from Andy Mitchell trying to figure out what on earth to even call him.

There was a knock on the door. One of our team members stepped in after I acknowledged the knock. They needed additional hands on the floor. I told them I'd be out in less than a minute then turned to face him as they skedaddled.

"So, Judas."

"Nope. You absolutely don't get to call me that."

"Mr. Mitchell, I need to help my staff. Do you mind waiting back here while I step out for a moment? We can continue this meeting once all is clear if that's okay with you."

"That works just fine for me Miss Oakley."

"Give me about twenty minutes and I'll be back."

"Certainly."

JASON

I sat in her office hoping everything would sort itself out, trusting that everything would sort itself out. She had the info now. It was her choice what to do next. I wasn't in a rush for her to decide. I knew this was something that might take a while to sift through.

Thirty minutes passed. Then forty. After we hit fifty minutes I stepped out of the office to see what was going on. That jont was packed full of people and the staff looked stressed. Oakley's face was scrunched up as she was preparing drinks left and right. There was a line of cups and mugs that just kept growing because the line didn't seem to stop. Every time they took an order the door swung open and two more people came inside.

I locked eyes with Oakley as I grabbed an apron, then headed towards the overflowing tubs of dishes hanging out above the trash cans. I grabbed a bin and took it back to the sink.

"Is there anything specific you want me to do as I load these into your dishwasher?" I asked her. She didn't say a word, just tilted her head towards the non slip mat on the floor.

I made sure to stand on it while I loaded the blue tray as full as possible, then used the sprayer to free the food and coffee stains from the dishes and flatware - sending it through the conveyor belt. Rinse and repeat, literally until the bin of dishes was empty. I looked up at Oakley once it was and she nodded towards a button just beside the sink. I flipped it and a garbage disposal began to whir. I ran some water in it until it sounded clear of food. Then I went back out to swap out a full bin of dirty dishes with an empty one.

By the time I came back to wash more dishes, the first load of dishes were done. I looked at Oakley who motioned towards the hand washing basin. I washed my hands and began to unload the trays. Once those dishes were put away, I got started washing the next round. This became my unofficial job for the next 6 hours. She never said a word. Only quick nods to let me know what I needed to do.

For six hours. I waited until the rush had dwindled down, finished and put away the last set of dishes, hung up my apron and grabbed my coat. I nodded towards Oakley and hit the door.

After a few hours like that I knew that their staff would be exhausted. They were able to rotate 15 minute breaks in a couple of times, but thirty minutes isn't enough to help you recharge your body. That's some tough work. I went across the street and ordered some lunch to be delivered to their small team, then I hopped in my car and drove into the office.

OAKLEY

He just hopped in and helped. I didn't have to ask. He just figured out where we were short handed and provided two helping hands. To top it all off, when I thought he was gone without a word, he actually ended up sending lunch for the team. When I needed him, he went above and beyond to help out. I thought about it all day and sent him a message when I got home.

"Thank you for your help today. Let's talk compensation."

"You're very welcome. No compensation needed, but thank you for the offer."

"I'll find a way to repay you, Mr. Mitchell."

"You'll cheapen it if you do, Miss Oakley."

"Everybody was talking about how you just jumped in to help and they appreciated the lunch."

He didn't reply. I guess there wasn't anything left to say.

Chapter Thirteen
JASON

Space. I wanted to give her some space. The last thing I wanted was for her to rush through all the stuff I dropped in her lap this afternoon. I kept thinking about how I'd have felt it if was me. I'd had some rough relationships but nothing quite like what she'd experience. She had a man promise to love her forever, then rob her of her financial security and leave her questioning her own self-worth. Then here I come dropping a bomb on her after she had begun to get attached to me. I tried to do it before, but maybe I was too patient to help with this specific situation. Maybe I should've tried harder to tell her. I tried to tell myself that I couldn't help it, but the truth was that I could. I mulled all of this over on my drive home from work, then again when I entered my house. I sat down on my couch and thought about my walk home this morning.

It only took me five minutes, but it was five minutes of

reminiscing that left me feeling open to all the possibilities that exist in the world. The last relationship I had been vulnerable and open. Too much for the other person according to what I was told. I tried to be accommodating and keep more stuff to myself, but bending who you authentically are for the comfort of others doesn't tend to work out. Not in business relationships. Not in personal relationships. And definitely, not in romantic relationships. By the time I unlocked my door I knew I definitely had to be honest and true to myself and whatever came of that, came of that.

My phone buzzed with a message. I looked down and read the text from Oakley. She thanked me for helping and tried to compensate me. There wasn't a reason for compensation in my mind so I told her that.

She said she'd find a way to repay me, but I didn't feel the need to be repaid for doing what felt right. I didn't do it for money. I didn't do it to show her anything. I just helped out because help was needed. Money or compensation of any kind would cheapen it to me. So I told her that.

She pivoted into talking about how everybody was gabbing about how I helped out. It felt excessive. I didn't know how to reply, so I didn't force it. I decided just to let it breathe so I could feel out how to respond. My eyelids felt heavy, so I figured I'd let them rest for a few minutes.

The next thing I knew I was waking up on the couch and it was dark outside. I thought maybe it was like 8:00, 8:30 max. No. It was almost midnight. I didn't take a nap. I went to sleep. I drug myself up off the couch and hopped in the shower to wash off the day. Some of my best ideas come when I'm in the shower. Apparently it inspires deep thinking.

This shower that was supposed to be just a short one so I could go to bed, turned into a recap of this wild day. I laughed at the fact that I woke up half naked in her bed. I rolled my eyes at the fact that I slipped out of her house without at least hugging her goodbye. My heart rate pulsed as I thought about the walk back to her office and how she lured me in. I was concerned about her reaction to me sharing the reason we initially met. And every time I thought about her shifting her position so quickly because I'd helped her with something my stomach turned a little. I didn't want her to cave so quickly. I wanted her to take some time to process the info. But maybe what I wanted was unrealistic. Maybe what I wanted for her and what she wanted for herself were two different things. Maybe I needed to step back for me and not out of some lofty idea that I was somehow doing her a service. I got out of the shower and dried off, then with my towel wrapped around my waist, sent her a text.

"My bad. Thought I was closing my eyes for a nap. Turns out I straight up went to sleep. I hope you're resting well. Give me a call tomorrow whenever you're free - if you still wanna talk that is."

My phone rang three minutes later. Oakley.

"Miss Oakley? Is everything okay?"

It sounded like she was moving around. "You sent me a

text yesterday that asked me to give you a call today when I was free. Well, it's today and I'm free."

I laughed as I realized that I sent the message at 11:59 pm.

"Miss Oakley - I meant in the morning."

"It is the morning, Jason. 12:04 AM."

"What the heck?"

"Is this a good time to chat?" She asked me, finally sounding like she had settled in one place.

"Sure. I just got out of the shower. Do you mind if I finish putting my pjs on right quick?"

There was a knock at the front door.

"Someone's at my front door. Why the hell is someone knocking on my jont before Jesus is up?" I tightened up the wrapped towel, slid my slides on and shuffled to a window to see who was outside my house. "Hold on, Miss Oakley."

I stuck two fingers between the blinds then split them apart, leaving a little gap so I could see and not be seen. I could only see two legs in some joggers and boots with the fur.

"Jason, it's January in Kansas City." There was an echo. I heard her voice outside before I heard it on my phone.

"Are you outside my door?" I asked, suddenly feeling myself get excited at the thought of reeling her in for the hug I ran away from when I started the day. I rushed towards the door as quickly as I could without leaving a slide behind.

"Uh huh. I hope that's okay," I heard her say from behind the front door as struggled to unlock the deadbolt that sometimes got stuck when the temperature change shifted the position of the door. Once I finally got it unlocked, I opened the door in a hurry. That crisp January breeze shocked me back into reality, quickly remembering I only had on a towel and my body was still a little damp from the shower. And there I was staring at Oakley, who had a sultry grin on her face. My grip instinctively tightened around the towel without realizing the after effect that would have on...

"Well, hello, Jason. Are you happy to see me or..."

"Stop." I wouldn't let her finish her statement.

We just stared at each other for a few seconds before she spoke again. "I started walking when I got your text. I followed the same route you took last night. I hope," her voice trailed off as her eyes dropped down to the front porch. It looked like she might have had second thoughts about her plan as she said it out loud.

"It's cold out there. Are you coming inside?"

Her eyes immediately found mine again and I held her right hand with my left, the non-cinching hand, and guided her into the foyer, then closed the door behind her.

"So two nights in a row you've seen me half naked. I'm starting to think this is how you prefer to see me," I said with a chuckle.

Her grin returned. "Jason, I should've asked first before just coming over here. I'm sorry about that."

"It's okay, Miss Oakley. Have a seat. Can I get you some water or anything?"

"Do you have anything stronger than water?"

"I have good ole KC tap water. That's stronger, right?" I asked, then watched her face light up in laughter.

"Water is fine, Jason." I could feel the towel move around my legs, but my hand hadn't lost its grip. That smile of hers was setting some things in motion and I needed to put on some clothes. ASAP.

"Okay, well since you're here, I want you to make yourself at home. The kitchen is right through that doorway. Bottled water is in the fridge door. Filtered water can be poured through the tap on the door. Or there's ice in the freezer and you can put the strong stuff on the rocks straight outta the faucet."

"You going somewhere?"

"Well it's January, in Kansas City, so I need to put on some lotion before my legs start to look like they're covered in flour." Her laughter was contagious and I found myself smiling at the glee on her face. "I'll be right back," I said as I shuffled back towards the bathroom to finish getting dressed.

"Jason, wait," she called to me. I turned to face her, my face asking the question so my mouth didn't have to.

She didn't say anything, just looked me up and down, locking her gaze on my eyes. Swimmin in 'em. Lord help me.

I smiled at her as I turned back towards the bathroom and finished what I'd started to do. I closed and locked the door then proceeded to moisturize the ash away like I was being baptized in holy water. I'd just finished putting on my shorts, t-shirt and socks when I heard her giggle in the living room.

I stepped out of the bathroom feeling less like my skin was gonna crack if I moved too fast, and walked towards the sweet sound of her laughter. I leaned up against the doorway, watching her peruse my family photos that were on the bookshelf and piano top.

"Your face hasn't changed at all, Jason."

"Miss Oakley," I called to her, then waited for her to turn around.

"Even here, you still look like the man who's standing in this room but you were so little. What was this, third grade? Fourth grade?"

"6th grade. I was a tiny kid. Then I hit a growth spurt and I've been the same height since my first year in college." I paused then spoke again. "Miss Oakley, what's going on?"

She turned around and looked at me. The smirk still present even though the towel had been replaced by something far less skimpy. "Still sexy," she whispered loud enough that I could hear it - even though I don't think I was supposed to.

"What's that?" I asked her.

"Sorry, Jason. Can we talk?"

"We can." I said as I pointed towards the couch and sat only after she had begun her free-fall into a spot - my favorite spot, the place in the corner where the cushions hug you. It's the same place where I had lulled myself into a long nap earlier. "What are you drinking? The hard stuff or is it a cocktail?"

She laughed again, "it's definitely the hard stuff. Straight from the tap is my preference but not everybody drinks it straight like that."

"I don't know why. It's better that way."

"Agreed."

"So, what's going on Miss Oakley?" I asked her again.

Her face softened. "Well, Jason, I wanted to come

apologize to you for earlier today."

I nodded as she continued, "I knew the world was small, but I found out just how small today when you share bombed me at work. It was a lot."

"I know it was. I hadn't thought about the fact that I shared that with you while you were on the clock until just now. My timing wasn't good there. I apologize for that."

"In all fairness you'd tried to tell me before, but I wasn't listening. I only heard the part where we had something in common," she paused like she was stuck in her own world.

I extended a hand in her direction when I realized she had tears streaming from her eyes. She held on and continued, "I replayed the times that you tried to tell me on a loop all day as I was making coffee. I felt so out of it. Things were busier today than a pig race at the fair and you were right there when I needed you - in spite of the fact that I hadn't held space to hear you out."

"My God that was country," I said as I started to laugh. "I'm sorry, Miss Oakley. I heard everything you said, but 'pig race at the fair' just sent me."

"Jam."

"I'm sorry, you're gonna have to give me a minute here," I said between shallow breaths.

She waited patiently for me to get my shit together,

but eventually that laughter took over her soul as well. We giggled together like two kids on the school yard. She leaned her head onto my shoulder as we laughed together. My head nestled on top of hers. For a solid ten minutes we had a laughing fit that caused my side to hurt. I yawned in an attempt to stop it, but she read it as time to go.

"Oh, you were getting ready for bed when we got on the phone."

"I was."

"I can go so you can get some rest. I just wanted to come apologize."

"I appreciate your apology but none is needed."

"Okay, well let me grab my coat" she said before I held onto her hand again.

"You're welcome to stay here tonight if you'd like. I have a comfortable new mattress and apparently this couch isn't too shabby either, considering."

"The couch sounds good."

"No, I'll be sleeping on the couch. You'll be sleeping in the bed. What kinda dude do you think I am?"

"Will you show me the bedroom?"

"You're at home. Just poke around until you find it. I'm gonna shut the house down and grab an extra blanket and pillow so I can sleep out here." She took my advice and went on a self-guided tour of the house, finding the main bedroom and stopping in the entryway. "You okay, Miss Oakley?"

"This bedroom," she mumbled, "it looks just like mine."

"I know. That's partially why I was so weirded out this morning and left without a hug or anything. I couldn't see that last night when I went to bed. But when the sun came up I thought I was in my house, then you were in my arms and I was trying to figure out when you came to my crib."

"Oh, Jason - this is a first for sure."

"Well, at least it looks familiar, right?"

She nodded, then asked for a hug goodnight. I moseyed in her direction, determined to keep it PG tonight. That hug felt like I was drinking a warm mug of cocoa while snuggled up under a blanket near a fire pit with my love. It was cozy and nurturing. Affirming. I just wanted to stay in it.

Her words softly cut through the contented silence, "Will you lay with me tonight, Jam?"

I didn't say a word. I simply walked us into the room far enough to clear the door, closed it, then kissed her widow's peak.

"I could stay here forever," she murmured into my chest.

"Big spoon or little spoon tonight?"

"BIG SPOON ME!" she joked as we found our way to the bed and I tucked her in for the night.

I walked around to the other side of the bed and said a quick prayer before hopping in and pulling the covers up.

She spoke softly, almost like the sleep had hit her instantaneously.

"Goodnight, Jason Andrew Mitchell."

I whispered. "Hey, can we set some ground rules for tonight?"

She nodded in response, her eyes closed, breathing heavier than normal. I knew I only had a few minutes before she was knocked out.

"Only spooning. No kissing. Hands above the belt."

She smiled, "Protect yourself at all times. Now touch gloves and head to your corners." I squeezed her hip and chuckled. "Above the belt, Mr. Mitchell."

"You're right. My bad," I said as I moved my hand to her stomach. "Good night, Miss Oakley," I whispered as I kissed her on the cheek.

She grinned. "That's two of your own rules broken. Were those meant for you or for me?"

"My bad. Both of us. Go to sleep."

"You go to sleep!"

We both laughed at the absurdity of the conversation.

"Good night for real this time Miss Oakley."

Four words and she was knocked out, "Good night, Mr. Mitchell."

I watched her body relax into the mattress, her face softening with each and every breath. I felt it coming. It bubbled up and over before I could stop it. In the literal blink of an eye I whispered in her ear, "I love you so much."

Chapter Fourteen
OAKLEY

I had drifted off to sleep in his arms. In his bed. In his house. When I woke up that morning he was gone. He wasn't in the bathroom. He wasn't in the kitchen or the living room. He was gone gone. I walked around the house softly calling his name, hoping he wouldn't jump out of a closet or a room and scare the bejeezus out of me again. But there was no jumping to be had. I checked the garage and his fancy car wasn't there. It wasn't parked on the street. It was only 5:00. I didn't know where he could have possibly gone on so little sleep, and so quietly that I hadn't heard him leave.

I sent him a message, "just woke up excited to see your face this morning..."

He replied, "Good morning! Glad you're up. Went to the gym. On my way home now."

"There's a perfectly good treadmill sitting in the corner of your bedroom...it's the same model as the one in my room, except mine apparently is the closet edition."

"Also doubles as clothes storage?"

I laugh reacted to his message and was typing a response when I received another one from him.

"I didn't want to wake you up. I wasn't sure what time you were planning to get up today and waking you up to ask that seemed rude af."

"I appreciate the consideration. I'm in your space though. Do whatever you need to do and I'll adjust."

"I hear you"

"But...???"

"I'm driving with Focus turned on. I'll see your message when I get where I'm going."

I headed into the bathroom to wake up and let things flow. I was in the middle of washing my face when I heard a door open and close in the house. I splashed water on my face to remove the rest of the soap, then wiped the counter clean and opened the bathroom door. I figured he'd probably be a sweaty mess, ready for a shower and I wanted it to be open to him when he was ready.

He dropped his gym bag on the floor in the bedroom then looked over his shoulder at me. I stood there in the doorway, wondering what he was thinking. He smiled, stood upright and turned to face me, moving slowly towards the bathroom, his arms open for a hug.

"There she is," he whispered as his arms enveloped me gently.

I immediately felt like I was at home, right there in his non-sweaty arms.

"I thought you were at the gym," I said to him, puzzled about the fresh scent I could smell tickling my nostril hairs.

"I showered before I left."

"You must be exhausted. Can I fix you something to eat?"

"Where did you come from ma'am?"

"Arkansas. We covered this already."

A throaty chuckle escaped his mouth. "We did. You're right."

"You know about my family and everything. Hey, you're supposed to tell me about your nickname."

"I am. You're right," he said while still holding me in his arms. "Can I fix you something to eat?"

"How did things get reversed that quickly?" I asked

before he leaned down and kissed my widows peak, then released his hug. I looked up into his eyes and he shook his head.

"Ahh. There you go again. It's too early for me to get suckered into your stare."

I watched as his pupils dilated again and smiled.

"Saucers."

"Look. I already told you why they look like that. I stand by my words from Saturday." He went and sat on the edge of the bed and patted a place for me to sit down beside him. I followed his lead and leaned into him - still a little groggy from the short night of rest.

"What's up?" I asked him.

"So I was thinking while I was at the gym..."

"Yes?"

"I don't think I can ethically keep you on my caseload."

I was nervous for what that might mean for the business. I was slow to respond to their correspondence and because of the agency, they already had history with me and questioned my ability to exercise good judgement. I turned my head sharply in Jason's direction. Tears automatically welling in my eyes.

"Why?"

"You were already sleep last night when I told you the reason why," he said while rubbing the back of his head.

"If I was sleep, then how could you possibly expect me to remember?"

"I don't. I just can't tell you yet. It's a good reason though. I need you to know that much. I'm also gonna ask you to trust me. I know that might be a hard sell given what just happened yesterday. But I'm trusting that somewhere in there, in the place where you know who I am, you trust yourself enough to give me the benefit of the doubt."

I dropped my head on his shoulder and he let his fall on top of mine. "I trust myself enough to do that, Jam."

"Okay. I need you to also trust that my next words are going to help us in the long run." He reached out and held my hand, our fingers intertwined and mine held on for dear life. I was bracing myself because it felt so big. That's the only way I knew how to describe it in that moment.

"Okay, Jam."

He took a deep breath and silence filled the room for an excruciating hour. It was probably closer to ten seconds but it felt long enough for me to run home and get cleaned up, then come back. I could feel my heartbeat pulsing in my throat.

"You've got my blood pressure up, sir. Please just say whatever you need to say."

"Miss Oakley, I feel like we're moving too fast."

It was my turn to be silent. I squeezed my eyes shut as tightly as I could so I could sear this image in my memory. I wanted it to be readily available the next time I closed my eyes. I wanted to see it again. I wanted to feel it again. I wanted to hold this love inside my body so I could return to it whenever I needed it - because it felt like we were about to go on a break.

"I don't know what to say."

"I have this tendency, Miss Oakley."

"What tendency, Jason?"

"...to eat the sugarplums first."

"What kinda..."

"Hear me out. Please."

"Okay."

"The sugarplums are so good that I binge eat them. I almost always find myself finishing up the last one and thinking there's still like 3 or 4 in the cup. Then I'm upset at myself for not being present while I'm eating them. They're so good I just keep mindlessly popping them into my mouth."

"Do you feel like that's what you do in your relationships too?" I asked as he nodded.

"I want to savor this one. I want to slow down and feel everything that's happening. That's why I sniffed your hair the other night. It's why I hold you in my arms so gently. It's why I allow myself to get lost in your eyes. I wanna feel all of it. I don't want to lose a second of it."

"Can I look at you?"

"Not right now. This is my back to back moment."

"Okay," I softly spoke as I sat still and stoic to listen to the rest of what was on his mind.

"I wanna court you Oakley Brooke. That's why I was trying to slow down our date count. You've already undressed me and we've slept in the same bed together twice in two nights. And I just don't want to mess this up. We have forever and a day."

I could hear the emotion in his voice.

"Jason, if we have forever and a day, then everything we do will be in perfect order."

"I hear you, Miss Oakley. Really I do. But let's imagine the shoe was on the other foot. Let's say you were the one who wanted to slow things down."

"Enough said," I reassured him.

"There's so much coming for us that I can already see, that I can already feel. I wanna savor it, Oakley Brooke. I wanna taste every ingredient of what we're creating."

"I hear you Jason Andrew."

"Will you help me savor everything?"

I reached across my body and his and gently stroked his beard and chin. I looked up at his closed eyes and smiled at how he leaned his face onto my hand like he was trying to use his cheek to feel the way my hand moved.

"I can help you do that, Jam," I said. He kissed the top of my head and then took one slow and methodical inhale. I exhaled slowly with him. "Is that why you set down ground rules for last night?"

"Yes. You just showed up on my doorstep and it was cold, and I didn't want to leave you out there because undressing you to keep YOU warm would've been more than I could've handled. I'm just being honest."

"I can imagine."

"So can I take you out to dinner on Friday?"

"What do we do about the days in between then?"

"What do you mean?"

"I mean, I slept so much better being near you the last two days."

"Same."

"Do I need to wait for better sleep like that again?"

He didn't answer right away. I could feel his knee shaking as his foot was tapping away on the floor. It stopped suddenly right before he spoke. "We can lay some ground rules if it helps to keep things clear."

"What kind of ground rules do you have in mind, Jason?"

"I want to be a good neighbor and I don't want to overstay my welcome."

"Wait, I'm in your place right now."

"I know, and I want you to feel at home here."

"I do, and I want you to feel at home in my place too."

"I do, Miss Oakley."

"Okay..."

"Just hear me out. Please."

"I'm sorry."

"You don't need to apologize for that. Just, listen. I don't want us to feel irritated with the fact that either of us is in our space when we don't want it. So I'm proposing no more than one night in the other's house per week to start. If we want to change that later as time passes, then we can revisit the ground rules."

"Time has passed," I said. He erupted in laughter.

"Let's give it at least two weeks, Miss Oakley."

"Starting when?"

"Starting from this past Saturday."

"Sir."

"Ma'am?"

"We've already hit the cap for this week."

"We have."

I don't know where they came from, but tears filled my eyes so quickly they caught both of us off guard.

"What's this? What's going on?" He asked me.

I whispered past the lump that filled my throat. "I don't know where they came from, Jam."

"Whatcha feelin right now?"

"I'm feelin like I wanna call in sick today."

There was a twinkle in his eye. "When was the last time you had a day off?"

"Sunday."

"I mean when the shop was still open."

"Hasn't happened."

"Who could you give the keys to today and trust that they'd handle everything?"

"My assistant manager could handle it."

"What time are they coming in today?"

"She's actually opening the store for me. I asked her last night if she could."

"What would happen if you asked her to manage things for the entire day?"

"I'm...I don't know what would happen."

"You wanna try it and see?"

I gazed into his eyes, trying to decide if I was willing to ditch my staff in favor of this man in front of me. I'd spent years building this business and one customer, one cup of coffee could be the downfall of everything - but that was true whether I was there or not. I nodded in the affirmative.

"Was that a yes?"

"Mmhmm. I'm gonna text her right now."

"Great. So are you hangin here today or at your place?"

"We aren't hanging together today?"

"I have to hand your file over to someone today."

"Is it a physical file or a digital file?"

"Yes. Are you asking me to play hooky today?"

"What would we do if you did?"

"Well..."

"What am I saying, Jason? I can't do that! I need to go into work today."

He let go of my hand and wrapped that arm around me. "Miss Oakley, did you know that you were serving customers in your sleep for the last two nights?"

"I did what?"

"I think you need to take a day off. Maybe that's today. Maybe it's a different day, but you need a minute."

"Jam! Was I really serving customers in my sleep?"

"Mmhm..."

"What in the entire heck!"

He closed his eyes and pretended like he was sleep so he could imitate me. "Wayell good morniiin! Wha-canna get started for yew tuhday?"

"Oh good gracious."

He chuckled, "It was cute. The first night it startled me. I thought you were talking to me."

"What did you do?"

"I told you that you knew my order but I wasn't ready for that yet."

"Oh Lordy."

"Yeah, then I realized you were talking in your sleep and I just went back to sleep. Last night when you said it, I just rubbed your back."

"I'm so embarrassed."

"I hear you. It's still cute though."

"Jason."

"So we're calling in sick today, right?"

Chapter Fifteen
JASON

One day off. We were up at the butt crack of dawn and the whole day was in front of us. I asked her where she'd like to go and she limited her range to things in Kansas City.

"Well, we could go to the art museum or go window shopping out in the burbs."

"Dream bigger."

"Bigger?"

"If we're playin hooky, let's *play hooky*. Where would you like to go?"

That question seemed to stop her in her tracks. She looked at me, as if she was about to try my limits.

"Beignets on Bourbon Street."

"Consider it done."

"What?"

"If you go home and get dressed - pack a personal item for a one day road trip, I'll get our tickets and travel together. I'll text you what time we're leaving as soon as I get the tickets."

"Jason, are we really going to New Orleans?"

I nodded and checked my phone, "It looks like it's supposed to be sunny and in the upper 60s there today."

"Jam."

I leaned over and kissed the top of her head and encouraged her to, "go get ready."

"You just said we need to slow down and now you want me to hop on a plane and head to New Orleans with you?"

"Yes."

"How is that slowing down?"

"It's not," I said while looking up flight info on my phone.

"Jason."

"Oakley," I said turning my attention back to her face - her sweet angelic face. I stuttered when I initially tried to speak and had to blink my way back into focus. "Y-you. The uh...the tickets. The flight. The next flight out of here leaves in 2 hours. We can make it if we leave here in 15 minutes."

"So are we taking it slow or no?"

"Yes, we'll be in New Orleans, not either of our houses. And we'll be back tonight and you can sleep in your house, and I can sleep in mine. And - if you're up to it, I can take you out to dinner on Friday."

She studied my face as I spoke, her eyes staring into mine, almost as if she were trying to decide if I was telling the truth.

She spoke softly, "Am I coming back here with my bag or are you picking me up?"

I kissed the top of her head once more and told her I'd be there to pick her up in 10 minutes.

"So I have five minutes to pack?"

"What do you really need that we can't get down there?"

"Nothing really I guess."

"Can you shower in five minutes?"

"I can today," she said confidently as she rose from

the bed. I walked her out and secured our tickets, then grabbed my backpack and hopped in the car to head her way.

She was waiting for me when I got there. Backpack in hand, winter coat on. When she got in the car her spicy perfume filled my nose and I reminisced on the pantry and those phantom sugarplums she wanted me to get from the top shelf. I felt a half smile begin to peek through my face and as she kissed my cheek, it bloomed to a full on cheese. I felt like such a simp but I didn't care. I could feel that pulsating energy just hovering between us.

"Are we still gonna make it to the airport on time?" she asked me, her voice full of hope.

"It's early enough that the traffic should be pretty light. I think we'll be just fine. You have your ID right?"

She nodded and I checked for mine, then we pulled out of her driveway and headed towards the highway. The sun hadn't even started to show itself yet and traffic was even more light than I thought it would be. So it was easy cruising to the airport up north. They had started construction on the new airport terminal to replace the one that felt like it was stuck in a time warp. I couldn't wait for it myself, but locals thought it would be a problem. They were used to convenience.

I guess it was kind of nice to pull into the short term parking and only have a short covered walk to the building, but I was open to the idea that something new could potentially be better.

We rode the escalator to the main floor and then walked the circle until we found our boarding area and the TSA screening station for it. We were traveling super light so that took little to no time at all, and by the time we got through airport security, our flight was boarding. Fortunately because of the airport layout we were basically already at the gate.

They screened our passes and let us board. She reached for my hand as we walked down the breezeway. When I turned my head to look at her I got a glimpse of her face, all of her childlike innocence oozed out of her pores. She was almost skipping.

"You excited?" I asked her. She nodded in response.

"What seats are we in, Jason?"

"Seats 3A & 3B"

"Three?!"

"Mmhm. Do you prefer a window or an aisle?"

"Window? Is that first class?"

"That's all that was left, Miss Oakley."

She stopped walking and I nearly plowed into her. I couldn't read her facial expression.

"What's wrong?"

"I can't believe you."

"You still wanna go?" I asked as I started slowly walking again, my hand on the small of her back. She nodded as her legs moved with excitement.

We greeted the crew and took our seats.

Bags stowed safely under the seats in front of us, she was staring out the window as I spoke. "When was the last time you were on a plane, Miss Oakley?"

Her face danced as she tried to recall the last time.

"College."

"So that was what about 5 years ago?" I joked to lighten the mood. She looked tense.

"Only 3 years ago sir," she joked in return.

"Where did you go?"

"Atlanta with some friends. The tickets were dirt cheap and so was the hotel."

"Hmm...tell me about the trip."

Her face scrunched like she was hesitant to speak.

"I'd rather not."

"Was Jensen one of the friends?"

She nodded. "It's okay to talk about him with me, especially if it helps you get out some of the hard stuff that's still lingering."

"I appreciate the offer, I'd just rather enjoy this time with you."

"Okay, well if you change your mind. Just say the word," I said and watched her eyebrows drop in relaxation.

She buckled her seat belt and asked only for water when the crew came through to ask about our pre-flight drinks. She paid extra special attention to the flight attendants during their emergency procedure demonstration. In that moment it struck me that what I thought was a hesitancy to leave her business might actually just be some pre-flight jitters.

I opened my hand for her to hold. She laced my fingers with hers and held on tightly as we backed away from the gate. I leaned over and kissed her widow's peak as we waited in line for our turn on the runway. "We're gonna be just fine, Bunny."

"Bunny?" she asked right as our jet turned onto the straightaway.

I pointed to her legs, both of which were bouncing rapidly. She buried her head on my shoulder and giggled as the plane barreled down the runway and I rested mine on top just as we went wheels up.

I spoke softly as the plane continued to climb, "How

you doin?"

"I'm okay."

I whispered, "You sure?"

She nodded, her head still resting on my shoulder. When we reached cruising altitude I heard something that made me chuckle.

"The word."

I raised my head and turned towards Oakley who was looking up at me with caution in her eyes.

"Atlanta. That trip. That was where he first told me he loved me. That was when he talked about our future together. The last time I was on a plane I was with a man who had made so many promises and I had no idea that he'd shatter all of them and my heart in the process. Ever dropped a mirror? You can find all the big pieces and put them back together but there's still always gonna be a crack or some gap where a tiny sliver is missing."

"Does it change it from being a mirror?"

"Well, no. I guess you can still see yourself in it."

"You can."

She paused and thought about it. I continued following my train of thought. "And while it might look like a broken mirror to some, it might look like a piece of art to the right person - someone with a discerning eye."

A tear filled her eye.

Her voice was soft but crystal clear, "I don't want to slow down, Jam." I didn't have a response. I just sat still, caught yet again in her gaze. After sitting in silence for half a minute she spoke again, "I didn't want to say that earlier this morning, because I was afraid of what would happen if I did. I didn't want you to think I was pressuring you because that's not my intent. I didn't want you to think I didn't hear you because I did. I don't think we're gonna mess this up Jason."

"You know that how?"

"I feel it in my soul. It's deep down in there. I told myself I wouldn't get on another plane with a man unless..."

"Unless what?"

"Unless I knew him."

"And you think you know me?"

"I know I do, Jason. And you know me too. You already said it."

I nodded.

"I've been on some long road trips but not another plane until today. Charlie asked me to come see him when he lived in Chicago - before he moved to Kansas City. He asked me to fly back with him a couple of times. I wouldn't do it. I knew that it wasn't him."

"Wasn't him what?" I asked her. The flight attendant stopped by with our boxed breakfasts. "Wasn't him what?" I asked again as I handed her the box of food and snacks.

She thanked both the flight attendant and me, then opened the box and looked inside.

"Wasn't him what?" I asked once more.

"He wasn't my person," she said as she studied my face then directed her attention back to the box. "Ooh, look Jam! A baby bearclaw, and it's warm."

"Miss Oakley. You're not about to just switch subjects like that."

"I'm afraid it's too late. We're talking about what's in the box." I blinked slowly in her direction. "What's in yours, Jason?"

I opened the box and struggled to pull out an invisible object that I held in my hand and presented to her. "Oh look, it's the last subject we were talking about."

She giggled, "Jason."

I smiled at that laugh, "Oakley."

"Jason. All I'm saying is I'm on a plane with you right now."

"Is that why you were so anxious and nervous earlier? Is that why you stopped in the breezeway?" Suddenly it all made so much more sense. She wasn't afraid of flying. She knew that she was stepping into the promise she'd made herself and she had to trust what she was feeling.

I knew I had to do the same.

"Oakley Brooke."

"Jam?" she asked as she stared at me with so much emotion in her eyes.

"I love you so much."

Chapter Sixteen
OAKLEY

I couldn't believe it. The way he looked at me confirmed exactly what I'd been wondering about for months. Those eyes. That piercing stare. So loving. So open. Then he said it...and I felt like I was the only person in the world at that moment.

He told me he loved me, and I shoved a piece of my bear claw in his mouth. I don't know why, so don't even ask. I just forked it over to him and he chewed it up while looking at me with those big loving eyes. I whispered, "I know your heart, Jam."

I mean really? I couldn't say it back? I didn't say it back. I could have - but I didn't.

I leaned in and lowered my forehead until it touched his, "Jason."

He whispered, "Don't say anything."

I considered staying silent. I considered holding my tongue. But the thought of me not telling him how I felt didn't sit right with me. I spoke softly, our foreheads still kissing. "I need to tell you something."

"Miss Oakley. Bunny."

I shook my head and opened my mouth to tell him anyway. Before I could get any words out of it, there was a piece of bear claw entering my mouth. He chuckled and kissed the top of my head.

"Here," he said handing my glass to me, "drink some water."

I took a swig and washed down the tiny bite of bear claw. The flight attendant who was walking through the cabin checking on all the passengers, stopped to ask us a different question. She leaned on the seat in front of us. "Y'all have some serious chemistry. Newlyweds?"

We both chuckled and shook our heads.

"Engaged?"

Jason chuckled and raised one eyebrow at me before turning his attention to the flight attendant. He slowly shook his head.

"Uh oh, did I just blow up your proposal plans?" she asked him.

"No, we're just on a little getaway today. Finding a new way to relax and explore the world."

"That's goals," she said as she winked at me and turned to continue her trek down the aisle.

We were goals. Triggered. I'd felt that before from people who saw the façade of a relationship I'd had with Jenson. In one two-word sentence she'd tripped that thin thread of trust that I was holding tight to, forcing me to completely let go.

The chill of the airplane window reminded me of the biting cold we'd left behind for something much warmer, something I could feel blossoming in my chest as I looked into Jason's eyes, something that didn't exist before him. It wasn't just the promise of beignets that beckoned like a sweet escape from the routine of my coffee shop filled life.

I began to settle into my seat. Eyes closed, the rhythmic hum of the engines provided a comforting backdrop to the whirlwind of thoughts racing through my mind. His voice had been so soft and sincere. That declaration just hung in the air like a delicate promise. The weight of his confession was inescapable. And still there was a yearning in his eyes, a vulnerability that filled those saucer sized pupils. It was that vulnerability that warmed my soul and opened me up to the possibility of what life could be, what this day could be.

Those five words echoed in my mind as I was nudged awake by Jason.

"We're about to land, Miss Oakley," he said, that yearning still present in his eyes.

New Orleans welcomed us with open arms and a burst of warmth, a stark contrast to the frigid world we'd left behind. It was still early enough that it felt like the promise of an extraordinary day. Jason had ordered a ride-share for us that was waiting upon our arrival. Within 10 minutes we were whisked away to a bustling cafe on Bourbon Street, its vibrant road alive with music and color. The intoxicating aroma of beignets guided us inside and Jason, ever methodical, insisted on turning this simple act of indulgence into an art.

"Close your eyes, Oakley," he told me. "Describe it to me, the smell."

"It smells sweet - like a donut. Lightly fried. My mouth's watering, Jason."

"Goooood," he said as I heard the clink of a fork on a plate. "Can I feed it to you?"

I nodded and waited for a fork to find its way to my mouth.

"You're probably gonna have to open your mouth a little wider for me."

"Wider?" I asked, wondering how the heck he needed more room for a fork.

"Wider," he said. A slight chuckle trailing on the end

of the word that woke up parts of my body that I thought I'd put in hibernation mode. His voice and that word just rattled around in my mind.

Wider. I parted my lips some more and waited for the fork. Just as I was questioning whether or not I'd opened my mouth wide enough, I felt it. Something warm and soft touched my lips. The powdered sugar on the top made the pastry glide across my top lip with ease. My tongue responded automatically, mimicking the men on the airport tarmac, guiding the planes to the right gate.

His voice, soft and low. "Describe the taste, the texture," he urged. His methodical approach to enjoying life intrigued me.

I took a bite and chewed, "It's warm." I paused and chewed some more. "Thick and delicate. Not too sweet." I swallowed my first bite. "Fried to pillowy perfection. Was that cinnamon?"

"Mmhm," he said. His words sounding like they were accompanied by a smile. "What do you hear?"

"The zydeco band in the distance, the coffee maker behind the counter, your breath."

"You can't hear my breath. Can you?"

"Maybe that was mine," I joked as I opened my eyes. A mischievous glint in his eyes lingered as he chuckled with me.

"How was that?"

"Overwhelming...in a good way." He nodded, his eyes filled with adoration again. "Jam?"

"Yes, Bunny?" I looked down to find my legs bouncing again just as they had on the plane.

"Why now?" I wondered aloud, my voice barely above a whisper.

His response was sincere, his eyes reflecting a depth of feeling that transcended the confines of this quaint cafe. I was rooted by his response, Small Business Saturday, the sugarplums on the side, and the silent courtship that had unfolded on his thrice weekly visits in the quiet corners of my coffee shop.

His exercise in methodical eating was a practice in mindfulness that leaked into our conversation. The intonations and inflections in his voice as he spoke, his body language, the scent of his cologne mixing with the beignets - all of it fed the story that was unfolding in my mind. The softness of his skin mixed with the strength of his hand as evidenced by the veins that were present when he held my hand. I saw it all. I absorbed it all. I felt it all. I lived in it.

Thank God for the flight attendant. Had I not been triggered, I wouldn't have pushed myself to be as open on this trip. I would've missed so much. I would've missed the connection.

Our conversation lingered into our stroll down Bourbon Street, just two souls on a journey of discovery. This trip wasn't just about beignets. It was about learning to relish all of life, appreciate it for what it was, one moment at a time. We browsed through titles and and chose a book for each other to read while we were in a quaint bookstore and then popped into a hidden art gallery. The air inside was filled with the scent of old canvases that seemed to insulate us from the bellowing bands outside. Paintings adorned the walls, each telling a story of its own. As we strolled through the intimate space, Jason's eyes sparkled with an infectious enthusiasm for the unexpected. We stumbled upon a secluded corner where the hair on my arms began to raise. The energy got stronger with each step we took. A small sign confirmed what I felt in my soul, "Emmaline's Free Readings," flanked the doorway of a closet-sized room with a table.

She appeared abruptly, a petite older woman with long flowing gray locks, then disappeared as quickly as her arrival. A smile on her face, her wagging finger beckoned us to the back. I looked at Jason, whose facial expression said he was game if I was.

"Let's see what she has to say," I said as I felt my body relax into the moment. Jason placed a hand on the small of my back, his body positioned to cover me just in case something got weird. The soft jingle of a bell announced our presence just beyond the entrance to this mystical portal.

Emmaline welcomed us with an air of mystery. "You found each other again," she said with a knowing smile as if she were privy to a secret only the universe held.

I exchanged a curious glance with Jason. The psychic beckoned us to sit, drawing out a deck of tarot cards. There was a quiet intensity that hung out between us as she laid three cards on the table, each flip revealing symbols and images that danced with unspoken meaning.

"The threads of your lives intertwined in the past and fate has brought you together again. A connection that transcends time and space."

Jason and I gazed into each others eyes again, a shared understanding of the serendipity that had led us to this moment. Our psychic friend continued, "You both carry scars from the past, but this journey between you is an opportunity for healing and growth." She looked up from the cards as though something had struck a nerve, "Who is Jenson?" I blinked rapidly, she was reading me and not the cards. Nobody else I knew of had met a person with the name Jenson. My pulse sped up when I realized she had the potential to spill all the beans, including the ones I held onto the tightest. "You just let him go on the way here. And Charlie?" I blinked and nodded. "He was meant to lead you back to your love," she said as she waved towards Jason. "Embrace the uncertainties. The universe conspires in your favor," she told me with such a serious look on her face. In the blink of an eye the glum was followed by a glimmer of light in her eyes. "His heart is pure."

I glanced in Jason's direction. His smile, reassuring. His loving gaze had returned. He was steady and calm. In the blink of an eye, I was as well. They say that home is the place where you live permanently, and he was definitely that for me.

The psychic continued, "Her soul resonates with yours but it's fragile. You know this though. You know each other well from before but it's important to learn each other in this life." Jason, still gazing my way nodded without speaking a word. His eyes though said everything that needed to be said and then some.

Emmaline had more information to share about our work lives, about our personal lives, and about what we would build together. By the time she was done speaking, I felt like she had stitched together a quilt of our past, present and future selves. She whispered something to Jason on our way out and I watched his face scrunch in confusion as he hustled to catch up to me.

Leaving the art gallery, the words of Emmaline lingered in the air, adding a layer of magic to our day. As we stepped back into the vibrant streets of New Orleans, the city seemed to whisper secrets of its own, echoing the promise of a newfound connection. Our silent walk took us from block to block, past colorful buildings with French influenced rod iron details.

Jason's words cut through the silence that hung out between us. "Miss Oakley," he began, his gaze steady, "I want you to know that I'm here for you, no matter what. I've told you before that I want us to move slowly. It's just because I know that trust takes time and I'm willing to wait."

His words were a balm to my mending heart. In that moment I was able to admit to myself that part of the rush was because I didn't want to lose him. But rushing through things had the potential to do the very thing that I didn't want to see. I exhaled softly, my body relaxing into his.

In the soft glow of the setting sun, Jason and I continued our adventure, hand in hand. The weight of his earlier confession still lingered and when mixed with the message from the psychic I couldn't escape the vulnerabilities it unearthed within me. The day in New Orleans had been a rollercoaster of emotions, stretching the boundaries of our budding relationship. We ventured back to the airport and waited at the gate for our flight to board. In the quiet moments between us, I felt a connection that stretched beyond words.

On the return flight, as the plane descended back into the wintry embrace of Kansas City, Jason reached for my hand. No words were necessary. I was tuned into the entirety of his message, body language included. The warmth of his touch and the sincerity in his eyes reassured me that this impromptu adventure was just the beginning. As the snowy landscape greeted us, I couldn't help but feel a shift. Something changed during that single day in New Orleans and I was left with a sense of anticipation for whatever was ahead.

He escorted me to the car, opening the door and guiding me inside to safety, then retreated to his side. I watched him move methodically, patiently, as though he were stalling. Once he was inside the car he pulled the seatbelt across his body and paused, gazing into my eyes wantonly.

"Whatcha lookin for in there?" I asked him.

He shook his head as if he were breaking out of a trance then fastened his seatbelt, a sly smile in the corner of his mouth.

I placed one hand on his before he could ignore the moment and drive away. The words exited much softer than I thought it would, "Jason, sir..."

"Miss Oakley?" he answered.

"Thank you for today," I said, waiting for his eyes to return to mine.

When they met across the cabin of the car, he nodded, "You bet, Bunny."

My leg was bouncing again. Uncontrollable.

I ran my left hand across the side of his face, memorizing every curve, every freckle, every beard and mustache hair. I was soaking in the moment when a wave of emotion hit me and I said exactly what was on my mind. No filter. No pretense. No beating around the proverbial bush. Just raw unfiltered emotion.

"Jason," I let his name linger on my tongue as I summoned the courage to speak life to the words that were burning a hole in my chest. "I love you and there's nothing you can do about it."

Chapter Seventeen
JASON

I leaned across the car and kissed her. I couldn't stop it. She had just told me that she loved me and that was the only response I could muster. When she'd tried to tell me on the plane I stuffed some pastry in her mouth. This time I used my tongue.

What a day. What a freakin' day. When she came to visit me last night I didn't know we'd end up in New Orleans for beignets. I didn't know we'd meet a psychic who would read our energy. I didn't know I'd tell her that I loved her and I fasho didn't know she'd tell me the same thing.

We weren't even a full week into the new year yet. I held her in my arms as best as I could with that seat belt holding me hostage and took in every detail there for me to feel. She was soft, physically and emotionally. And I sensed that she hadn't been the latter in a very long time.

That made me want to take my time with her even more than before.

I pulled away from that kiss and stared into her eyes again. The love was so deep I could feel it in my veins. "oooooooOOOOOOO!! What have you DONE to me woman?!?"

Her laughter brought a smile to my face - one that couldn't be wiped away like the lipstick her thumb removed from my lips.

"What have I done to YOU? What have YOU done to ME, sir?" she asked me.

I tried to shake it all away so I could drive, but there was so much joy in my soul that I couldn't stop smiling.

"Okay, neighbor. I need to get you home."

The silence was awkward. In my head it didn't sound the way it did once the words left my mouth. She snickered. I shook my head again.

"Well that didn't come out quite right," I told her as I put the car in drive and pulled out into the garage. We drove away in contented silence, on our way back to the neighborhood. Instinctively I thought to take her back to her house, just like I would after any normal date. But when I pulled up in front of her place she wouldn't get out of the car. I offered to walk her to the door. Nope. I held her hand and waited for her to move, but her eyes told me that she wasn't ready to say goodbye. That leg just bounced up and down with even more fervor than it did on our travels.

"Bunny, this has been one of the best days of my life."

"The best one for me, Jam."

"I can't wait to see what our next date brings."

"Me too," she said as she stared deep into my eyes and ran her fingers across my palms.

"In order for us to have a next date," I paused and took a deep breath. When I exhaled, I finished my thought, "we have to finish this one."

She whispered, "I know. I've tried to move about 5 times now, but my legs won't do anything except bounce with anxiety."

"What are you anxious about?" I asked her.

She didn't answer. I placed a hand on her leg to try to soothe whatever she was struggling with. I waited for a few minutes before I assured her, "I'll be right around the corner."

I almost wasn't finished with the statement before she asked, "Will you stay with me?"

"One day you won't even have to ask me. One day we'll have rings on our fingers and we'll be building a life together."

Her voice was soft. "One day?"

"One day, Bunny."

"But not today?"

"No ma'am. Not today."

She whispered, "Okay."

"Can I kiss you goodnight?"

She nodded and waited for me to unbuckle my seatbelt and lean across the car. It was supposed to be a sweet peck on the cheek to end the day. She apparently had other plans and turned her face to meet mine. Those lips. Those damn lips. She pulled me in. We were makin out in the car again. I don't know how much time passed before I actually was able to pull away from her and get out of the car. I took my sweet time walking around to open the door for her.

She didn't get out right away, so I held out my hand to help her out, closing the door behind her. She reeled me in for a hug and I held on tight, waiting for her to let go. She didn't. This was the type of hug I'd longed for in a partner. One that would be present with me, holding on for as long as they wanted without fear of meeting some sort of manufactured "appropriate" social constraints.

I whispered in her ear, "We're definitely back in KC. It's colder than a..."

She giggled. The warm air from her nostrils tickled the side of my neck and I kissed her. Again. In the cold night air. We were outside the car staying warm like two people in puppy love. I needed to walk away, but I couldn't help myself.

She pulled away, looking at the sidewalk. I nodded, knowing exactly what she needed. I slowly caressed the underside of her chin with the back of my index finger.

My words, barely audible, "Can I walk you to your door?"

She whispered, "We both know if you walk me to the door that you're coming inside."

I giggled. "No ma'am. I'll be good," I said as I interlocked my fingers with hers and started walking towards the front door. We got halfway there before she realized she'd left her bag in the car. "I'll go grab it. Meet you on the porch." I hustled back to the car, hoping to catch back up to her before she got to her front door but I wasn't fast enough.

When I grabbed her bag and turned around, she was already inside the house. In that moment I knew that I only had one option. Toss the bag and run. I'm kidding of course, but I was definitely nervous for the greeting that awaited me. I crept up to the door and rang the bell. She hollered from the hallway near the bathroom.

"Be right out!"

I wanted to tell her that I'd leave the bag on the couch

and call her when I got home. Instead my feet were cemented in place right there at the threshold of the door and I held my breath waiting for her to come back. I heard the door open and she peeked down the hallway.

"It's cold in this house. Can you close the door please?"

I shook my head no, not wanting to risk the decision to leave vs. staying.

She chuckled, "So you're just gonna run up my heating bill then?"

I shook my head again, then closed the door behind me. I could feel my heart beating in my throat. Anticipation of the unknown was gettin to me. She stepped out into the hallway, her coat no longer on.

"Thank you for grabbing my bag, Jason."

I nodded, my feet still stuck. There was a longing in her eyes. For what, I wasn't sure, but I knew if I had a chance of getting out of there tonight, I couldn't feed into the temptation to kiss her again. That would surely send us spiraling down a path that I wasn't sure I was ready for. Once we start that, I become the rabbit. Hungry. Ravenous. Insatiable. A subject change was required.

"So what made this your favorite day Miss Oakley?" Her face lit up as she told me about the best parts from her perspective; creating distance from work, being intentional, trusting herself, and Emmaline, the psychic.

"It's like she was looking into my soul, Jam," she uttered with wonder filled eyes. I couldn't agree more. She'd definitely read my ass.

"When she said your heart was fragile, it - it confirmed my thoughts."

"Which thoughts?" she asked as she held my hand and guided me towards the couch.

I took in her face before I answered. So open. So curious. "...to slow down." She nodded and tugged on my hand but I wouldn't sit down. I wanted to respect her space, her healing heart. She tugged again, a bit more firm this time but I didn't budge, which caused her eyes to meet mine.

She stared up at me like she was attempting to read my thoughts, then spoke. "Do you have time to sit down?" Her eyes lowered, almost as if in shame. "I know you've been with me all day, so if you need to go I understand."

Her guard looked like it was down and her face - so soft, sullen almost. She was completely vulnerable in that moment and I knew that's something she was working through. "I can create a few moments," I told her. She raised her eyes to meet mine again and I felt like I must've been lookin at galaxies or something. Life swirled all around in there. I was caught in her gaze. Again.

I sat down on the couch, leaving a bit of space between us but still connected through our touch. "I just wanted to talk to you about today," she said.

I nodded and waited. She was quiet. Almost like she wasn't sure where to start.

"Quite the day, huh?" I said attempting to lighten the mood. The corners of Oakley's eyes crinkled as she smiled.

"Definitely more than I bargained for when I woke up this morning," she shared, her tone offering hints of surprise and contemplation. Her eyebrows matched the latter.

I wanted to dive deeper, to understand what she felt about us, about me. But I held back, mindful of the delicate balance between my feelings and her need for space. The air in her house was thick with unspoken words and lingering thoughts.

A smile tipped the corner of her mouth before she spoke again. "I have so many things I want to say. So much to share, but I just realized how sleepy I am."

I stood to my feet, "I understand. I'd better head back home so you can get some rest. I know you'll be up early tomorrow to get back on the grind." She stood to her feet as well, those eyes looking me over like she was sizing me up. I started walking backwards towards the door, mindful of the furniture so I didn't trip over an end table and wind up on the floor. She tracked after me, slowly, methodically. My back finally pinned against the door, I fumbled for the knob to no avail.

"Can I kiss you goodnight?" she asked me.

I nodded, giving up the search for the doorknob and focusing my attention on my love, standing right in front of me. I hoped for a sweet kiss goodnight but her lips were soft. Her kiss, sensuous. I longed to keep kissing her. I needed it. My body craved it. I wrapped my arms around her waist and pulled her in as close to me as possible. She melted in my arms. Her weight came crashing down on me and as reckless as it sounds, it was much the opposite. She was cautious and prudent, not throwing caution to the wind but instead giving into her vulnerable side and allowing for a deeper connection in the process. It only took one sniffle to make me stop, drawing my face back to assess the situation. There wasn't sorrow in those tear filled eyes, but release. She had allowed me into her heart and I knew from that moment that I wanted to honor and protect it as much as she would allow me to.

I wiped the tears away and gazed into her eyes. There were still things to learn about each other but I was ready and willing.

I whispered, "I see your heart, Bunny."

She nodded and leaned back into me, whispering a message that struck me in my core, "I yearn for you, Jam."

It was at that moment that I was grateful to have been sandwiched by her and the door. I'm sure I would've dropped both of us because my knees buckled. Strong as I am, steady as I can be, I was wooed by her words. I've wooed others but I've never been wooed myself. I knew she was special when I first laid eyes on her and here she was proving it over and over and over again.

"You have no idea what you do to me, woman."

"I mean I can feel a lil something, sir."

I laughed heartily.

"I don't mean physically. I mean emotionally. And I want to preserve that. It's special."

"Is this good bye?" she asked wistfully.

I nodded, "For tonight."

"Just hold me a little longer please?"

I nodded. "Until you're ready to let go."

The door held onto us into the night until she convinced herself that it was okay to let go.

"Thank you, Jason."

I nodded and turned the doorknob, knowing if I was going to leave the house that this was the moment. She held onto my hand and nodded.

"Goodnight Miss Oakley," I said as I let our touch lapse one finger at a time.

"Goodnight Jason. Call me when you get home?"

I nodded and smiled at her attempt to extend the night anyway that she could then turned towards my car. The reluctance to part was shared, loaded with unspoken emotions and ripe with promise.

That trip around the corner to my house was much faster by car than on foot. I called her within a minute and assured her that I would text her when I was ready for bed. Back in my own space, the quietness felt so much more pronounced. Just this morning she was in my house with me and now I found myself wishing she were here and wondering how we would bridge our two worlds.

I sifted through the mail that had come in, placing one handwritten envelope with familiar penmanship aside to read later, then hopped in the shower to wash off the day. Once I was in bed I sent Oakley a text, "Goodnight Miss Oakley."

She replied, "Goodnight, Jam."

"Sleep well, Bunny. I love you."

Her reply was instant, "I love you too."

In bed, I reflected on our time in New Orleans. Emmaline's words echoed in my mind, a mysterious affirmation of our divinely timed connection. "You found each other again."

I wondered if it was the same energy that had pulled me away from Baltimore and led me to this moment.

I promised myself that I'd visit Oakley's coffee shop the next day. Not just as a gesture but as a step towards weaving our stories together. I wanted her to feel, to know, to trust that I was more than my past and ready to embrace whatever our future held.

Drifting off to sleep I held onto hope. I knew our journey together wouldn't be easy, but I was no stranger to challenge. I knew in my heart that this path, though uncertain, had the potential to lead to something beautiful - as long as that handwritten envelope didn't hold the wrench of a message inside that I anticipated it would.

Chapter Eighteen
OAKLEY

I leaned across the counter to serve up an order when the door opened and in walked the most pleasant surprise. My heart began to soar like a hawk eagerly waiting for the right moment to pounce on its prey. Not that I was stalking Jason, nor was he my prey, but my heart had definitely taken flight.

Last night was different. I'd grown accustomed to him snuggling me in the night. Sure it was just two nights in a row, but I missed him last night. I found myself lost in thought, trying to figure out what the psychic meant when she told us that we'd found each other again. Just me and my thoughts, hanging out in bed, trying to get some rest. I managed a few hours of sleep before I needed to get up. I got in earlier than normal because I wasn't sure if they closed the shop the same way that I did. Only a few things were different but it didn't require much more effort than usual.

I thanked each member of our team for their work in my absence yesterday and then jumped in on the floor to help them the same way I typically would. Now there he was, in my coffee shop, lookin like a model, certainly not any actuary I've ever seen. That smooth skin. That smile. Those eyes. Those damn dimples. That heart. Those lips. Sheesh. Those lips. He didn't do anything but walk in the door and all I could think about was leaning over the counter to greet him.

He waited in line like everyone else and pretended he was a normal customer. When it was his time to order, our cashier recited it with him which made me giggle. I had already started warming up his bear claw so it was ready for him by the time he paid. I gazed deeply into his eyes as I slid the pastry across the counter to him. His hand lightly grazed the top of mine as he reached for the plate. The touch was electric and I looped my pointer finger over the top of his thumb to brace myself. We held onto each other for just a blip of a second. But apparently it was long enough for our barista, Sophie to take notice.

She cleared her throat and asked me if I could share the magic remedy for my 24 hour bug. "I think my throat is starting to feel a little itchy," she joked. Jason chuckled, gathered his order and balanced it with the small notebook he carried in with him, then headed back to his regular booth. With a steady flow of customers getting back to his table might be more challenging than I'd like, but my determination was strong.

Every now and then I'd glance back to his table and he'd flash a boyish smile in my direction. Other times I'd notice a look of consternation on his face as he held an envelope in his hand. His eyebrows would scrunch as he'd look at it between sips of coffee and bites of bear claw. Those sugarplums had long disappeared. He set the envelope down on the table and patted it, pushing it away from him. Then brought it back to himself and raised it up high. Inspecting it. I nodded in his direction and he nodded in return, finally opening the envelope.

I watched his face shift uncontrollably between care and concern, then finally discontent. I don't know what news he'd just received but my glances in his direction increased in frequency, checking to ensure that he was okay. I excused myself and headed back to my office for just a moment to send him a text.

"Good morning, Jam - I don't know what's happening, but if you need me, blink twice the next time you look in my direction."

I went back out to the floor but he was gone. His tray was gone. His table had been cleaned. His notebook and the envelope were gone. There was no sign of him.

Sophie noticed my look of slight panic and pulled me aside.

"He cleaned his table and left quickly like there was an emergency."

I nodded, concerned about the possible emergency

that he faced when she added one more thing. "There was a woman who met him outside."

"Thank you, Sophie," I said as I slipped towards the back to check my phone for a reply. There was one waiting for me.

"Sorry, Bunny. Had to get to work. Call you soon."

It was seemingly such a small thing that set off a chain reaction of epic proportion. My body was fighting for what felt like survival. Something, a gnawing, nagging pull in my gut told me that wasn't the full story. In my head there was a wrestling. My tendency to withdraw and rebuild my wall of protection was being challenged and I didn't know how to respond to it. The walls felt like they were starting to close in on me and I...I just needed some fresh air.

I grabbed a nearby brick and propped the delivery door open on the back of the shop and stepped outside. The chill of the air snapped me back to the present moment, just long enough for me to see it. Jason, standing with his hands in his pockets while a gorgeous brown skinned woman with long straight, flowing hair rested her hand on his shoulder as she spoke. Her face was a glow and she lovingly caressed the roundness of her stomach, just below her belly button with the other hand. Her smile was warm as she gazed down at her body and back to his face. I turned my eyes to Jason and waited for his response. He was frozen in place, hands still in his pockets, his eyebrows furrowed and his face greying from what appeared to be shock.

The brick failed me. I heard it wobble then fall. The heavy steel door swung fast behind me and the loud squeal drew their attention in my direction. I couldn't reopen the it without the key that was sitting on my desk, just 5 feet away, inside the coffee shop. So I was stuck. In place. In a moment that felt like I wasn't supposed to be privy to. And all eyes were on me. I averted my gaze in an attempt to disappear.

His voice usually soothed me. This time it irritated my entire soul, "Oakley. Bunny."

His curvaceous friend sounded hurt as she spoke, "Bunny?"

Now that both of them had spoken, I knew I couldn't wish myself to another location. I opened my eyes, and Jason was just a few steps in front of me, arms outstretched - reaching to comfort me. He seemed to instinctively know how to show up for me. But in this moment, I was struggling to trust - not just him, but myself.

I curled into a ball inside his arms and sobbed. "I'm so sorry. I can explain, I promise. It's really not what it looks like. And I know how bad it looks."

I wasn't ready to hear him yet, I was too hurt to hear it as it was. I needed a minute - some distance so I could actually hear what he wanted to say. I shrugged out of his embrace, my tear stained cheeks facing him head on as I spoke.

"I can't have this conversation right now, Jason. I'm not

in a place where I can listen to you yet."

His hands returned to his pockets and his eyebrows furrowed as he nodded. "I want us to come back to it though. Promise me we'll talk about it?"

I nodded as quickly as I could. Every fiber of my being yearned to get back in the store. I pounded on the door, hoping that someone, anyone, heard my not-so-silent plea.

The door opened just as quickly as it closed and Sophie was my savior. She looked at me, then trained her eyes on Jason and his mystery guest, then back to me. I nodded and followed her inside.

"Promise me, Oakley?" he gingerly asked. I turned around to face him and controlled the weight of the door with my hand as it slowly slid in my direction. His face was serious, he was pleading. Not pleading his case, but pleading to be heard. I wanted to hear him out, but not right now.

"I'll text you at the end of the day, Jason."

He nodded, his face suddenly more optimistic and hope-filled. But that shifted in an instant. The last thing I saw before the door closed completely was her hand on his shoulder and his apologetic eyes.

Sophie spoke quietly as the door closed, "You okay?"

I shook my head no and slumped down in my desk chair. My hands covered my face as the tears came back to cleanse my eyes again. She placed one hand on my shoulder as she told me that she'd take care of things on the floor. I thanked her as she slipped out of the office and returned to the front of the shop.

There are two kinds of silence. The first still allows you to hear the other things you're currently co-existing with - the HVAC system, deep freezer, the muted but bustling conversations happening on the other side of the door. The second type of silence mutes all of the extraneous sounds and leaves you only with your thoughts.

I was fully involved in the latter but with just one thought, "You can't listen with a closed heart." I knew I needed a break from thinking about it, so I washed my face and hopped back out on the floor. I was ready to let the time pass like a rabbit or a turtle, however it felt in the moment. I was determined to rest and reset so I could listen with an open heart.

Chapter Nineteen
JASON

Damn. Damn - damn - damn.

It all happened so fast. I was there to get my morning coffee from my favorite coffee shop owner and before I knew it I got caught up in a shit-filled hurricane. One handwritten envelope and one random text sent my world into complete and total chaos.

When I grabbed that envelope from the mail, I immediately recognized the handwriting. Tina. The one who wanted to win me. I loved her, but I couldn't let her desire to control everything taint my world anymore. She's the main reason I stayed in Kansas City and here she was sending a hand addressed letter to me. I took it with me that morning, convinced that being near Oakley would somehow make it easier to read whatever was on the inside of the envelope.

Her text came in while I was staring at it. "I'm here in KC. Headed your way. We need to talk."

I opened the envelope and lost my breath. She'd sent me a letter and a photo of a child. I should've opened it at home. I shouldn't have taken it with me that morning. I looked towards the counter where Oakley was. I needed her reassurance. She was gone. Ghost. I got up to clear my head and get some air when I saw her at the door. Nope, not the woman I was just looking for, but Tina. She was right there waiting for me.

I asked her to walk with me, I wanted her as far away from the coffee shop and Oakley as possible. I couldn't stand the thought that she could muck this up for me. We were supposed to be building trust. I couldn't risk it. She'd even gone so far as to send me a text checking on me. I replied that I had to go to work and I'd hit her back as soon as I could.

When Tina tried to joke with me, "Hi Jason, it's good to see you too!" I grabbed her by the elbow and started walking around the corner. Where I was going, I had no freakin clue. I just knew it wasn't here and certainly not now.

"How in the actual fuck did you know where to find me?" I asked, my legs carrying me down the street and around another corner.

"You know your location is still available to me right?" She asked, trying to keep up with my harried pace.

"So you decided to use that to stalk me?" I asked, stopping abruptly in the alley, finally turning to face her.

Her arms folded across her chest, "We need to talk, Jason. I just used it to come see you so we could talk."

"What is this shit?" I asked her, pushing the envelope onto the folds of her arms.

"You calling your child shit?" She unfolded her arms and the envelope did flips on its way to the pavement.

"How old is that child, Tina?"

"Old enough to be yours, Jason!"

I shook my head as I looked at the picture poking out of the envelope on the ground. Maybe they had my eyes. I couldn't tell for sure. I was too angry to see straight at that point. With the exception of a couple of months ago, we've had two Presidential cycles since I'd seen her. This child would've been nearing the end of elementary school. Nothing made sense in that moment. Absolutely nothing.

Tina stepped closer, resting one hand on my shoulder. "She has your eyes, doesn't she? You see it, don't you?" I looked closer at the picture and placed my hands in my pockets as I realized she did.

My voice was humbled into quietude. I spoke softly, "Why did you wait so long to tell me?"

She rubbed her belly, "This one's yours too."

I had visited my family in Baltimore two weeks before Thanksgiving and I somehow thought things would be different with us. Tina and I never had a problem with physical chemistry. There was definitely a chance that this unborn life she so lovingly held in her belly was mine. But I couldn't figure out why she hadn't told me about the older child then. I opened my mouth to ask when I was startled by a squeaky, slamming door. Shit if it wasn't her, the woman of my dreams, standing there with her eyes squeezed shut like she was trying to be invisible.

"Oakley? Bunny!" I ran to her.

Tina sounded confused, "Bunny?"

I held her in my arms and she sobbed with an intensity that caught me off guard. I asked her to let me explain. She shirked away and pounded on the door. Told me she didn't want to talk about it now. I asked her to promise we'd come back to it soon. The door opened. I asked her again to promise me. She said she'd follow up with me tonight. I nodded my head, relieved that she was open to talking about it. Just as the door closed, I felt Tina's hand on my shoulder. I'm almost 100% sure the last face Oakley saw was one of sheer horror. I'd forgotten that Tina was there and that I might be a father.

I didn't want to turn around. "Who is she, Jason?"

I didn't respond. I just stood there staring at the closed door hoping the last thing she saw didn't change her mind. "You ran to her," Tina acknowledged. "You hid me in an alley."

I nodded, still not turning around.

"I know how much I love her," I told Tina.

"You love her. Mmhmm," she caught her breath then continued. "How long, Jason?"

"You're not gonna believe me when I tell you," I said, finally pivoting to face her.

"How long, Jason?" She asked again, her arms folded across her chest.

I shook my head, knowing how wild it was gonna sound when I told her the truth. "You're not gonna believe me. It's gonna sound crazy."

The question was gone. Only her demand for an answer remained. "How. Long."

"Five days."

"Five..." she laughed, "five, hah!" More incredulous laughter, "Five days?"

I was stoic and serious, "Five days."

Her voice dropped. Her eyes widened, "Five days? You knew you loved her after five days?"

I could feel a soft smile crest the corners of my mouth. I tried to stop it but she was asking me about the woman I loved. I couldn't help myself, "I knew I loved her when I first saw her face."

She sucked her teeth in disbelief. "So what happened to November?"

Everything that came out of my mouth was so matter of fact. Not much emotion, just strictly business. "I came in here a couple days after Thanksgiving and she got me."

Tina rolled her eyes and smirked like she had caught me in a lie. "But you said, five days."

I was stoic, "I did."

She shook her head back and forth like the math wasn't mathin'. "That's like five weeks though."

My lower lip almost disappeared as I mumbled, "Mmhmm."

Her eyebrows scrunched in discontent. She wasn't happy at all with the way this conversation was headed. "So is it 5 weeks or 5 days, Jason?"

I didn't mean to roll my eyes. It just happened. "It's 5 days, Tina. Days. Today is January 5th. Five days." I counted them out on my fingers, "The first, second, third, fourth, and fifth."

Her face looked ghostly. It was like she'd lost all blood.

"Humph" she paused and looked me in my eyes. "Were you ever that sure about me?"

I looked away at the door, then back to her hopeful face. "You don't really want the answer to that. Do you?"

She heaved a sigh so heavy I thought she'd been carrying something I couldn't see. "So that's a no then?"

I took a breath, staring directly into her right eye. "I ain't never been this sure about somebody in my whole entire life, Tina."

She pouted, "We have children together, Jason."

She stoked the fire and I was hot, "Children I just found out about today! Why the hell didn't you bring up the older child when we were together the last time I was at home? Does this child even exist?"

She handed me the envelope and I pulled the photo all the way out to look at the child again. Either it was Ai generated or she gave birth to a child that was part alien. The fingers are always a dead giveaway. Eight long and slender fingers on one hand was far too many to be convincing. In an instant, not only did I deny this computer generated kid, but I also had high doubts that the one in her belly, if there was one at all, was mine.

I stuffed the photo back in the envelope and placed it in my pocket.

My stance was firm and confident. "When was she born again?"

Her weight shifted from one leg to the other, "I told you

when she was born."

My feet were rooted in place. "You didn't. You only told me she was old enough to be mine."

She stuttered and stammered. Couldn't find a lie fast enough.

I spoke before any stories could come flowing out of her mouth, "I'll take a paternity test when you're ready. For both of them."

Her weight shifted to her heels - she looked like she was about to flee the scene, "You don't have to take a paternity test. I know they're yours."

I still hadn't moved, not one single inch. "I just want to confirm it for myself."

She straightened her coat, her hands brushing down the front of it. Her shoulders turned in my direction as she leaned forward ever so slightly. Her eyes fixed on mine looked up at me like a puppy dog. "Will you move back to be with me when we confirm it?"

That used to sucker me in. In fact, that shit worked on me in November. Not today though, "I ain't movin' nowhere near Baltimore. My family knows it and so do you. When we lost my sister, that was more than enough for me to stay away. If they're mine, I'll let my family know so they can get to know them. I'll fly back to visit them regularly. We'll figure it out remotely."

Those soft shoulders squared off in front of mine, "But you'd have me."

No dice. My smile was broad, "If I'm living in Baltimore, you better believe Oakley'll be there with me." I couldn't see myself there without her.

"Bunny?" she lambasted. "What makes her so special anyway?"

"Shit, what doesn't make her special? Look, I was on my way to work. I still need to go into the office. If you need something related to the test text me. If I'm available, we'll find a time to talk. But I gotta go."

I walked past her and kept moving, even when she called my name and eventually my phone. I walked back around the corner to my car and looked through the window of the coffee shop towards Oakley. She was staying busy but I could tell by her body language that something was bothering her and she was working through it.

I opened the door of my car and waited, hoping to catch her eye just once. Waiting. Just once. Waiting. She looked up in my direction and I just nodded. She shook her head from side to side and I got in my car and drove to work.

It wasn't lost on me that I was driving into work at the building where she used to be employed, likely from the same office. Today was the day I got to follow up with the team to transition her file to someone else. It felt like a conflict of interest because I replaced her. Add to the fact that I was in love with her and that could possibly set her up for additional scrutiny down the road. No. I had to transition her case to someone else and I knew exactly who it should go to. I had already emailed her about Oakley's situation before the year changed. I think I knew even then that we'd have a conflict of interest.

Michaela was just a few years out of school and was eager to help her fellow sistas out. She was big on equity and deconstructing white supremacy culture from within. We've had some deep conversations in the last few months. It didn't matter what it was, the conversational tides always seemed to point towards the need for change. When I talked to her about Oakley's coffeeshop and all of the ways she supports local artists and creatives, Michaela was excited about the prospect of helping her expand her operations.

I knocked on her cubicle wall and she turned around to greet me.

"Goodmorning, Andy! 24 hour flu all gone?"

I chuckled, "Feeling better. Not gonna lie." One quick flashback took me roundtrip again - New Orleans to Kansas City. I could see her angelic face smiling as she told me she loved me. Man I hoped this morning didn't fracture the trust we started to build yesterday.

Her eager voice snapped me back to reality, "Did she love it, Andy?"

I fought back a smile, "You'd have to ask her."

"Maybe someday I will."

"Maybe. Listen, here's the file I emailed you about yesterday."

"Ahh, thank you!"

"I'll email the two of you today, making the connection and completing the transition."

"Sounds good."

"Thanks for taking this one, Mickie."

"Yeah, no problem. Here are the two cases, I told you about."

"Got em. I'll have these closed out before the week is done."

"That soon?"

"Yep. These shouldn't take long. Honestly, that one wouldn't have taken long either, but uhhhh..."

"You fell in loooOOOooove."

"Hush." I said to her as Michaela giggled and nodded. I stood still, knowing she was right and feeling grateful for the newness of this year. "Alright, let me get to it."

"I can't wait to be in a relationship with a man who looks at me with half as much love as you do when you think about her. Let's be honest though, I'm never getting married."

Here she goes.

"American Marriage is a social construct of white supremacy culture."

"Oh boy."

"It is! Historically, the woman became property of the man, hence why she took his last name. Who benefits from a woman squandering away her talent and tending to the cooking and cleaning? White men were given the freedom to be and do whatever they want. Meanwhile women were held captive by financial rules that wouldn't allow them to leave even the most oppressive situation. And let's not even talk about their rules prohibiting the enslaved from getting married. They rolled all of it together into a tight little package wrapped in religion."

"Well Michaela, thank you for that retrospective on the institute of marriage."

She chuckled, "Seriously, Andy. I'm just sayin, if you love her the way you look like you do, take her last name."

"I'll take that into consideration," I said as I tapped the folders on the side of the cubicle wall and headed back towards my office. "Have a great day!"

"You too!"

I walked into my office, sat down in my chair and spun around to the computer. I clicked open the mail client and started drafting an email between Michaela and Oakley. An email that should've taken no more than 20 minutes to draft and send ended up taking an hour and a half because of all the co-workers who stopped in to wish me a Happy New Year.

They had taken vacation. I didn't. They had spent time with family. I hadn't. They found work-life harmony. I now understood why someone could want that. Before, work was priority for me because it kept me busy. I didn't have to think about being so far away from my family. I didn't have to think about the dates that were few and far between. I didn't have to think about all of the things that were missing from my life. Now I had something real, something tangible, someone real that let me feel the weight of more than work. I'd prioritized life over work more in the last five days than I had in the last five years.

Two quick knocks on my door then a flurry of words. Typical entry for Christopher. "Jason, Happy New Year! Got your email on the Butterfield's. Great work sir."

"Hey Chris! Thanks man. Good to see you this year."

"So what's new? Somebody said you had the 24 hour flu yesterday." He looked at me like he knew a lady was involved. "Are you contagious?" he joked.

"Nah, I'm good," I laughed. "Thanks for asking." A smile that would rival a toothpaste model was spread wide on my face.

"The New Year looks good on you man. Whatever you're doing differently, whoever is giving you that glow, keep it in your life."

"Aight man, let me get back to this email. I got some work to catch up on from yesterday."

"Yep. I'll be ready for our 3:00," he said. I nodded as he walked away.

I was reviewing the email draft when I heard a familiar voice, "Knockity, knock!"

I spun back around to greet Brian. "What's good man?"

"Ayooo, 24 hour flu looks good on you dude."

"Ahhh...funny."

"So the wife and I are having a couples night this weekend..." he side eyed me, a smirk filling his face before he continued. "Can we count on the two of you to join us?"

"The two of us?"

"Yeah, you and Tami?"

"Tami?"

"Tamiflu?"

I spun back around in my chair and laughed. "Man, get outta here with yo corny jokes."

"She's got that good good, huh? Cured you right on up," he said walking into my office and plopping down in the chair across from me.

"Aye, lemme send this email right quick, bro."

Brian nodded, "Dear Tami, you got the cure."

"Bruh." I typed out the rest of the email and clicked send, then looked up at Brian, who was batting his eyelashes in my direction. "What?" I asked him. He batted his eyelashes again. I laughed, "Whaaat ninja?"

"So who we invitin' to couples night?"

"I'll tell you later man. Let's link for lunch or drinks or something soon."

"Yep. Tomorrow maybe? I know you have your big 3:00 today."

I reached across the desk and dapped him up. "Two big cases to close. But soon though."

"We'll figure it out," he said as he stood up to leave.

"Yep."

"Aight man," he said as he left me with my work.

Playing catch up on work meant the day flew by. I was able to get on the calendar of both clients I'd traded with Michaela. Then right before I was on my way to the big

3:00, I received an email reply from Oakley.

"Andy, thank you for everything you've done thus far, and for connecting Michaela and I via email. Michaela, I look forward to working with you. I've enclosed my availability below."

On my way to the conference room for my 3:00, I thought about how weird it was to have her call me Andy and not Jam or Jason. It was weird to have her be so formal. But it needed to be that way for the sake of protecting her business. I was content with the transition and held that confidence as I walked into the 3:00 meeting and outlined the plan for Q3 and Q4 of this fiscal year. I walked out of that meeting and headed straight into my supervisor's office per her request.

"So Andy, it looks like you've set us up for a strong finish to this fiscal year."

I nodded, my hands folded across my lap, waiting to find out why I was called into her office spur of the moment.

"I know you're wondering why you're sitting in my office when there wasn't an official meeting request sent to you."

I nodded again.

"I've received an anonymous tip that you've been inappropriately engaged with a client."

"I transitioned the file to Michaela today as soon as I got into the office."

"I understand that and do truly appreciate your swift attention to rectifying your misconduct. But this is still a case of your misconduct."

My stomach was filled with knots, "I understand."

"We've terminated people for less. This is a direct conflict of your agreement. I've spoken with the Board and we're all in agreement on the next steps."

"I'll pack up my office immediately."

"We're putting you on probation for the next 4 weeks."

I shook my head in disbelief, "I'm sorry?"

"Not even one tiny blip of misconduct or error, sir."

"Can do."

"Alright. Keep up the phenomenal work sir. I'm trusting you'll do what's best for yourself and the company."

"Yes ma'am," I said, feeling overwhelmingly grateful that I still had a job. What struck me the most as I walked out of her office was just how quickly I was okay with the notion of losing my job over Oakley. I could start again somewhere else. None of that mattered in the moment. Had you asked me if this would've been my response in October I would've laughed at you. There would be no way I'd so easily sacrifice my job without a fight. Now look at me, ready to give it all up in a heartbeat.

I was lost in thought walking down the hallway to my office, sitting in my office replying to emails on auto-pilot, when my phone buzzed on the desk. I turned my head in its direction and noticed it was from her.

"Hey Jam, just met with Michaela. You okay?"
"Hey Miss Oakley, I'm good. One month of probation."

"Because of yesterday?"
"Umm, no. Long story. How are you?"

"I'm okay. Long day. Cook you dinner tonight?"
"Can we cook it together?"

"Sure. 6:00?"
"Yep. What can I bring?"

"The truth."
"You got it. See you at 6."

Oakley L. Powell-Mitchell liked your message.

I couldn't help but think about the way this day started and here she is checkin on me to see how I'm doing. I couldn't wait for 6:00. I didn't know what her meeting with Michaela was like, but "long day" felt ominous.

Chapter Twenty
OAKLEY

My Ring doorbell sounded at 5:55. If he was going to be nothing else, Jason was going to be on time. I was still washing my hands in the bathroom at the time so I answered it on my phone.

"Hey I thought I had 5 more minutes."

That endearing smile appeared again. "I can run around the block if I need to."

"You don't have to run anywhere. I can give you the code."

His head shook adamantly. "No ma'am. You're not giving me the code. I'm a patient man. I can wait in the car."

"I'll be out sooner than a chicken lays an egg."

His body leaned into laughter, "I have no idea how soon that is Miss Oakley, but I'll be out here when you're ready for me."

I spent the next four minutes talking myself into letting him in instead of hiding away in my self-induced hermitude. Deep in my gut I knew the conversation we were about to have was going to force me to be vulnerable and bare my soul. While there was a knowing reassurance that I'd be okay, my brain was working overtime to sabotage it all.

At 6:01 I opened the door. Jason waved from inside his car, fully entrenched in his car karaoke set. He was gettin it to the 6LACK verse on the I Want You Around remix, choreo and all. I returned the wave then motioned for him to come inside and walked away from the door. The way he was enjoying the music I didn't want to interrupt.

He waited for that verse to finish then came to the door humming the song loud enough for me to hear it as soon as he stepped out of his car. The closer his voice got, the more anxious my brain became. The more anxious my brain, the more tense my muscles. I stood in the kitchen, fighting my reflexes so I could unclench my jaw. When he knocked on the front door, a wave of calm spread over my body. Everything relaxed. The door swung open before I could answer it and he sauntered inside. His scent. Intoxicating. I wasn't ready have this conversation under the influence. But here I was, tipsy - from his scent, and from the familiarity of Jason letting himself into my house.

In that moment it very much felt like he was coming home - to me. The ease of it all had me off-kilter and out of my head, at least for the moment.

I turned in his direction and smiled as he locked the door. My senses on overload - it felt like I heard every pin fall into place within the lock. The silence that filled the room was heavy, but my heart was light. Jason regularly brought a calming presence with him and I could feel the shift as my house once again transformed into a home.

That deep rumble returned as he turned to face me. "So chickens must take a minute to lay eggs, huh?" he said as he opened his arms to greet me. I felt myself wrapped up within them before I knew it.

I don't remember my feet moving, but I went from the doorway of the kitchen to the front door in what felt like the literal blink of an eye. I needed him and my body did what was necessary to meet that need. My heart felt better when he was near, and when he wrapped me up in a hug there was a depth of love present that I hadn't known before we met in this lifetime. He didn't have to say a thing. I could feel every word right there in that embrace. Everything that I am was welcomed with his gentle presence. And he just held on, chest to chest, heart to heart, cheek to cheek, no motion to let go. Just waiting, for as long as I wanted, as long as I needed while the slow burning fire roared between us.

I leaned in hard, absorbing his love as I felt it creeping in. That nagging voice of doubt questioned whether or not I deserved to experience love like this. I gasped ever so slightly, but he knew what I needed well enough to squeeze just a little bit tighter.

His voice, a near whisper in my ear, "What is it Bunny?"

I already felt tipsy but there was something about the care and concern in his hushed voice that brought on a full blown SWV episode. My knees got weak. I could hardly speak. The blood was racing through my veins and something came over me. I nearly passed out. "I need to sit down," I whispered.

Jason walked me over to the couch and sat down with me, the heft of his arm wrapped around my back, soothing me like a weighted blanked. Those internal thoughts were starting to overwhelm me. I lay my head on his shoulder and his head lay on top of mine. We sat in silence while he loved me slowly. I lost all track of time because of his endearing patience. I vividly remember the clock reading nearly 6:30 when he began to softly hum the song he was listening to in the car. The love within his tone felt like he was pouring a magic potion into me - and that elixir was liquid courage.

I felt it coursing its way through my body. I took one deep breath and exhaled my fears. Tears trailed down my cheeks as I spoke. "I don't know that I deserve your love, Jason."

His voice, tender, "What do you mean?"

"The way I treated Charlie, I'm not sure if...I guess I'm waiting for..." I let my words trail off and Jason just waited patiently.

I wiped the tears that rolled down my face and couldn't believe that my right mind was leading me to admit such a deeply personal fear. But I felt safe enough to let it out and well, the wheels were moving faster than the car at that point. It felt like I didn't have a choice. My lips parted and out flew my thoughts, "I don't feel like I'm good enough to receive a love like yours."

He shook his head, not saying anything in return, just looking lovingly into my eyes. I started to speak again and his index finger quickly found and pressed up against my lips as if to shush the words that were about to bumble out.

"You, Oakley, as you are right now, are unique and mysterious, and funny, and beautiful at your core and on the surface. I know your big heart was hurting when you made the choices you made in the past. But those choices only define you if you let them. You will always, ALWAYS, be lovable and valuable and worthy of love. But only when you forgive yourself will you let the goodness in."

One hand to my face, he wiped the tears from my cheek then kissed my widow's peak as I nodded. I could feel my heart expanding and growing as he spoke more life into my world.

"I wish I could take those thoughts and make them disappear, but all I can do is continue to remind you that I'm here and I love you, as you are. There are no conditions on it. This isn't some car offer with hidden clauses. This is the most pure love I've ever felt for another adult in my life. And I'mma be here when you're ready for me."

I couldn't squeak any words out. Just a nod or two, then he continued with words that broke me wide open, "And if at the end of all of it, I've loved you and you find yourself somewhere other than with me, that's okay too. I don't want you to think that you have to be with me because I love you so deeply. I just want you to know that my love is unconditional and I'm here for as long as you'll let me share your world."

I nuzzled my face into his neck and kissed him. It was the first part of him that I came in contact with and I didn't mean to start something, but when I felt his fingers run through my hair I knew I had inadvertently set a five-alarm fire. He didn't kiss me in return, but his leg started bouncing with vigor like he was fighting it - hard.

I whispered to him, "Kiss me if I'm wrong, but dinosaurs still exist, right?"

He grabbed my waist and pulled me onto his lap, kissing me so deeply I couldn't decipher where his soul began and mine ended. I melted into him, allowing myself to get lost in however long the moment was. Jason was home. I was safe. And that combination allowed me to let loose in a way I hadn't yet experienced. He loved me through my guarded heart and created a space for me to be soft and gentle. I quietly snickered and Jason, while still sucking on my lower lip, chuckled and told me, "that felt like a trap."

"I just wanted you to know it was okay to kiss me. That's all. I know you're trying to be patient, Jam."

He moaned and "Mm mm MMMphed" his way through the next 15 seconds of blissful contact, at one point mumbling that he, "almost forgot to breathe for a minute."

I didn't know up from down and I don't know what got into me. Maybe it was the warmth of his kickstand that I could feel pulsing beneath me, but I couldn't be stopped. I broke away from those luscious lips just long enough to catch a breath and call for him, "Jason?"

"Mmhmm?" He asked, pulling me back to him. We called timeout to regroup, resting forehead to forehead in contented silence, catching our breaths and considering all of the options on the table.

I lowered my voice and spoke as softly as my heart felt in that moment, "Are you gonna take me back to the bedroom or do I have to lie to my journal tonight?"

"Oh Shit..." he said as he pulled his face away from mine and stared into my eyes like he was trying to decide if I was serious. The look in his eyes mirrored my own feelings—desire, love, and an undeniable connection. His mouth hung open slightly and I wiped away as much of my lip gloss as I could. "But we...we're supposed to be making dinner together right now."

I bit my lower lip as I tried not to laugh at what I was about to say, "I mean, I have some dinner for you if you want it."

His dimples resurfaced as he gazed into my eyes. My hands cupped his face, my fingers resting behind his ears and my thumbs caressing the cheekbones that were covered by the sudden rush of blood that flooded upwards. He let out a shallow exhale before he spoke. "How bout this..."

My chest heaved - passionate, labored. I waited impatiently to hear his proposed plan. My front teeth slowly grazed across my lower lip and his lips parted like he was aching to kiss me again. He forced a blink and shook his head to refocus as I ran my fingers across the buttons on his crisp white collared shirt.

"Okay. Okay. Okay," he said as he finally released his full grip on my waist and used one hand to stop my fingers from undoing the first of several buttons.

"How bout what, Jam?" I asked, the passion surging through my veins.

His eyebrows danced like he was sifting through his options. He nodded, firm in whatever decision he'd landed on. "Fuck it. Let me make you dinner tonight."

My face grew warm in anticipation, a smile breaking through the butterflies, "Wait, you're gonna make dinner for me or you're gonna make me dinner?"

He stood to his feet with me in his arms, my legs wrapped around his waist, "Yep."

I giggled into his ear as he walked towards the bedroom,

his sexy musk wafting through my nostrils, "Oh my!"

He snuck a quick glance at me, "Behave now."

"It's far too late for that, sir," I said as I started to remove the hoodie I had thrown on after work. I dropped it on the floor as he opened the bedroom door.

"Save some for me please?" he asked me. I nibbled on his ear. "Oh shoot, woman. You're not playin fair," he said as he walked to the edge of the bed and playfully patted my butt so I'd drop my feet. "Let me look at you."

I struck the goofiest poses I could muster as he visually took me in from head to toe. His smile was wide, dimples on full display, and those eyes – they caught me yet again.

"Can I take your shirt off, Miss Oakley?" He asked with a sincerity that stopped my goofy antics in their tracks. I nodded. The sensation of his fingers caressing my shirt covered back as his hands tracked their way to the hem made my heartrate skyrocket. His gaze never faltered, even when the shirt crossed in front of us on its way over my head. I tried to fix my hair and he swatted my hands away with a look of adoration in his eyes. We stood still, taking each other in, mere inches apart, in silence, simply enjoying each other's charged presence.

"Can I touch you?" he asked, waiting until he had a response from me before moving a muscle.

"Yes, Jam," I affirmed. A shiver ran down my spine at the gentle touch of his hands on my bare skin. They coursed from my neck across my shoulders and down my arms, letting his fingers play with mine for a minute, that gaze still locked in. I was lost in what felt like a million lifetimes of love. He guided my hands behind his head and neck, and I felt his strong hands gently tracing my back again, methodically exploring every inch with deliberate care. My labored breathing had slowed as I absorbed every millisecond of his loving touch. My heart though, experienced a surge, its beat quickening as the warmth of that touch stoked a fire within me. The space between us charged with a magnetic energy impossible to ignore. The tension coiled in my chest.

The world outside ceased to exist as we lost ourselves in each other. I let my fingers roam, making their way to the buttons of his shirt, pausing to seek permission first with my eyes. He nodded and stood stoically while I freed each button and removed the shirt from his shoulders, untucking it from his pants and slowly letting it drape onto the bed. His chiseled chest radiated strength and vitality, commanding attention. My hands surrendered to the pull, tracing the lines that seemed to request my touch with gentle reverence.

"Can I take this off?" he asked as he ran a finger underneath the shoulder strap of my bra. Not the cute bra, ladies! The one you put on so you won't be tempted to reveal it anyone else. I didn't care. He made me feel like it didn't matter. Not the way he looked at me. He wasn't paying any attention to that.

Still caught in his gaze, I softly whispered "yes" as I leaned into his chest so he could unfasten the hook and loop. An empowered sensation coursed through me as he slid each strap off my shoulders. Embracing an unrestrained freedom, I leaned back and let gravity do its job - a release from all constraints. He finally broke our gaze, his eyes leaving mine and slowly traveling down my body with a reverent curiosity, taking in every curve, tracing the unfamiliar and inviting lines as if he were mapping his path to pleasure. I stood still, my power amplified by his awe-struck exploration that seemed to wrap me in a light that was lit from within.

"Jam?" I called as his hands followed his eyes on their journey to discover every uncovered inch of my body.

I could see the desire growing within him - a smoldering intensity, bubbling beneath the surface, ready to burst. "Yes ma'am?" his smoky reply. I found myself gripping his shoulders, grounding myself as the magnetic pull between us amplified in strength. I reached out to caress his face, guiding his eyes back up to mine.

I don't know where it came from or why I thought it was good to ask, but it came flying out faster than a pig at chow time. "What's your favorite part of me?"

His answer stopped me in my tracks. "Your body or your soul?"

I didn't have a response - the words, caught in my throat.

He chuckled, and answered his own question, trapping me in a sensual gaze that took my breath away, those fingers spread wide, gripping my back. "Your soul's energy feels healing. Your light is so full - and bright." It was in that moment that I had completely come undone. I buried my closed eyes in his neck. He tilted his head to meet mine as he continued, "And, well, I've only seen 50% of you so far, but you have this peak on your upper lip right in the middle where the two sides meet that I adore."

As if I weren't already deeply in love with this man, the fact that he'd paid such close attention to my face, to really see me, made me feel valued and appreciated in a way that turned me out. He could see me in ways that others hadn't bothered to and I was totally his, however he wanted me. This love of ours was either going to give me life or completely wreck me in the best way possible.

His fingers tugged at the waistband of my joggers and slightly twisted, the tension, the pull, the anticipation turned up the temperature another notch. I moistened my lips with the tip of my tongue, letting it linger, letting it take its time, pretending it was him. The natural reaction below the belt creating a slick warmth that made me self-conscious. I lowered my head feeling that vulnerability take charge. His head tilted until he caught my gaze again, a wanton twinkle in his eyes as he whispered his request. "Can I see the other half of you Miss Oakley?"

As if things weren't already a steaming sauna down there, he was about to be met with the metaphorical flood of Babylon. His touch made me feel whole and free and I had a deep-seated feeling that the level of debauchery that was about to go down would be one that would cleanse our souls and somehow ironically restore us to the most pure form of ourselves.

All of this rolled through my head as I slowly nodded at my love. Again, his eyes stayed locked on mine as he slowly removed my pants and supported me as I stepped out of each leg. His hands slowly trekked a route from my ankles to my calves and shins - eventually making their way to the back of my knees which made me want to pull him on top of me. Those strong hands found their way up my thighs and around to the fold of my rear where he gently gripped and kneaded - only for a moment. That irresistible force drew us together, our movements fluid and instinctual. The moonlight streaming through the windows bathed the room in a soft glow, casting shadows that danced across our intertwined bodies.

I reached for his belt and tugged, asking with my eyes if I could remove it. He nodded and I listened to his keys as they hit the ground, still buried within his pants pocket. There we stood, me on top of the bed, nothing protecting me but the panties I usually wore when I was doing laundry, him on the floor, wearing nothing but socks. Apparently I had grabbed more than his pants. He didn't flinch. He was unapologetic in both his nakedness and what greeted me as a result. It was time for my eyes to roam, to trace the outline of his rigid frame, my hands following suit as I pulled him closer to me. Time seemed to stand still.

There in that moment, as he bared all of himself to me, the superficial barriers around him now gone, I felt grounded within. These knees still wobbled though. I ran my fingers underneath his chin and whispered, "I know you." He buried his face in my stomach and kissed my belly button. A shockwave raced the entirety of my spine and my weak knees finally buckled.

"Come here. Lay down," he insisted. I complied without hesitation or question. His hands guided me gently to the bed, my hips positioned close to the edge of the mattress. He lifted my arms above my head and slid a pillow vertically from my shoulder blades to the top of my head, then guided my hands beneath the pillow and kissed me softly.

"Can I see all of you?" he asked as I nodded eagerly - mostly ready for him to no longer ogle the final hour draws that I was currently sporting. His hands lifted my waist off the bed as he peeled the final layer from my body, revealing everything I was born with and some that joined me a little later. The floodgates were now officially open. "Damn," he said as he licked his lips, ready to make good on his promise.

Chapter Twenty One
JASON

Everything I ever wanted was right there within my arms as I greeted her at the door. She floated in from the kitchen and nuzzled in for a hug that felt calming. I didn't know what the evening had in store for us, but each moment with Oakley felt like it lasted forever, so this relatively short relationship felt more like a lifetime to me.

I could feel her about to break before she told me what she feared so I held onto her, patiently pouring as much comfort as I could in her direction. As soon as I told her what I saw in her soul, she attacked me. She didn't really attack me, but passion sent her for the jugular and she definitely hit the spot that turns me into the hulk. Remember the bags of chips that I devoured without savoring? She flipped that switch as she nibbled on my neck and I was well on my way to another impassioned zone out with Oakley as the target. I had been ready to talk about what happened this morning and with the rest of her day. I didn't think we were goin there tonight. It was the farthest thing from my mind. But the more she teased me, the stronger the urge. I tried so hard to fight it. I really did. But every single time her lips moved across my skin that craving built within me - called to me, until it was so strong that all I needed was a hint of a reason and everything would be different.

She asked me to kiss her. That was it. I couldn't fight it anymore. My lips craved her, a blend of tenderness and urgency that elevated the intensity. I needed to be as close to her as physically possible and she went with the flow as I pulled her on top of my lap. I'm a patient man but she gave me the green light over and over and over again. The more we kissed, the more certain I was that tonight was about to be the night I loved all of her, if she was all in. I felt the passion building all through my body and before I knew it, I was carrying her off to the bedroom. I watched her wriggle, then ducked as she tossed her hoodie on the floor behind us. I wasn't the only one feelin the urge and I could see it as I lowered her to her feet on the bed.

Her eyes drew me in and said yes, but I didn't want to make any assumptions. I wouldn't touch her until she gave me consent to love her, slowly. Every time she said yes, every little bit, every little 'more,' every teeny ounce of resolve that was left started to melt away. You only get one set of firsts with someone and I was trying to savor the moments before we entered the phase of no return - the last of the physical firsts.

Every inch of her body responded to my touch.

Goosebumps and hair standing on end, and all of it drove me to touch her just a little bit more, let her feel me, slowly. We stood just an inch between us, held together by a heavy energy that felt familiar even though I hadn't felt anything like that before. She undressed me and my restraint was in tact until she ran her fingers through my beard and told me she knew me. I kissed the closest part of her body to me and caught her as she relied on my hands to hold her up.

"Come here," I told her, knowing good and well that what I was about to do to her would take her breath away. "Lay down," I urged, my hands guiding her towards the bed. She didn't say a word, just followed instructions while gazing into my eyes.

When I asked to see all of her, a knowing smile cracked in the corner of her mouth. Did I mention she was perfect? Every single solitary wet inch of her being was perfect. "Damn." It was the only word I could conjure up in the moment. I just stood there in awe of her glory, eager to taste her. Eager to satisfy her. Eager to help her feel what I felt for her.

The moonlight bathed her skin in a glow that damn near robbed me of my voice. I could only manage a whisper. "Can I touch you?"

She clenched her lower lip between her teeth and a slow nod preceded her breathy response. "Wherever you want, however you want, Jason."

"Wherever?" I asked as I caressed her ankle. She

nodded. My voice soft and low, "However?" I asked as I kissed the top of her thigh.

She squirmed, her face a mix of anticipation and pure lust. She licked her lips and repeated her words, this time through shallow breaths, "Wherever you want, however you want, Jason."

I dropped to my knees, almost in worship of her, wrapping her legs around my back and pulling her close to me. "Wherever?" I asked as I ran my hand from her knee up to the top of her thighs, across her inner thigh, and watching her shudder as she felt my thumb caress the soft folds of her temple door.

"Mmmmmmm...mmhmm."

Just a little bit more. If I had anything to say about it, I was about to guide her to a level of satisfaction she'd never felt before. That was my goal - to love her completely and thoroughly.

I whispered, "However?"

She cupped my face and pulled me up for another kiss, her hands roaming down my back and pulling my body in until all of our body parts were introduced to each other. She was warm and inviting, everywhere, so I asked her again - I'm sure she could sense the passion building within me, "However, Miss Oakley?"

"Love me," she panted, "touch me however you want."

I nodded, wearing only a mischievous smile. "Be back in a moment," I told her as I kissed my way from her face down her torso, returning to the door to all the hidden treasure. "You look so sexy, laying there, waiting for me to ravish you."

One long lick must've been the code to unlock the next level. Her legs opened wide while her hands gripped the back of my head. She tasted as sweet as I thought she would and the deeper my tongue explored, the more flavors I got to taste. Her body worked to feed me just as fast as I could eat it. She got louder with each stroke of the tongue and I wanted to take her right to the edge.

"I love it when you moan, Bunny. Don't hold back." Her hips began to grind into my mouth until we caught a rhythm. She was letting me see all of her and it had me ready to go. "How's that feel? Tell me what you like."

"Aaaaaaaaaaaaaaaaaaaaaaaaaaaah - aaall of it. You...I... shit...I can't talk. Mmmmmmmmm." I watched her eyes roll into her head and felt her body begin to shudder. I had to time things just right, I wanted to stop right before she started to quake. My lips smacked and lapped and tried to keep up with the floodgates but I couldn't. The more furiously I tried, the closer she got to the edge. "Jaaaaaaay. Jaaaaaaaaaaaaaaay."

"Mmm hmmm?" I asked still devouring her.

"Don't stop, Jam." That was my cue, she was writhing and about to burst. I licked her slowly one more time then pulled away. She touched herself while she waited for me to finish licking my lips as clean as they could be.

I gazed deeply into her eyes, waiting for just the right time to speak. She was working herself into a frenzy and it was like watching Beethoven create a sonata. "I wanna come with you. Can I..."

"Please," she interjected. "Uh huh. I want you inside me."

I shook my head as I rifled through my pants. I didn't have any protection with me. Then it hit me. We were gonna fix dinner and have a hard conversation. I wasn't supposed to be hard and having her for dinner.

"I don't have a..."

She reached in her nightstand and grabbed a handful of condoms, sifting through the sizes as she ogled my dick.

"This one," she said as she handed me a magnum. "Are you allergic to latex?"

"No ma'am, I'm good." I told her as I rolled the condom on.

"I bet," she said, chuckling as she gazed into my eyes.

"Well, shit," I said, feeling like I had a lot to prove.

She reached down for me, stroking me and gently guiding me closer to her. I got lost in her eyes as she began to tease the tip with her temple gates. I closed my eyes and shook my head, knowing that I was about to go off the rails with this one.

She guided me inside and I stopped breathing. It felt like I was connected to the source of the universe and my body was responding in unexpected ways. I felt a tear roll down my cheek and her hand caress it away. I couldn't even begin to find a stroke, let alone one that would let us climax together.

She whispered, "Can I take us there?"

I nodded and grabbed her hips, rolling with her as we switched positions. "I can't feel my fingers. Everything's hot."

"Me too. What's happening? Why does it feel so good?" She asked as she rode me slowly.

It was a symphony of shared passion, each stroke a note resonating with the depth of our connection. "Oh shit," I felt my eyes roll into my head. "I dunno." Our music beginning to quicken in tempo. Accelerando.

"Jam you feel so good."Mezzo forte.

"Yo. I am not in control of my body right now," I loudly writhed. The music, Forte.

"Let me love you through this, Jason," she said - our bodies tied together. Legato.

Everything was happening so swiftly. I couldn't explain

it. "Are you doing this to me?" The music repeated itself, building to a breaking point.

"Uhn-uhn this is different." Her stroke game continued, "Never felt this before."

I held her hips and watched as she shifted gears on me. Slowly. Faster. Slow. Fast. My body was confused and I loved every second of it. "Damn woman!" The energy and zest increasing, Energico.

She bucked and shrieked, holding onto my chest for balance. "I can't hold on much longer, Jason." The crescendo.

It felt so good she had me sucking air through my teeth. "Mmmmm. Shhhhhit, me either!"

Her walls gripped my dick and any control I thought I had flew right out her bedroom window. I sat up in bed and held onto her as I dropped the kids off in the condominium. Each pulse inside her drained me and sent her into a spiritually charged orgasm. We held onto each other, sweaty and empty, but somehow I felt cleansed and renewed. Our connection seemed to transcend the physical. Descrescendo.

Time seemed to stand still, her body completely relaxed into mine, love wasted. Her craving and mine contented. My heart, full. She sobbed into my shoulder. "Talk to me Oakley." I kissed her forehead and tried to catch my breath. "What's going on, love?" Decelerando.

Her face still buried, "You're not gonna believe me." She sobbed some more.

"Try me," I said lifting her face and looking into her eyes. I nodded. "Try me."

She lay wrapped within my arms and took a moment to gather herself. "I feel like I just made love to God himself." I definitely didn't see that coming out of her mouth.

"Wait - what?"

"See. I told you." She chuckled through her tears.

"No," I panted, still out of breath. "Tell me more."

"There was a, a white flash of light that was coming from your body as you were, you know."

"I thought that was you," I told her. I'd seen it in my mind as I closed my eyes and held on for dear life.

She stared at me, her face serious. "Jason, who are you?"

"Who am I? Miss Oakley. Did you feel the way your body pulsed around me, held onto me, pulled me deeper into you? Who are you?" As soon as those words left my mouth, I felt her again, gripping me, and then I realized that I was still inside her temple. The more she teased me, the faster I was ready for action again.

"Jason, I don't know what happened," she said

attempting to be coy. "I do kinda wanna see if that was just a fluke."

The thought of it brought me back into my body. "You tryin to go again?"

Her gaze was focused. "I am." She nuzzled her lips into my neck and nipped my skin with her teeth. The passion went zipping through my body like a bolt of lightning.

"I'm afraid I'm gonna need a new condom for that," I joked.

"Can we roll over to the nightstand?" she asked, her eyes full of hope.

"Ummm...as full as this thing probably is, I don't think it's a good idea for me to be on top of you."

She smiled at me like a proud parent, "Okay, I'm gonna hop off and grab you a towel real quick."

I steadied myself for the shock and shuddered when her lips rolled over the head. She nearly sent me into another galaxy and I collapsed in heaven on the bed. While she ran into the bathroom to grab something, I lay as still as possible, trying to figure out what the heck just happened. She came back in, a warm wet washcloth in hand and proceeded to stroke me clean.

"You sure you wanna go again?" I asked her, just making sure she was still interested. Before I knew it her mouth was full and my head dropped back on the pillow.

"Oh shit."

"This okay?" she mumbled.

"Oh, shit." Those seemed to be the only two words I could get out.

She sucked and licked and stroked all at the same time, her body worked in sync to bring me to the brink of collapse. Just as I was about to burst she backed up, looking me in my eyes and smacking her lips, "You want me to finish you like this?"

A chuckle built inside my body because of how forward she was, how comfortable this moment felt. "No ma'am." I propped myself up on my elbows in an attempt to catch my breath, "We're supposed to try again remember?"

She opened her hand and unwrapped another condom, then slowly rolled it down around me. I wanted to try things a slightly different way this time. "Let me see if I can lead this time?" I joked as she nodded and hopped on the bed on all four.

I knelt behind her, caressed her back and ran my hands down to her waist, not stopping until I could grip her ass. I wanted to gaze into her eyes but part of me wondered if that'd been the reason things felt so different the first round. Just checking a hypothesis, that's all.

She reached between her legs to find me then guided me into her warmth, slowly, a fraction of an inch at a time. I got a solid three strokes in when she arched her back, sending me into the deep end and spiraling back to the world we'd just left. My body raced to bring her satisfaction and every feature in the room got erased from view. Even the bed was gone. It was just the two of us, in white space, connecting in the holiest of ways. My grip tightened like I was bracing for the inevitable. My body felt like it was about to betray me. I closed my eyes for a moment to slow down and regain my composure. She felt so damn good. I opened my eyes - still just us and nothing but a blanket of pure white.

Her breath was shallow. Her voice, sweet, "Jaaaaaaaaay." She spoke softly like she had a secret for only me, "How? How do you already know every spot?"

It felt like an out of body experience, "Mmmmm...it's happening again, Oakley."

"Go deeper, Jam," she urged as her hips began to slow wind.

Those sexy legs spread wider as I pushed further in. "Damn. I can't feel my fingers."

A chorus of moans escaped her mouth in rhythm with each stroke. "Oh God. Ohhhhh...kay. Mmmmmmmmm." I was good as long as she didn't say my name. Every time it graced her lips in passion, my body shifted gears. It didn't matter how loud, but those whispers sent me somewhere else, "Ahhhh...Jason."

"Everything's hot again," I said as I pulled her back to me, watching her ass bounce against my lap with each fervor stroke.

"Me too. What's happening? Why does it feel so good?" she asked as she found a way to ride me slowly from the front.

"Oh shit, I dunno."

"Damn you feel so good, Jason," she whispered as she began to grip me again.

A new level of passion unlocked. "Yo. I am really not in control of my body right now," I told her, thrusts getting stronger with each breath I took.

"I can't control myself around you," she breathed. "Fuck me, Jason."

As if I wasn't already locked in, her raw passion amped up my intensity even more. I was committed to thoroughly testing my theory. But everything was happening so swiftly. I couldn't explain it. "Are you doing this to me?"

"Uhn-uhn. I'm just...oh no. I'm already...I'm about to..."

I held her hips and watched as she took over and shifted gears on me. Slowing down. Speeding up. Slow. Fast. "Damn woman! It's happening again."

She bucked and shrieked, somehow raising upright and wrapping one arm around my neck for balance. "I can't hold on much longer, Jason." I wrapped one arm around her from behind and pressed my cheek against hers as I let my body continue to do what it naturally yearned to do. We were perfectly in sync, rocking to a syncopated rhythm all our own - one we created and one we sustained.

It felt so good she had me sucking air through my teeth again. "Mmmmm. Don't hold on. Just let go baby." One more stroke into her blissful abyss and, "Shhhhhit, I'm bout to..." My body rocked and shuddered in time with hers. We held onto each other, pulsing and throbbing through our rapturous passion.

This time it was me who cried as the room came back into view and welcomed us back to this dimension.

"Jason, what happened?" she asked as my shoulders heaved through sobs and laughter.

"Damn it. What the fuck was that?" I asked as I pulled out and collapsed into a confused seat on the bed.

"What'd you see Jam?" she asked as she curled into a ball and rested her head on my thigh.

I ran my fingers through her hair, sweeping the lose strands away from her sweaty forehead. "I don't know where we were but the room went white. It's like we were in another dimension and we were in charge of generating love for the whole world. I could only see you. Nothing else was there." I gazed down into her eyes and got lost in another universe, "I kinda feel like I was just reborn."

She nodded. "Same. We were floating in an empty space - no walls, just us and a sea of white."

I tried to ease my own tension with a joke, "Can we google this after we get cleaned up?" She was already on her phone trying to figure it out. I looked over her shoulder and noticed the time. "That can't be right!"

"What's that?" she asked softly.

I could feel my eyebrows scrunching in disbelief. "What time is it?"

She seemed totally unfazed, "According to the phone, almost 9:00."

"No freakin way. Where the heck did we go? I was over here feeling bad for not lasting more than 5 minutes."

Her giggle made me smile. "What time did we..."

"I got here at 6:00. By 6:30 you were sharing your fears and maybe fifteen minutes later we were in the bedroom. That's a big maybe."

She smiled up at me, "So let's say 6:45 to..."

"It's almost 9?!"

"Yeah, I don't know how to explain that. It definitely felt like a solid 10 minutes each time."

I laughed, "That's generous."

"That last time though...Jason." She placed her phone on the bed beside me.

I didn't say a word. I just waited for her to share her thoughts.

"I felt like I came apart, like my body exploded into tiny pieces and the universe put me back together again. I've never experienced that level of bliss and euphoria."

"Damn."

"I've never had sex and felt like my soul had been cleansed after."

"Shit. What have we done?" I laughed.

She smiled and chuckled, "I think maybe we ripped a hole in the space-time continuum."

"That's entirely possible and maybe the best description for what just happened."

We stared at each other in silence and just laughed for no reason.

That smile of hers was beaming. "I honestly can't believe I'm sittin' here naked with you and feeling like I'm fully clothed."

"Yeah, I was just thinking the same thing. And also, I feel like I should probably go take a shower."

Her eyes were playful, "Do you want to shower with me?"

"Yes, and also, no." I watched the laugh lines crease near her eyes. "I feel like we'd get frisky and I'm not willing to risk electric shock with the water and all. Plus," I paused and marveled at the way her face lit up, "we'd look up ten minutes later and it'll be midnight!"

"Fair point."

"So we're supposed to fix dinner, you still wanna do that here? I can shower at my house, grab a change of clothes and come back here - in like 30 minutes. Or..."

Intrigue was written all over her face, "Or?"

I felt myself fighting my own smile, pretending like this was a serious option instead of one of debauchery, "Or we can head to my house and shower together to see if there's just some weird portal over here."

"Jason...tomorrow we'll be at your house. Tonight, I want to cuddle up with you here in this bed, where we made love and broke the universe."

"Want me to door dash some food for us while you hop in the shower?"

"Yes. And pack multiple changes of clothes in a duffle so you can have some over here next time and you won't have to go home."

"Yes ma'am," I said as I saluted her.

She sat upright. "Jason, I love you so much."

"I would love to kiss you right now but I'm sure I still have your juices on me."

"Really, Jason?"

"I love you, Oakley Brooke...more than you'll ever know."

I hopped up and started to get dressed again while she turned the shower on.

She peeked out from the bathroom door. "Go out through the front door and lock the doorknob. Come back in through the garage. 1-1, 2-8, 2-0."

I found myself gravitating towards her, "That's the same code as my phone. Is that why you looked at me like that?"

She nodded. "It's the first day you walked into the coffeeshop."

I stopped at the bathroom door, "It's the day my world changed."

She smiled as she opened the shower curtain and hopped in. It only took a second for me to reconsider my first response. "Miss Oakley," I called to her.

Her voice carried above the sound of the flowing water, "Yes, Jam?"

"I uhhh - I think I do wanna join you in there."

"You're willing to risk it?" she joked.

"Yep. I'm gonna go grab some clothes and come right back. Give me 5 minutes."

"If you say so."

I dashed out of the house, locking the doorknob behind me and hopped in the car - racing around the corner to my house. I let myself inside, dropped my amazon package on the floor and threw some random clothes in my bag along with my laptop, just in case I needed to handle some work at a random hour.

I was back at her house in 4 minutes, unlocking the garage door with the code she gave me. She was still in the shower when I kicked my shoes off at the door. She called to me when she heard the door close.

"Yes, ma'am?"

"I can't wait to see what time it is when we get out of the shower."

I stripped in record time, leaving a trail of clothes on the floor to mark the path behind me, then peeked behind the curtain. The world felt like it stopped as soon as I saw the water cascading off her back. I wanted to drink from her skin, touch every inch of her again. I took a deep breath in and exhaled slowly, trying not to come across too eager. But damn was I ready for round three.

The baritone in my voice shocked me when I spoke,

"Can I join you?"

She bit her lower lip and nodded at me. "Yes, but see what time it is first?"

I looked at the watch I had forgotten to take off and told her, "It's five after 9,"while quickly removing it from my wrist so I could join her without regret.

I stepped into the shower and was greeted with nearly scalding water. I forgot about the heat as soon as she laid a passionate kiss on me and covered me with a soapy loofah that scrubbed my chest and back. She handed me the body wash and I lathered it up and rubbed her back. She leaned under the water and let it rinse her clean, then returned the favor to me. I lifted her up against the shower tile and tossed one leg over my shoulder to brace her as I devoured her yet again. I remember hearing the doorbell ring and saying, "dinner," out loud. Her laugh made me realize how bad the timing was. I hadn't intended on making a joke but that didn't stop it from being funny.

She had me in her sights yet again. I'd grabbed some condoms from the house before I left and reached out to pluck one from the bathroom counter as we got down for Round 3. New location, same result. Tingling fingers. The room disappeared. It was just the two of us, swirling around each other until I couldn't take it anymore. Five minutes. Max.

I folded like a bad hand in poker. She collapsed onto me. We cried with each other this time. No explanation needed to describe the unfurling of each layer that made us uniquely us.

We took turns washing each other's physical bodies in the same manner as we had just metaphysically cleansed ourselves yet again. I loved this woman inside and out and my whole world had been flipped upside down by her presence.

"Alexa, what time is it?" she called out between sniffles.

The mechanical voice replied, "It's 11:22 pm."

"Fuuuck." I gazed into her eyes, trying not to get lost again while wondering what the hell was going on.

A slight chuckle escaped her mouth before she shut it down. "Jason."

"Sorry."

"No, don't. It's just -" I wiped the tears from her face, "what happens when we make love?"

I shook my head in her direction. I didn't have an answer to that at all.

She continued, "Where do we go?"

I shrugged. That shit felt just as mysterious to me as it was to her. I turned the water off and handed her a towel and the lotion she requested. I put on my sweats and hoodie and grabbed the food from the front porch. When she came into the kitchen I laughed and told her it was a good thing I'd ordered salads because, "if these were fries, they'd be no good right now."

"I'm kinda not hungry."

"Yeah, I'm only gonna take a few bites so my stomach doesn't growl in the middle of the night."

She nodded, "that's probably a good idea."

We ate those crunchy salads in silence, just the sounds of forks piercing lettuce and teeth mashing leaves to watery bits. Every now and then a snicker would escape as we looked at each other still baffled by the trifecta of confusion.

"So - we still have a bit of unresolved stuff to talk about," I finally said, breaking the silence.

"Does it honestly even matter anymore, Jason?"

"What do you mean?" I asked, hoping what she meant aligned with what I thought she meant.

Not an ounce of funny in her bones when she spoke, "We are clearly meant for each other. Whoever, whatever comes up we can face it better together."

Somethin' about her answer locked me in for life. She just didn't know it yet - or, maybe she did. "I fuckin love you so damn much, woman."

Her face lit up and I could see both rows of teeth as

she grinned, "I love you too, Jam." My body felt warm from the inside, like I was at home. "Can we go to bed now?" she asked me.

"Yes ma'am."

I cleaned up the salads and turned off the lights in the rest of her house, then led her to the bathroom to brush our teeth and carried her off to bed like it was my place. I watched her stretch out across the bed and then make space for me. I nodded and followed her under the sheets.

It was nearly midnight as the bed welcomed us home and at least 12:30 before I drifted off to sleep. My dreams couldn't beat out the night I'd just had. From sun up to sun down, this was a day that would go down as one of the most memorable on record for me. From a surprise visit and paternity claim from an ex, to nearly getting fired at work, to galactic sex with my soulmate - aside from a wedding or the birth of an actual child, I don't know how you could top it.

Chapter Twenty Two
OAKLEY

Jason grinned through the night and seemingly slept like a baby. I, on the other hand, woke up at least three times from wild dreams, trying to decide what part of my life was actually real. If I tried to explain that experience to my therapist she probably would've had me committed, or at the very least, tested for drugs. The room disappearing? Jason shooting white beams of light from his chest? The two of us floating in white space? No. Nothing about that seems reasonably sane. My dreams were equally as out there. I knew we had to talk about some stuff this morning before either of us went to work, but how do you even begin to have a conversation like that, how do you even wrap your head around it when you're just flat exhausted?

I closed my eyes and tried to calm my mind long enough to drift back off to sleep for thirty minutes, or before my alarm sounded for the day. Meanwhile, Jason was immovable - stretched out across the bed on his stomach, his head facing me, one leg draped across mine and one arm reaching out towards me. He was so still I found myself randomly checking to see if he was breathing. Then, when I discovered that he was, I was envious of the amount of deep rest he was getting.

Just as I could feel that good sleep coming over my body, my alarm sounded. I knew if I didn't get up in that moment, that I'd miss another day of work. It was rare that I missed one, so two in one week probably would've had my staff thinking something was seriously wrong with me - instead of seriously right. I sat up on the edge of the bed and slowly readied myself to get up. A quick toe wiggle as I stretched and swayed like the top of a tree in the wind. Then recovery slides on my feet and up for the day. It only took me a few steps to get to the door, but when I turned around and saw Jason enjoying his slumber, you could've convinced me that I'd walked miles from the bed. I wanted to be there beside him, but resting. I tripped over thin air on my way to the bathroom and I heard him ask if I was okay from the bedroom.

"I'm fine," I lied as I hobbled the rest of the way down the hallway. I knew that I probably needed to gather myself and make sure that my face didn't look completely exhausted before I walked back to the bedroom. Before I glanced at myself in the mirror I realized there wasn't really anything I could do about that so I just peeked to see what the impact of a couple hours of sleep looked like on me. But instead of being greeted with circles and bed head, my skin was glowing and I looked completely rested. In fact, I was hesitant to admit it, but I looked younger than I did at the start of yesterday.

I splashed some water on my face, thinking there must've been something in my eyes. Maybe it was the lack of sleep that had me hallucinating. But when I dried my face with the towel and looked again, it was very much the same thing. In fact, I looked even younger than before I rinsed what little sleep I did get off my face. Everything was confusing to me. Something had fundamentally shifted my entire world. What was impossible before now felt completely doable. What was improper felt right. What was old and weary was made new again. I was thoroughly confused as I walked down the hallway to greet Jason.

I leaned on the doorway and peered inside to find that he was already awake - his eyes bright and ready for the day as he lay in the bed and said, "Good Morning."

"Good morning to you, too!"

"You look well rested this morning. How did you sleep?"

I chuckled, "I do? I didn't really sleep all that much."

"You didn't?"

"No sir. I only slept in 15 to 20 minute sprints, roughly once or twice every other hour."

"That sounds brutal."

"It felt brutal."

"Why do you look so well rested?"

I shrugged my shoulders. "I think maybe it's something related to what kept happening yesterday. My face..."

"You look about- I'm sorry, I just realized that I cut you off. Go ahead."

"No, what were you about to say about my face?" We laughed.

"Just that you look younger today than you did yesterday. I'm not sayin you looked old. I'm just saying you look noticeably younger this morning."

He patted the bed for me to come sit down and I smiled and shook my head, knowing full well if I sat down on that bed near him that I'd be tempted to lay down and snuggle up. That's probably what I needed to help me rest last night, but he just looked so peaceful.

He stood to his feet and walked to the doorway to hug me. I totally and completely melted in his arms. When he kissed me on my widow's peak and I heard his morning voice, "I'm sorry you didn't sleep well," you might as well have started the clock for Round 4. If he did anything else remotely sexy, I wasn't gonna make it out of the house.

"I'm sure I'll be able to take a nap this afternoon or something. How did you sleep? Are you hungry? I feel a little rambly today."

His throaty chuckle made me smile. "I'm surprisingly

not hungry and I don't remember sleeping at all."

"You were pretty still last night. A few times I had to check to make sure you were still breathing. I didn't want to wake you up because you looked so peaceful."

Still hugging in the doorway he asked me, "Did you need something?" I nodded and he continued, "You could've woken me up."

"You looked so content."

"I felt pretty content. Well what did you need? Is it something I can get you now?"

"I needed you."

"Just for clarity sake and the sake of the little guy in my pajama pants that's starting to wake up..." he leaned back and popped an eyebrow at me. "...in what way?"

"I just needed your arms, that's all. I just needed some snuggles I think. It probably would've helped me drift off to sleep."

"I got you tonight. I'm not sure how you didn't just completely pass out like me. Three rounds of mind blowing...well, wait. It was mind-blowing for me. Was it that for you?"

"Mind blowing doesn't feel big enough, Jason."

"It doesn't?"

"No."

"What does?"

"Mind-bending. Life altering. Psychedelic."

"Psychedelic?"

"Moving. Heartbreaking."

"Heartbreaking? Oh no!"

"Yes. Now that I know this level of connection and beauty is possible, how can I live in a world where other people don't get to experience it?"

"Damn. That is kind of heartbreaking. But how lucky are we that we know what can be?"

"I feel pretty damn lucky."

"Me too. Oh shit. I think I know what she was talking about now."

"Who's that?"

"Emmaline. She whispered something to me when we were leaving and it didn't make any sense until right now."

"The psychic? What did she say?"

His smile was wider than I'd ever seen before, "She said..." he laughed like he couldn't believe it himself. I waited for him to fill me in. "I love you so much, Oakley." That didn't sound like something a psychic would say, so I looked up at his face only to find him wiping the tears that fell from his eyes.

"You okay Jam?"

He nodded, "Good gracious she was right."

"What did she say, Jason?"

"She told me that we didn't just happen to meet in November. We've been loving on each other this entire lifetime. That the whispers and the longing were us calling to each other and that once we were together, nothing else would exist in the world, that I would find God again through you."

"Uhhh...what? Wait, you lost Him?"

"That's how I felt when she said it. I mean, I've been questioning a lot of things here recently and that was one of them. But the last thing she said to me was, 'you'll see tomorrow - when your souls merge and higher consciousness will strip you naked. She,' and she pointed to you when she said this, 'she will make you pure.' I didn't understand how anybody was gonna be stripped naked or how you were gonna make me pure."

"Whoa."

"Right? Kinda makes me wanna go back and see her again."

I was gobsmacked, "Emmaline!"

His body was unmoving. "Yep."

I teased him, "You feel naked, Jason?"

He nodded adamantly, "Yeah, but not ashamed of it."

I felt his stomach growl between us and walked him to the kitchen without another word, guiding him to a seat in the same chair where we'd eaten dinner earlier in the week. SO much had changed in less than 7 days. So much was different and yet so much was still the same. What I knew for certain though, I was likely gonna be an immovable force because of one wild night and a soul-changing encounter with the man who took over my job and came in to fulfill his assignment.

Neither of us knew at the time that it was so much more than work, but that was beyond evident and clear in the wee hours of the morning as I served him a cup of black coffee with sugarplums on the side. I didn't know what was next for us, but I knew that we were on this ride together. That whatever "assignment" was next, for us, would be one we'd tackle together in this new version of life that we'd gotten a glimpse of last night. The preview was spectacular. I just hoped the movie lived up to the hype.

A contented sigh slipped from Jason's mouth as he smiled across the table at me. I thought I could read his mind, but he caught me off guard.

"So let's talk about yesterday morning."

Chapter Twenty Three
JASON

With the two clients I'd received from Michaela all wrapped up in less than 24 hours, that left me with a lot of time to think about what went down on Thursday night. I wanted to move slow, but there was no containing the energy that was created between Oakley and I. It's been clearly evident since we had the chance to officially meet each other and I'm sure it was there way back in November. Yesterday was like a combustion engine though, and I highly doubt I'll ever connect with someone like that again.

Just like I knew when I'd had my last cigar, I could also feel that she was the last person I'd allow in my life in that way. There wasn't a worry or a stitch of concern about me. I just felt settled. Not like I was settling, just resolved. Content in my bones. Growing up I had this fear that I'd be missing out on something if I settled down. I used to wonder if that same fear kept me out of relationships that could have led to marriage. What I know now is that those relationships just weren't for me. They were seasonal in the same way I was to them, but this one just felt different. I felt like not being with her would be the biggest mistake I could ever make in my life. Oakley and I - we were the same. At least, we were very similar and I knew for a fact that she and I would make a dope team. Insert random flashbacks of last night into these emotional thoughts about our future and my morning was 90% consumed by thoughts of her.

I was never so excited to grab lunch in my life. Brian's infamous knock on the doorframe brought me back to the present. "Knockity Knock!"

"B. What's good sir?" I greeted him, trying my best not to look like I'd just had the best sex of my life the night before.

His neck slow rolled and his head snapped in place, "Oh no. What's that shit eatin' grin on your face from?"

"Shut up."

"Hell no. Am I driving or are you?" he asked as I hustled to grab my keys so we could get out of the office as fast as possible. The rumors had already started to spread and I didn't want anybody to overhear anything that could add to the gossip.

I walked past Michaela's cube and listened as she "ooooooo"ed at me like I was a child about to get in trouble. "Jason, did you get to those accounts yet?" I assumed she was trying to stall and slow me down so she could be nosey and somehow flip the convo back into white supremacy culture. I'm not sayin she was wrong. I just didn't want to hear it today.

I answered without turning around so she couldn't kill my vibe, still beelining it to the elevator, "All wrapped up this morning Michaela!"

I mashed the button at least 10 times in a 3 second span to call the elevator. I knew it wasn't gonna make it come any faster, but I was in a hurry to get out of there. "Where y'all going? Can I come too?"

"Grabbin' lunch. Want me to pick you up something?"

"Nah, I'll grab something later. Thank you."

I waved as we hopped into the elevator and the doors closed.

"So you got some last night?" Brian asked immediately.

I couldn't do anything except laugh.

"You ain't slick Jason. You just thought you were gonna sneak that past me, huh?"

Still no words. I couldn't do anything except laugh.

"Bruh?!" he asked through an expectant chuckle.

I shrugged my shoulders and continued to keep my lips

sealed shut. What we'd just experienced wasn't a random occurrence. It wasn't your normal everyday sex. I wasn't about to tell him that, but he looked like he was expecting some sort of response. I decided to wait him out.

The elevator doors opened and we proceeded to walk out of the building towards the small cafe down the block where we'd occasionally meet to vent. My body braced itself for combat the entire 3 minute walk. Shoulders tight. Back stiff. Fists clenched. Everything was tight but that was a stark contrast to how loose I felt inside. Everything within me felt at peace and relaxed, but I'm sure I didn't look like it.

We sat down and ordered and I tried to open the conversation, "So what's good with you, B?"

He shook his head ferociously and chuckled incredulously. "Nah, son. You're not about to pretend like nothing's happening in your world."

"Who said I was pretending?" I asked him.

"You need to unclench those fists. We not boutta fight."

I looked down at my hands and let them relax into the present moment.

"So tell me about Tami."

"Ayooo. Who the hell is Tami?" Those fists clenched right back up.

"Son."

"You got one more time to 'son' me, B."

"Okay Baltimore, tell me about Tami."

"Who in the hell is Tami?"

"Who in the hell is Tami he says - Tamiflu son."

The waiter brought our food to the table just as I was about to reach across the table. Brian erupted into laughter.

"Ahh...funny." I shook my head at his attempt at a joke and reached for my lunch.

"Nah, but seriously. Tell me about this woman you're willing to risk it all for."

"B." I couldn't get any other words out. Just thinking about where to start had me feeling like a giddy kid. I couldn't stop the grin from spreading across my face so I just grabbed a french fry instead.

"That's all I get?" Brian asked as he took a bite of his sandwich. His mouth was full but that didn't stop him from following his thoughts, "You almost lost your job bruh. What happened? I mean obviously we ain't linked in a minute but I thought you were getting back with Tina."

"It's been more than a minute if you thought I was gettin back with her."

"Okay well then catch me up."

"Tina felt familiar. I thought there was a chance but I remembered why we're not compatible and I apologized to her. Then yesterday out of the blue she showed up with a picture of this child with 8 alien lookin fingers on one hand, claiming it was mine."

"Wait, yesterday?"

"Mmm hmm. In the morning. Then I get to work and I thought I was about to get handed a box to go pack my office."

"Wait, she just showed up yesterday?"

"Yes. I was at the Fresh Grind and - "

"Terrible name for any business that's not a nightclub by the way. Did you tell Tami that? Sorry, carry on."

"Nigga."

"My bad."

"Yes, I told her that. So anyway, Tina showed up to her coffeeshop and she saw the whole thing go down in the back. The picture. Her rubbing her belly and telling me that the baby's mine."

"Wait, Tami saw that?"

"Yep. Within about 2 hours I went from being happier

than I've been in a long time to feeling like I was hit by a dump truck and was clinging to life support."

"Shit. What did she say?"

"Who? Tina or -"

"Tami."

"If you don't stop calling her Tami."

"What's her name then?"

"Oakley."

"Okay, what did Oakley say?"

"She sobbed in my arms."

"Okay wait - but you - yesterday - was it Tami, sorry Oakley or Tina?"

"Was what Oakley or Tina?" I asked him, knowing full well what he was talking about but testing to see if he'd just outright say it or try to find another way to beat around the bush about it.

"The late night snack."

"The what?"

"You know what I'm talking about. Who was it?"

I just grinned.

"Tami. How the hell?"

"I don't know man. I wasn't expecting it. I didn't see it coming. It just happened."

"You just magically fell in?"

I couldn't hold my laugh anymore. So I chuckled and dipped a fry in my ketchup and chomped away.

"Bruh, I'm gonna need you to write a handbook."

"I didn't want it to happen. I mean I did, eventually but I was trying to get us to slow down."

"Said no man ever."

"Let you tell it. But I was. It hasn't even been a week yet and we've already spent the night with each other multiple times, went to New Orleans together - "

"Wait, what?"

" - faced a few major misunderstandings. It feels like a year crammed into about 5 days."

"Go back."

"To where?"

"New Orleans."

"What about it?"
"Is that where you were on Tuesday?"

I coughed into my hand.

"So you. How. Who bought the tickets?"

I coughed into my hand again, then reached for my bottle, "Phew! I think I need some water."

"You bought two last minute plane tickets?"

"First class."

"Oh, my bad! You bought two last minute first class plane tickets to NOLA. Did you stay overnight? No. You couldn't have flown back that quickly and had all that other stuff happen. Let me revise. You bought two last minute, round trip, first-class plane tickets to NOLA for you and a client."

"I mean when you call her a client it sounds shady af."

"She is a client."

"Was a client."

"And when did she no longer become a client."

"New Year's Day."

"No, yesterday nigga!"

"I mean officially sure."

"Son!"

I shrugged.

"I think we both knew pretty early on that - well, shit wait."

"Wait what?"

"She didn't know me as Andy at first."

"Holy shit."

"What?"

"You, motherfucker."

"Me what?"

"Write the goddamn manual already!"

I dipped another fry and shook my head.

"It's already bestseller."

"Bruh."

"How in the hell—"

"Every damn day it felt like she unlocked another part of me. She needs to write the book. Not me."

"What?"

"She sees me - right through all the surface shit. She's changin' me."

"Time will tell."

"You're right. But she opened up parts of me that I never let anyone touch."

"In a week?"

"In one touch. Shit was instant."

"Maybe she does need to write the book, 'cause what?"

"Every damn day. She's everything I need. I have no doubt at all that we'll always find a way."

"To what?"

"Back to each other."

"Y'all ain't even had time apart yet."

I shrugged my shoulders and suddenly out of fries, picked up my burger.

"Are you sayin she's the one?"

"B. Ain't no doubt in my mind that it's her."

"In less than a week?"

"Instantly."

"You and I, we've known each other a long time bruh."

"College."

"I ain't never in my life seen you talk about a woman like this. Not even Tina's Ai-baby-havin-ass."

I nodded.

"So wait. Is there really a child on the way and could it be yours?"

"If there is, there's definitely a chance it's mine."

"And Tami knows this."

"We talked through it this morning." I said and was instantly transported back to the kitchen and the look on her face when I blurted out, 'So let's talk about yesterday morning.'

> Her face looked hesitant, like she wanted to have the conversation but was a little bit unsure about what would come of it. I rested my hand on top of hers as she looked down at the table.

> She spoke softly, "Yesterday?"

> I caressed the back of her hand, "Yesterday."

> Her eyes met mine, "Okay."

I nodded, "I'm sorry."

"For what Jam?"

"I know we kinda talked about her before but I apologize for not telling you about the last time I saw Tina."

Her breath was shallow. Her soft hand tightened into a rigid ball. "Well tell me about it now. When was it?"

"A couple of weekends before Thanksgiving. I had gone back to Bowie to visit my family."

Her inhale was sharp. Cutting. I felt rushed to fill in the details.

"She wasn't there with them but she saw me running an errand and. She umm. She just felt familiar. I remembered the good times when I saw her and we fell into our old habits again."

"So that could be your baby she's carrying?"

I nodded. "I used protection but it was hers and-"

She held up a hand for me to stop talking and I hushed immediately, trying to read the room.

"I just need a minute," she said as tears began to fill her eyes. I nodded, still silent and afraid to speak. The quiet hung out with us, filling its own seat at the table, the awkward third wheel. I hoped it would disappear if I ignored it. Eventually it got up and left as Oakley cleared her throat to speak.

"I don't even know why I'm crying right now. I know you had a whole life before me." I nodded, still being patient and just listening. "I just didn't think there was someone else so close to that day."

"I understand."

"When was the last time you talked to her, Jason?"

"The day after Thanksgiving - after I had already flown back home. That's when I apologized to her for what happened."

"How did she respond?"

"She didn't."

"She didn't?"

"No. No response. No comment. No contact. I assumed she was pissed and blocked me and it made sense that she would given what happened."

"So then you saw me and what happened - because you'd just had sex with your ex?"

"My whole world stopped when I saw you."

She nodded.

"I was drawn to you in ways I couldn't understand or explain and I didn't know what to do with it. So I didn't do anything. I didn't say anything. You were supposed to be a client. I wasn't supposed to let you in. I wasn't supposed to adore you. I wasn't supposed to fall."

"Jam."

"Miss Oakley, I'm sorry."

"What are you sorry for now?"

"If she's really pregnant, then my choices will likely have an impact on us. On you. You didn't ask for any of this."

"If she's pregnant and the baby is yours what's the plan?"

"I don't want any child of mine to grow up not knowing me."

"Would you move?"

"I don't know. I can't see myself-" My words got caught in my throat. I could feel the tears building in my eyes and just let 'em fall.

"You can't see yourself moving?"

"Without you. I can't see myself without you."

"Jam, you don't even know me."

"Don't I though? Don't you know me? In your gut, what do you feel?"

"I know you."

"And I know you. I also know that I don't wanna build a life without you."

"This is crazy."

"Life is crazy."

"We could move together - I mean if the baby is yours, Jam."

"I wouldn't ask you to do that. You can't leave your business."

"We've clearly seen that I can."

"I hear you but-"

"Stronger together, Jam. Remember that?"

"Damn." She hit me in the feels again. "Stronger together."

She stood up from the table and made her way over to me, turning me into her seat. She rested her forehead on mine and closed her eyes. I closed mine and let the feelings wash over me like a tsunami.

"I love you Oakley Brooke."

"I love you too, Jam."

"What time you gotta be at work today Miss Oakley?" I asked as I picked her up and carried her towards the bedroom like she was my bride.

Brian snapped his fingers at me, willing me back to the present time.

"What's good?" I asked him.

"Where the hell did you go?"

"Just lost in thought."

"Tami?"

"Stop."

"She must've put it down."

I closed my eyes and shook my head, thinking back to this morning post-breakfast. Five minutes. Tingling fingers. Faded room. Just the two of us, gettin it in like we were trying to make a baby of our own. She arrived at the coffee shop nearly an hour later than normal when I finally dropped her off.

Brian's laughter brought me back again. "Did you just bite your lip? Bro! What is wrong with you?"

"Ain't nothin' wrong," I said while crackin a smile. "Everything's right, B."

"Everything?"

"I told you I just wanna go slow with her."

"Mmm hmm. There's that word again. Slow. But y'all did the complete opposite of that. Turbo relationship havin ass."

"I'm taking her out on a date tonight."

Brian's head cocked to the side, his lips twisted in disbelief. I fought for my life to keep a straight face. Neither one of us won that battle and we doubled over in laughter. My side hurt from all of it. Just as I regained my breath, an older man approached the table. His salt colored hair and wrinkles gave us a general idea of his age.

"You young fellas have it right. Live in your joy. Don't let the world take it away from you."

"Yes sir," I said to him as Brian nodded.

"So which one of you is in love?" he asked us.

Brian's head snapped in my direction and I raised a single finger in the air.

"I knew it. It's all over you. I could see that even through my cataracts." He lead us in laughter then looked me over. "This is a new love."

"Yes sir."

"Embrace every moment you have with her." I nodded at the wisdom that I knew was forthcoming. "I wanted to take it slow with my love and she thought I didn't want her."

"Word?" Brian asked.

"Yessir. I spent the rest of her life showing her how much she meant to me."

I felt his words like a punch to my gut. "I'm sorry for your loss. I can see how much you love her."

His face softened, "We had a baby girl and my wife Brooke, she didn't make it through the birth."

"Aww man. I'm really sorry to hear that." We sat in shared silence as he looked down at the table, like he was longing for one more moment or maybe remembering the last one.

"Life sometimes comes atcha faster than a freight train."

"I hear that."

He looked up at me and studied my face before speaking again. "So this love of yours. What's her name?"

I smiled at the thought of her. "Oakley, sir."

"Well hush my mouth." His face twitched slightly before he smiled and continued, "If you love Oakley the way your face says you do, you go whole hog!"

"I'm sorry?"

He chuckled, "Make sure she knows it from the time the rooster crows until the wolf howls at the moon."

"Sun up to sun down," I nodded. "Can do."

His smile was warm, "Well okay then. I best be on my way."

I stood up and extended my hand for a shake, "It was nice to meet you Mr. -"

"Just call me, Pop."

"Okay, Mr. Pop."

He waved both hands in reservation, "Just, Pop." He shook my hand then reeled me in for a hug that oddly felt like home.

"Yes sir, Pop."

Brian stood to shake his hand and that's all he got. No hug. Pop nodded in our direction and headed for the door, pausing for just a moment to turn around and glance at me one more time. He tipped his head towards me, "See you sooner than a chicken lays an egg, son." And just like that, he was gone.

"He say, see you soon?"

"Yeah, and he called me son."

"So he can call you son but I can't?"

"B," I paused, "I think that was Oakley's Dad."

Chapter Twenty Four
OAKLEY

We're gonna have to get some things figured out because four times in less than 12 hours is borderline obsessive. Some might even call it diabolical. I felt altogether different walking into the coffeeshop that morning and apparently my staff could tell. They all nodded at me slowly, like they knew my secret and wanted me to know they knew but weren't going to tell anyone else about it. I just rolled my eyes at every single one of them.

Fridays were typically busier than the norm, and this one was no different. I spent most of my time helping out on the floor instead of replying to Michaela's correspondence. But when I caught a moment after our lunch rush and stopped to catch up on email, I noticed a message on my phone that was definitely unexpected.

"Hey Oakley Brooke, popped up to Kansas City to

surprise you. You weren't in at your usual time so I'll just hang out in KC for the day. I'll be back to see how things are going with you later. Dad."

I love that my Dad signs his texts. It makes me giggle in the best way. I found myself laughing at that text when he sent another one.

"Hey Oakley Brooke, I just met a handsome fella today that might be in love with you. Didn't get his name but he seems like a good guy. Dad."

Then another text. This one wasn't from Dad.

"Hey Miss Oakley. You've been on my mind a lot today. Looking forward to our date tonight. Grateful to spend some time with you outside of the house ;) I love you. Still want me to pick you up from work this afternoon? Also, does your Dad live in KC?"

Oh. Good. Gravy. How on earth did the two of them meet each other before I could set it up in a controlled introduction? I had so many questions and zero answers which helped me feel unsettled.

My phone buzzed again. Another text.

"Hey Oakley Brooke, just pulled up in front of your coffeeshop but I don't see your car. It looks open. Are you at work today? Dad."

I replied, "Hey Dad. I'm here! Come inside," then hopped out of my chair and ran to the front of the shop to see if I could catch him before he drove away.

He was opening the door just as I made it to the front. He hopped in line and placed an order.

"One black coffee. One bear claw, warmed up just a smidge. And can you put some of those Sugarplums on the side in a little bowl or something?"

Always a paying customer before he gave me a hug. That's the same type of support I got from him as a child. Mom was gone and he refused to bring another woman into our house. So it was just the two of us. They were older when they had me, so I always wondered if that's what happened to Mom, but I never felt a need to ask. He told me about her as often as he could. And when I did something excellent he always told me it was her genes and not his that allowed me to do it. That might have been partially true, but he was a great example to learn from. From middle school through college he dated, Ms. Jenny. They had a son together when I was 13. I called her Mom and even introduced her to friends and teachers as my parent, but Dad never proposed. I always wondered if he felt a bit of guilt. Again, I just never asked. I figured it was grown folks business and I was far from grown. So when the time was right, I'd find out.

He grabbed his food and plopped down at the same seat in the back that he always chose. Coincidently it was the same seat that Jason always chose too. I think it's probably because you could see the whole shop from that spot. I grabbed Dad's order and delivered it to his table with a warm hug.

"Hey Oakley Brooke! It's so good to see your face in person."

"Hey Dad! It's good to be seen!"

"You have some time to sit down?"

"I always have time for you."

I sat down across from him and watched a huge grin slide across his face.

"I met someone today."

"Oooooo. What's her name?"

"No no. Let me finish. I met someone today. I think you might be dating him but I didn't get his name."

"Can you describe him?"

"Oh, he's about yay tall and add some milk to my coffee to get his complexion. He was at lunch with his friend and they were just a laughing away."

"Yeah?"

"Mmm hmm."

"So how would you know he was dating me?"

"He told me so. He said your name when I asked him who was the woman he'd already admitted to being in love with. The boy had hearts in his eyes."

I grinned at the thought of them meeting by chance.

"He couldn't stop smiling, Oakley Brooke. I think he likes you the way I liked your mother."

"Jason."

"What's that?"

My grin widened at the thought of him. "His name is Jason, Dad."

"You love him too I see."

I nodded. "He feels like home Dad. Remember you used to talk about how Mom felt like that?"

Dad nodded too as I continued, "that's exactly how he feels to me."

"Ms. Jenny never quite felt like home. I loved her a whole lot and I love your brother a whole lot too. But I couldn't not have that in a relationship after having it with your mother."

"I can see why."

"Yeah. Well, Jason is it?"

"Uh huh."

"I think he's in it for the long haul. Has he told you that yet?"

My head bounced again as I answered him. "Yes sir."

"Let him lead, Oakley. I know you. You want things when you want them. But there's not much better than savoring something that's been slow-cookin all day long."

"I've stepped back Dad. We're piloting this thing together."

"Co-pilot then. I like it."

The bell for the door rang and before I turned around, I could feel him again. His presence strong. I was home again.

"Jason."

"Oh, y'all are just like your mother and I. You knew it was him and you're lookin at me."

"Dad."

"He saw you but he's going to the counter to order."

"One coffee. Black. One bearclaw. Warm. And a cup of sugarplums on the side."

Dad's mouth dropped open, "Is that what he orders?"

"Every single day he comes in." He was getting closer to

me. The energy felt stronger and more vibrant. The pulses beat in rhythm with my heart, or his heart, or maybe it was a combined beating that allowed me to feel it so strongly. Either way, I knew he was only a few steps away.

I turned around and glanced at him. Winking in his direction. He winked back and made a beeline for my Dad.

"Hey Pop! I guess those chickens must've laid their eggs."

Dad chuckled and stood up, reeling Jason in for a hug where the two of them held on for dear life.

"Had I known you were Oakley's father-"

"Don't say anything else, Son," Dad interjected.

"It's so good to meet you, sir!"

"Call me Pop!"

"I never gave you my name earlier."

"Ohh shucks. You didn't have a need to."

"Well, I didn't know I needed to," he chuckled. "Jason Mitchell, sir."

I teared up at the sight of the two men I loved the most, loving on each other.

"Well Jason Mitchell, I sure hoped it was my daughter

that you were smiling about this afternoon."

"It definitely was."

They let go of each other as they called Jason's name. His order was ready.

"I'll go get it. Sit down Jam."

"I can go get it, Miss Oakley."

I held his hand and ushered him into my seat, then went to grab his order. They were laughing away when I returned.

"Thank you! So hey, I thought you might be swamped again when you didn't reply, so I swung by to see if I could lend a hand. I hope that's okay."

"It's fine, Jason," I said as I slid into the seat beside him.

"You sure? I'm not trying to break up the family time."

"I'm positive. I'm actually really curious how you two met today." I said while rubbing Jason's back.

"I was at lunch with Brian and he was teasing me about you. Your Dad comes over to the table before he left to encourage us to keep the joy in our lives. He read me like a book."

"Whaat? Dad did?"

"Yep. He knew I was in love with someone. But he didn't know it was you. At least not right away."

I nuzzled my head onto his shoulder and he dropped his head on top of mine.

Dad smiled at the two of us. "When did you know I might be her father, Jason?"

Jason lifted his head, excited to share his sleuth-like skills. "You mentioned your wife's name and I thought it was a coincidence that it was Oakley's middle name. When you flinched a little as I told you the name of my love, I wondered if it was more than a coincidence. Then you told me you'd see me sooner than a chicken laid an egg and I thought there's no way they're NOT related."

"Have you heard her say that one?" Dad chuckled.

"Yesterday!" He laughed then grinned down in my direction. I tried to keep a straight face. Dad was watching us.

"That one. That one right there. That's the face he made in the restaurant Oakley Brooke."

"I've seen this face before, Dad."

"You have?"

"I have."

"When was the first time?"

"The day he walked into the coffeeshop."

He looked at me like he wanted to kiss me. I shook my head, trying to be respectful of my father, who could read the room.

"Go ahead and kiss her. I'm gonna slide to the indoor outhouse," he said on his way up and out of the booth.

Jason lightly traced his thumb across my right cheek, gazing lovingly into my eyes.

I whispered, "Hey Jam."

"Mmhm?"

Still hushed, "Are you gonna kiss me?"

He whispered, "No ma'am. As soon as I do your Dad's gonna come around the corner."

"What?"

"Just let this be my kiss for now."

I leaned my cheek onto his palm and closed my eyes for two seconds when I heard Dad's voice. "Was I gone long enough?"

"I couldn't bring myself to do it, Pop."

"Jason," he said. His voice, serious. "Sometimes you gotta risk it to get the biscuit."

The two of us laughed while Dad's smile of satisfaction filled his face.

I mentioned that I needed to get back to work and Jason asked if we needed to reschedule tonight. Dad nearly bit his head off at the thought of it. He asked if we could meet him for breakfast in the morning. Jason insisted that he could modify the plans for all three of us. I let them hash it out and told them to surprise me.

Chapter Twenty Five
JASON

I was planning to pick her up for a real date, not one where we linger in each other's spaces. But Pop was joining us. He wouldn't let me reschedule on her and I couldn't for the life of me imagine him driving all this way and not spending time with his daughter. So our plan was to arrive at her house at 6:30 and drive to dinner together. She had no idea.

I hopped in my car and drove around the corner to her house. Parked in the driveway was an old pickup truck. Pops opened the door and welcomed me inside. "Hey son. She's in the bathroom. Said she'd be out before you got here."

"I tend to show up a little bit early on the regular."

Pops laughed, "She said that too."

I had a seat on the couch and Pop sat down to ask me about what I do for work.

"So, Oakley hasn't told you the story about how we met yet, I see."

Pop laughed and shook his head. "Not yet. Why don't you fill me in."

Oakley popped her head out of the bathroom, "I thought I heard you talking to someone out here, Dad. Hi Jason."

I smiled at the sight of her beautiful face.

Pop turned in Oakley's direction, "Oakley Brooke, are you decent? Can you please get dressed, child?"

"I'm gettin there, Dad. Two minutes! I just wanted to make sure you weren't out here talking to the dust bunnies under the couch."

"You ready for a lifetime of this?" he said, his belly full of laughter.

I nodded, having already enjoyed my free preview of the movie.

"So about that story," Pop continued, waiting for me to fill him in on how we met.

Just as I opened my mouth to tell him, Oakley popped out looking as beautiful as ever. My eyes were locked on her. I could feel my heartbeat quicken but couldn't get any other words out. "Hi!"

She grinned in my direction, "Hi Jam!"

"Oh Lordy. I feel like I need to leave you two alone," her Dad joked.

Eyes still fixed on me as she inched closer to me, "Y'all ready?"

Her body felt warm in my arms as she welcomed me into her home. So soft. Naturally mine. My peace. I held her close, simmering in the moment, then pulled back to look into her eyes. Without hesitation I leaned in and kissed her, a gentle touch, not the hungry type that sent us down the rabbit hole yesterday. I broke from our embrace, suddenly remembering that Pop was in the room with us. Her eyes sparkled with life and light, as the world that had started to fade away began to return to focus.

"I think we better go," I softly spoke. She nodded in return.

Pop asked, "Are you sure you want my company?"

Oakley joked like she was reconsidering so I responded promptly, "Absolutely."

During the drive to the restaurant the conversation was shared and easy, just like the conversation at lunch and at the coffeeshop. Pop shared a few tales from when Oakley was a child. Hearing them from his perspective seemed to open Oakley's eyes to see them in a new light.

"I was quite a handful, Dad. Sorry about that!"

"No apologies needed Oakley Brooke. I wouldn't have it any other way. It's part of why you're such a strong woman now."

I nodded in agreement with Pop.

At the restaurant I held the door for both of them, a small gesture to show my respect and care. We were seated at a cozy corner table, the ambiance warm and inviting. Perfect for a date. Slightly awkward for a chaperoned date for two adults. As we looked over the menu, I felt Oakley's hand slip into mine under the table. It felt like a silent reassurance that she was content in that moment.

The food was delicious. The conversation, rich. I felt lucky to sit at the feet of a man with such homespun wisdom, who seemed to be okay with me dating his daughter. I felt grateful for the chance to get to know him better.

Throughout the evening, I kept stealing glances at Oakley, her presence a constant source of joy and calm. Her laughter was soothing, and this outing was a far cry from our first visit to a restaurant. Each time our eyes met, our otherworldly connection continued to grow stronger, erasing the slight apprehension that was present in my brain. Each time she reached out to touch me, fingers lingering longer on my skin, I felt more confident in our connection. And yet, there was still a nagging feeling that my brain was struggling to override. It was the part of me that tries to protect me and keep me safe from pain that was actively firing alongside all the good stuff.

I had planned to take her on a walk after dinner, and asked Pop if he was interested in joining us for that. "I'd love to hear some more of your stories if you're open to sharing."

"I don't want to impose on your night. I appreciate you sharing part of it with me."

"Dad, I'd love it if you'd join us."

His hands raised in contempt, "Oakley Brooke, dinner is one thing. A stroll through the park at night should be left to the courting couple. If you can drop me off at the hotel, I can get my car from your house tomorrow."

She smiled, but double checked to ensure he was serious, "Are you sure, Dad?"

His nod was heavy, "As sure as eggs is eggs and the sun rises in the east."

The ride to the hotel was quiet. Each of us was in quiet reflection, lost in our own thoughts. I don't know what was on their mind, but my amygdala was working overtime, triggering my stress response system. I hugged her Dad when we dropped him off and thanked him for sharing the evening with us.

He held me tight, the same way my Dad used to hug me when I was a child, "You take care of my girl, Jason Mitchell."

The emotions that squeaked out caught me by surprise. "Will do, Pop," I told him, a hint of warble in my tone. I cleared my throat.

"Feel it all. It's okay, Son. I'll see you soon."

I nodded, feeling overwhelmed with gratitude for the time I got to spend with him.

Oakley's sniffle brought me back into protector mode and I reeled her into the hug too. Pop encouraged us to continue the date so I backed out of the group embrace to give Oakley a chance to say goodbye to her Dad without my presence. I lingered by the car door so I could open it for her when she was ready to go. I tried not to eavesdrop but Pop had a booming voice that carried without much effort.

"He's a keeper, Bunny."

"I agree, Dad."

Wait, he called her by the same nickname I'd called her by on the plane. The alarms in my temporal lobe were going off like fireworks. **Danger! Danger!**

"Love you, Oakley Brooke."

"Love you, Dad."

"Love you, Jason Mitchell."

I was startled from my stress, "Love you, Pop."

She nearly ran into my arms and I held on while I watched Pop disappear into the hotel lobby. Faint whispers filled her ear, "Are you ready, Bunny?" She nodded and I opened the car door and ushered her inside.

We rode to the biggest park in the city. I opened the car door for her and held out a hand to help her out. It was a warm January day, a balmy 59 degrees. So we strolled through the park, hand in hand, the air cool and refreshing. A stark contrast to the temps that nearly killed me just a few nights ago. The stars twinkled above us and though I felt a sense of contentment wash over me, this night felt like more than just a date. This step towards building our future felt heavy - so heavy I stopped walking.

Oakley looked up into my eyes with wonder and concern.

"What's going on Jam?"

I couldn't get any words out. Her presence was reassuring, and looking into her eyes seemed to calm my nervous system, but the feelings were still there. Just lingering. Mocking me. It was absurd that such a good day could be clouded by thoughts that felt so misaligned to me.

Worry lines played across her forehead, "Talk to me, Jam."

I was having trouble breathing.

"Should we go back to the car?" she asked me. I

nodded quickly, not wanting the general public to see the meltdown that was pending.

Back in the car, the emotion swelled through my chest, rising until it exited through my face in the form of tears.

Chapter Twenty Six
OAKLEY

His tears flowed uncontrollably and it all happened so quickly. I didn't know what happened, what triggered it, or what to do other than reaching out to hold his hand through it.

"Talk to me Jason."

His body labored to slow down his breathing. I caressed the back of his hand with my thumb, hoping to encourage relaxation.

Finally he spoke, "My heart, my soul says this feels right. My brain is working hard to protect me."

I blinked out a tear of my own. I don't know if I was feeling his pain, mine or a combination of the sort. I didn't say a word, just nodded.

In hindsight I should've said something, but in the moment I didn't know what to do.

Exasperation was heavy in his voice. "Did you hear me?"

I whispered, "I did."

"You didn't say anything."

"I didn't know what to say. I understand the conflict."

His voice was soft, "That would be helpful to hear."

I continued to whisper, "Well you know it now."

"Do I?"

"I don't understand what's going on right now, Jam. What's happening in here?" I asked, caressing his temple.

His tears continued to flow as he spoke, "My body is in a battle right now. I don't think I can do this, Oakley."

I was hurting for him. I was hurting for me. I didn't want him to fight himself.

I spoke softly, "If you need to let me go, it's okay, Jason."

He gazed into my eyes like he was trying to find the answer to something. We sat in silence, his tears streaming down his face and my tears beginning to coat mine as well.

He cut the minute of silence with one word, "Why?"

"You want the truth?" I asked. He nodded.

I held his hand and held his gaze. "I have loved you from the moment I first saw you. It was the most pure unconditional love I've ever felt for another adult in my life. I tried to understand it but eventually I just stopped and accepted it for what it was."

He nodded, "What was it - is it?"

I caressed the side of his face, "I love you as you are in this moment. And in 10 minutes I'll love you as you are in that moment. In 5 years if we're still around, I'll love you in those moments too."

He wept in my arms.

"It's okay to let go. Your hearts been shattered before right?"

"Yeah."

"And it's never not come back together, right?"

"Always does eventually."

"Right. So just let go. Fall to pieces. I'll be right here to pick up all of them so you can piece it back together and create a masterpiece when you're ready."

He looked up in my arms and spoke from the heart,

"How do I let go?"

I took a deep breath, mulling over whether or not I really wanted to let these words out, "Maybe we need to take a break. You were trying to get us to slow down and we did the exact opposite of that. What if we take Saturday to just be?"

He nodded, "Maybe so." I held his hand and rested my head on his shoulder. He lowered his head to meet mine. We sat in silence for a while. I wondered if he was hesitant to leave the park because we were still together in this moment, while any move to our neighborhood would send us into unknown territory.

"Jam, Jason, I have something at the house that I think you should have. Can you take me home?"

"What is it?"

"One of them is the book I picked out for you in New Orleans. The other is, well, you have to see it. Can you take me back to the house?"

He nodded and I wiped the tears from his face. He reluctantly started the car, his eyes fixed on my face, taking me in before everything changed.

The ride back was quiet. The air heavy with uncertainty. It was such a stark contrast to the dinner with Dad. Everything felt like it was falling into place. My three worlds were merging harmoniously, or so I thought. Jason pulled into the driveway, opened the car door for me and walked me to the front door, but he didn't come in. He stood outside, his hands wringing. Eyebrows folded.

"I need to grab something from the house, Miss Oakley. I'll be right back, okay?"

I nodded and watched from inside the house as he walked down the street and disappeared around the corner, leaving his car in my driveway as a promise that he was going to return. I chuckled to myself as I looked at my driveway, full with vehicles that didn't belong to me, but rather to the two men I loved the most - and neither one was here.

I closed the door and retreated to my bedroom to grab the two things for Jason before he came back from his house. I sent him a text as I slid into the bathroom, letting him know that the front door was locked but he could let himself in using the code.

I was washing my hands as I heard the door to the garage close and listened as he called out my name.

"I'll be out in a minute, Jason!"

When I opened the door he was sitting anxiously on the couch, a light towel wrapped around something the shape of a book.

He stood to his feet when he saw me, "Here's the book I picked out for you in Emmaline's place."

He held his hand out and his fingertips lingered on my hand as he passed the book to me.

"Thank you, Jam. Here's two things for you." I handed him a small gift bag. "Do we open these now or do we wait?"

"I want to wait."

"Okay."

I sat the wrapped book on my coffee table and opened my arms for a hug. He wrapped me up and held on. I stayed right there, in my house, wrapped up at home in his arms for as long as he wanted. It was a perfect fit, and I trusted that he would find his way back. I looked up into his eyes and could feel the energy before he leaned down to kiss me goodbye. The world narrowed to just the two of us.

"Thank you, Jason," I whispered against his lips. "For everything."

I caressed his face, locking the feel of his skin, the scent of his beard, within my memory.

"You know where to find me when you're ready, Jam." He nodded. I walked him to the door and watched as he walked to his car, a lingering look of affection and hesitation before he got in, backed out into the street and disappeared around the corner.

Chapter Twenty Seven
JASON

The walk back to my house to get the book felt like a lifetime. Every step was heavy with the weight of the conversation from the park. Oakley's words echoed in my mind and I couldn't shake the feeling that I'd left too much unsaid.

As I entered my house I was greeted by the familiar smell of my favorite candle, a scent that usually brought me peace. Tonight it only intensified my turmoil. I grabbed the book I had bought for Oakley and headed back to her house, determined to explain everything I had left in the shadows.

I took a seat on her couch feeling the weight of the moment bearing down on me. As soon as she stepped out from the bathroom, her face compelled me to stand. I couldn't possibly sit on the couch with her, I knew it would distract me. Just sitting on it for the 30 seconds I waited took me back to last night and how we broke the universe.

As I passed her the book and her touch lingered, I lost all train of thought. Everything that I was supposed to say to clear the air got caught in limbo. Even a deep breath wouldn't let it escape There was so much to say.

She felt so right in my arms. I couldn't make sense of what my brain was doing. I knew it was supposed to be protecting me, but from what, I didn't understand. My heart knew. I was so sure about her, about her family. My brain was betraying me. I had been hurt before, she was right about that. But I knew I was ready for her. This was something special, something I'd never felt before. I wanted her help. I wanted to let her in. But I needed some reassurance that what I was feeling wasn't an illusion.

I got back to my house and stared at the gift bag, trying to decide whether or not to open it now or let things settle and open them in the morning. I left it in the living room and walked into the kitchen. I stared at it while I poured myself a glass of water to soothe this tension headache. I brushed my teeth, about to lay down for the evening and peeked out at it from the bathroom door, toothbrush dangling from my mouth. I turned off all the lights and retired to the bedroom, ready to lay down and go to sleep. I picked up the phone to send her a goodnight text but stopped myself. We were supposed to be slowing down and this was the opposite of that. I set the phone down and closed my eyes but all I could see was the bag, waiting to be opened. The anticipation got to me. I sprang from the bed and opened the door, peeking out at the bag waiting for me. One deep sigh and I shuffled out to the living room to grab it.

"I'll just open it in the bedroom."

I climbed back in the bed and held the bag in my hands.

"Please let it be a candle," I joked with myself.

I reached inside and felt three things, two flat and one round. I pulled out the round item first and chuckled to find she had given me a jar of sugarplums. I stared at them, watching them shimmer in the full moon light that was streaming through my window. I pulled out the second object, the book she had picked out for me in New Orleans, "The Seat of the Soul," a book that provides a spiritual framework for understanding relationships and destiny. An interesting and complementary choice with the title I chose for her, "The Soulmate Experience." Between the two of us we were committed to the idea of strengthening our destined connections. My brain started to calm down as I looked at these two things she had so carefully picked out and shared with me. Just as the smile started to return to my face I remembered there was another book in the bag. I reached in and pulled it out to find a journal. I searched for a pen so I could begin to write an entry about this day and how I was feeling in the moment.

When I opened the journal I found something unexpected. She had already written her own entries in it. This was her journal and the first entry was from Small Business Saturday from last year.

November 28, 2020

Today was one of those days where everything felt perfectly ordinary until it wasn't. The coffee shop was buzzing like a beehive with the usual Saturday crowd. Dad, who was visiting for the week of Thanksgiving, came in for his regular order, which always brings a smile to my face. There's something comforting about the consistency of preparing his order - bear claw, warm, coffee black, sugarplums on the side.

Just as I was pouring his coffee, I noticed a new face at the counter. Big brown eyes that held a twinkle, unlike anything I've seen before. He was tall and quiet, almost reserved, yet there was a warmth in those eyes that also caught me off guard. He ordered the same thing as Dad, which was not a common order at all. It definitely made me do a double take.

He didn't say much, but there was something about him that felt familiar, like a deja vu moment. I watched him find a seat and he chose the table right next to Dad's. They exchanged nods and I felt a strange sense of connection, as if the universe was whispering to me to remember this moment.

I hope this isn't the last I see of him. The cat's out of the bag and my curiosity is piqued.

Until tomorrow's entry. Oakley Powell.

She'd felt the same thing as me and reading this entry transported me back to that day. Suddenly I remembered Pop's face. We were definitely supposed to meet. There was an entry for every Monday, Thursday, and Saturday that I showed up and it was like an out of body experience watching her describe how the connection was growing through shared glances and an energy that seemed to pull us closer to each other as we went. There was an entry about Charlie's wedding to someone named Dr. Chris, who she seemed to adore. Then there was January 1st.

January 1, 2021

Today I met him. The man who's been coming into the shop since Thanksgiving weekend. Jason Andrew Mitchell. I've always been drawn to him like a magnet and now I think I know why. He feels like home. He looks at me with so much love. And of all the things for him to say to me, he told me he's never been so sure of something in all of his 44 years of life. He's going to marry me, he said. And the scariest part is I think he might be right. I promised him that he could have my middle name if he made it through the 5th date with me. If we're not already married before the 5th date that is. He calls me Miss Oakley with so much passion.

Apparently sometimes he calls me by the name I left in his contacts. I hope I didn't jinx myself. I'm gonna try to get some sleep so I can be well rested for tomorrow. I'm so excited about this date that I don't know how well I'll sleep. We're about to find out.

Needle in a haystack, found.

Until tomorrow's entry. Oakley B. Powell-Mitchell.

I was transported back to that day. I felt it within my bones. I was going to marry her. What was my brain trying to do? She was my wife. I kept reading. I couldn't stop.

January 2, 2021

Today was supposed to be magical, but it ended up being a disaster. Jason and I had our first official date—a brunch I was really looking forward to. But my own apprehensions got the best of me. Every little thing he did or said seemed to rub me the wrong way, and I couldn't understand why. I could still feel the energy, the connection. But my brain was in the way.

I kept overthinking everything, questioning his intentions, and doubting the connection I've felt since Small Business Saturday. My fears shaded everything, and what should have been a lovely morning turned into an awkward, tension-filled mess. Jason could tell something was off, and I hated that I was the one making it difficult.

I stormed out in frustration, but he was so patient even as he left. I need to figure out why I'm sabotaging something that feels so right. I hope I haven't ruined everything. It's like I'm barking up the wrong tree, and I need to get my head on straight.

Until tomorrow's entry. Oakley Powell (hopefully

Mitchell)

I sighed deeply after reading this one. I could feel my confusion all over again, but I could also feel my resolve. I understood it, in much the same way as she had understood it tonight. I was right there when she was ready to talk about it, the same way she said she would be for me.

January 3, 2021

After yesterday's brunch debacle, Jason suggested we have a redo. Apparently he lives around the corner from me. How's that for destiny! He walked to my house so we could continue the date. I wanted to treat it like its own date. There was something about being in this space that allowed us to relax and be ourselves. The weather was freezing, but his presence brought warmth. I showed him the sugarplums and we shared our first kiss. It made my knees weak.

He was going to walk home but he chose to go without a jacket. I felt his keys in the pocket and was going to rush them to him, but he scared me so much when I found him outside, confused and shivering cold. I thought I was gonna lose him and I was mad at the Universe for letting us find each other and only giving us 3 days. There was no way I was gonna let him go without a fight. We sat by the fire to warm him up and are currently cuddling in bed as he sleeps.

We ended the day on a much better note than

yesterday, feeling connected and hopeful again. As they say, every cloud has a silver lining.

Until tomorrow, Oakley Powell

She thought she was gonna lose me after 3 days. She felt the same thing I felt in that moment. Three days was not enough.

January 4, 2021

Today was a rollercoaster. I gave him my middle name today and then Jason revealed that he's the actuary who's been emailing me—the one I've been avoiding because I thought he had taken my job. I was shocked, then angry, then hurt. How could he keep that from me? It felt like a betrayal, like he was hiding a part of himself.

I confronted him about it, and we had a heated argument. I didn't know if I could trust him anymore. But then, when we were short-staffed and overwhelmed at the shop, he jumped in to help without hesitation. He worked tirelessly beside me, proving his dedication and integrity.

By the end of the day, my anger had subsided. His actions spoke louder than his words, and I began to trust him again. It was a challenging day, but it reaffirmed that he's someone I can rely on, even when things get tough. It's like the proof of the pudding is in the eating.

Until tomorrow, Oakley Brooke

As I read her entries it began to feel like a lifetime of love was lived within this week.

January 5, 2021

I went to see him last night after I wrote yesterday's entry. I couldn't stay away. Something pulled me back to him. This morning he suggested we play hookey from work and jet set to New Orleans. It was everything I needed and more. We ate beignets on Bourbon Street and he had me using all of my senses. Then we met a psychic named Emmaline, and her message struck a chord with me. She spoke of overcoming fears and trusting the journey, and it felt like she was talking directly to me.

Traveling with Jason was a new experience, and I was nervous at first. I had promised myself that I wouldn't travel with another man unless I could feel his love. Not only did he make it easy, fun, and safe, but I could feel his love in his actions. We explored the city, shared our dreams, and laughed like we'd known each other forever. The psychic's words stayed with me, giving me the courage to open up and embrace this connection fully.

I'm learning to let go of my fears and trust that the universe has a plan for us. He told me he loved me today and I felt every ounce of it. I love him too and part of me knows that I have loved him since November. This trip has brought us closer, and I'm grateful for every moment. It's true what they say, fortune favors the brave.

Until tomorrow, Oakley B. Powell-Mitchell

Sheesh! That day was life changing for me and to read how she felt in the moment is exactly what I needed. The more I read, the more my brain settled down. I was anxious to read the next entry though. That was the day we broke the universe.

January 6, 2021

Today was beyond words. Jason and I made love for the first time, and every time it happened, it felt like we broke the universe. Everything around us turned white, as if time and space ceased to exist. It was just us, lost in each other, in a moment of pure connection and love.

Afterwards, as we rested in each other's arms, the world slowly came back into focus. It was surreal and beautiful, and I've never felt so close to another person. Jason is my everything, and today proved that our connection is something extraordinary, something cosmic and divinely timed. As they say, love conquers all. We can conquer the world as powerful as ours is.

Until tomorrow, O.B.P.

Her everything. She said I'm her everything. I could feel the tears streaking down my face and I just let them joints fall. She was my everything too. I was going to write that on the next page, assuming she hadn't penned an entry from today. I was wrong.

January 7, 2021

Dad and Jason met today and my world felt complete. My heart was so full watching them together. It just feels right...to me.

I think Jason's brain is probably betraying him the way mine did during brunch. I get it. I know how much it hurts. I want to support him through this, to be there as he figures things out. But I also don't want to overstep. Our connection is strong and to me it's a matter of when this break will end, not if. So when he's ready, I'm here to remind him of our something special, our time bending, universe breaking love, and just how strong it is. I'm ready to fight for it.

Oakley B. Powell

p.s. You know how to find me when you're ready, Jam.

I did indeed. I knew where I needed to go, first thing in the morning.

OAKLEY

The door to the coffee shop opened and I was hopeful that it would be my favorite person on the planet. I turned my head in that direction and in walked Mandy and the party girls. They'd returned to get the dish on Jason and I's first date and I just wasn't sure what to share with them. If a week for most relationships was like a 5K, ours had run an ultra-marathon in the same timeframe.

"Soooo...we're here for the tea."

I laughed and told them we sold coffee.

"Really funny. Tell us about your first date."

They placed their orders and I delivered it to their table to walk them through the events of this week.

"Y'all are destined to be together. I bet he read the journal yesterday. He's got to come in today!"

"He just has to!"

Every time the door opened, they turned to see if it was him. The energy wasn't there and I knew it was someone else. So every time it wasn't him, they turned their heads back to me to find me with pursed lips, signaling that it wasn't him without even looking. I thanked them for coming back in and told them I would let them get back to their own gossip, then popped behind the counter to take care of some things.

There I was leaned up against the back counter, watching the news on the tiny tv in the far corner when my beacon started blinking. I felt the stirring and uncontrollably stood upright. It was instinct. My body was at the ready. The door opened. A well-timed gust of wind tossed some lingering leaves up into the air in a swirl, and in the blink of an eye there he was.

"Are you open?" he asked, hope hanging out in his punctuation.

I couldn't speak, a mix of emotions passed through me. Tears filled my eyes. A nod and a smile. That's all I could get my body to respond with. A nod and a smile. I met him at the front counter. Not sure how I got there because I don't remember my feet moving. His eyes remained fixed on mine the entire time. The rest of the world seemed to fade away and there we were, the two of us, stepping closer to fill the void of time and space that was needed to bring us back to each other. Our tight embrace lingered. He pulled back just enough to gaze into my eyes. His voice was soft and filled with sincerity.

"Oakley Brooke. My strength. My peace. Thank you."

Author's Notes & Acknowledgments

Author's Notes

From the last Author's Notes:
> "There was a teaser of another love story in this one that I'm hoping you caught. And don't think we're leaving out Oakley...she may need her own separate series."

Well, I'm still writing romance novels. Clearly Oakley was ready to tell the world her redemption story. There is definitely a series here, as I hope you can tell by the ending of this book. What happens after Jason returns to the coffeeshop that Saturday? What's next for these two? Is the baby real and is it Jason's? I promise I won't leave you hanging like that.

This story, like most of the stories in the Sugarplum Universe is about trusting what you feel and being willing to pour love into the world in spite of hurt, disappointment, and potential fear. The desire to hide, to run, to not trust what's in front of you because of past experience may be present, but so much joy is around us if we're willing to look for it, if we're willing to create it, if we're willing to live within a space where multiple things can be true at once.

Navigating the scars left by callous relationships is a heavy, painful thing to traverse. And while it's a hard thing to live and write about, its discussion is so necessary for healing. The undoing created by that type of loss leaves us with an opportunity to reconnect with what's truly important to us.

By leaning into the undoing, by walking with your fear, by having a solid network of support around you and trusting your gut, you have the power to stand fully in who you are and welcome in the type of love **<u>we all</u>** deserve.

The Sugarplum Series was an unexpected detour from my path as a children's book author, and one I have learned to embrace over time. They say authors write the stories that they need, yet I doubted that I needed a romance novel in my life. I was wrong.

These books were about so much more than Oakley, Jason, Marley, Jax, Dr. Chris, Charlie, Marlo, Steve, Sabrina, and any of the other characters who are included. They're far bigger than romance. They're about the sweet fruit that comes from nurturing healthy relationships; romantic, friendly, familial, collegial, whatever form.

Even when we think we have the answer, we only really possess a tiny fraction of knowledge compared to all the information there is to obtain. Through these books I've had the chance to connect more interpersonally with readers and friends, and while none of it was something I predicted for my life, I am grateful for every ounce of it.

Acknowledgments

To the Beta Readers, your patience, quick follow through and time is truly invaluable. I appreciate your willingness to ensure that this next book in the Sugarplum Universe lives up to the expectations left by the first three books in the series. I appreciate you more than you know.

To the friends and family who encouraged me to listen and share, I appreciate you and am tremendously grateful for your support. My most sincere thanks to the crew (you know who you are). I appreciate your time, your honest critiques, and the humor you leant to my writing process. Thanks for ensuring I remained human throughout the writing of this story.

To Kelly, Deborah, & JT, who were willing to read the spicy stuff and provide feedback on it - even if it was just an emoji - thank you for creating a safe space where I could refine and craft the content that was flowing through me. Thank You, thank you, thank you, a million times over for holding space for me when I needed it most. Know that your friendship is one I cherish, and the same is always here for you, regardless of the circumstances.

To Coach, thanks for the creative inspiration to FINALLY finish this story. Always grateful for your extra push and your light, whether it's intentional or not.

To my parents, siblings, and relatives, thank you for showing me what family can mean, in all its varied examples. It is because of how you love each other and others that I can write a story that displays the essence of relationships built with a strong and stable foundation. I love you to the moon and back!

Finally, to the enthusiastic readers of the Sugarplum series, thank you for sharing your love of this series. I hope this next iteration lives up to the hype (and doesn't shock you too much). If this is your first foray into the Sugarplum Series, welcome. Now that you've finished this book, you might give A Spoonful of Sugarplums a chance. It will help to fill in some of the details for you.

Remember always, there is at least one thing exists without beginning or end. Love is eternal.

About the Author

C. L. Fails is an author, story shepherd, joy sherpa, and an accidental educator; having served pre-school through college students in her hometown of Kansas City. An agent for equity, she has dedicated her career to helping others learn to follow their internal compass, and thrive despite challenge. She is currently Founder & CEO of LaunchCrate Publishing - a company created to help writers launch their work into the world while retaining the portion of profit they deserve. Outside of LaunchCrate she is an active advocate for education, serving as a former Girls on the Run Coach, on the Board of Directors for several nonprofits and is highly involved with several equity initiatives through her collegiate alma mater.

She is author of several books that inspire us to be bold, take risks, and learn from our mistakes. When she's not helping clients, hosting a podcast, speaking with audiences or working on her latest work in progress about building community, you can find her doodling on whatever object may be nearby.

Her favorite work is documenting personal narratives through the Modern Memoir service, and serving as a Story Shepherd to writers, working to launch their work into the world through Idea to Editor. Both services are offered by LaunchCrate Publishing. Check out launchcrate.com for more detailed information.